ISBN 978-1-333-28890-7
PIBN 10484206

English
Français
Deutsche
Italiano
Español
Português

www.forgottenbooks.com

Mythology Photography **Fiction**
Fishing Christianity **Art** Cooking
Essays Buddhism Freemasonry
Medicine **Biology** Music **Ancient
Egypt** Evolution Carpentry Physics
Dance Geology **Mathematics** Fitness
Shakespeare **Folklore** Yoga Marketing
Confidence Immortality Biographies
Poetry **Psychology** Witchcraft
Electronics Chemistry History **Law**
Accounting **Philosophy** Anthropology
Alchemy Drama Quantum Mechanics
Atheism Sexual Health **Ancient History**
Entrepreneurship Languages Sport
Paleontology Needlework Islam
Metaphysics Investment Archaeology
Parenting Statistics Criminology
Motivational

THE PRINCESS OGHÉROF.

A RUSSIAN LOVE STORY.

BY HENRY GRÉVILLE.

AUTHOR OF "THE TRIALS OF RAISSA," "MARRYING OFF A DAUGHTER," "MARKOF,"
"SAVELI'S EXPIATION," "A FRIEND," "DOURNOF," "BONNE-MARIE,"
"DOSIA," "LUCIE RODEY," "PHILOMENE'S MARRIAGES," "SONIA,"
"GABRIELLE," "PRETTY LITTLE COUNTESS ZINA," ETC.

TRANSLATED FROM THE FRENCH
BY MARY NEAL SHERWOOD.

PHILADELPHIA:
T. B. PETERSON & BROTHERS;
306 CHESTNUT STREET.

HENRY GRÉVILLE'S CELEBRATED NOVELS.

The Princess Oghérof. A Russian Love Story. *By Henry Gréville.*

"THE PRINCESS OGHÉROF," by Henry Gréville, is a thoroughly fascinating love story. Its interest is intense and sustained, and at no point does the reader find a dull line. It is purity itself, and there is not a word nor a thought in it which could harm the most innocent. The scene is laid in Russia, and the characters move in high society. The plot is well defined and strong, and in it is a pretty love romance, full of sunlight and joy. It will at once become vastly popular with the hosts of American novel-readers.

Lucie Rodey. A New Society Novel. *By Henry Gréville.*

"LUCIE RODEY" teaches a great lesson, which will be felt even by those who read it with breathless interest merely for the sake of the story. They will find the wife and mother "faithful unto death," though exposed to lots of trials and temptations.

Savéli's Expiation. A Pure and Powerful Love Story. *By Henry Gréville.*

"SAVÉLI'S EXPIATION" is one of the most dramatic and most powerful novels ever published, while a pathetic love story, running all through its pages, is presented for relief.

Markof, the Russian Violinist. A Russian Story. *By Henry Gréville.*

"MARKOF" is an art study, full of beautiful prose and true poetry, and such as could be written only by such an artist and genius as the author of "DOSIA" is.

Dosia. A Russian Story. *By Henry Gréville.*

"DOSIA" is a charming story of Russian society, is written with a rare grace of style, is brilliant, pleasing and attractive. It is an exquisite creation, and is pure and fresh as a rose.

Dournof. A Russian Story. *By Henry Gréville.*

"DOURNOF" is a charming and graphic story of Russian life, containing careful studies of Russian character, and character drawing, which are most admirable.

Marrying Off a Daughter. A Society Novel. *By Henry Gréville.*

"MARRYING OFF A DAUGHTER" is gay, sparkling, and pervaded by a delicious tone of quiet humor, and will be read and enjoyed by thousands of readers.

Bonne-Marie. A Tale of Normandy and Paris. *By Henry Gréville.*

"BONNE-MARIE" is a charming story, the scenes of which are laid in Normandy and in Paris. It will no doubt create a sensation, such is its freshness, beauty, and delicacy.

Pretty Little Countess Zina. A Charming Story. *By Henry Gréville.*

Zina, the Countess, bears a certain resemblance to Dosia—that bewitching creature—in her dainty wilfulness, while the ward and cousin, Vassalissa, is an entire new creation.

Sonia. A Russian Story. *By Henry Gréville.*

"SONIA" is charming and refined, and is a powerful, graceful, domestic story, being most beautifully told—giving one a very distinct idea of every-day home life in Russia.

Philomène's Marriages. A Tale of Normandy. *By Henry Gréville.*

The heroine's life is narrated in a most fascinating manner, and is an admirable picture of country home-life, full of wit, of a high moral tone, and full of interest.

Gabrielle; or, The House of Maurèze. *By Henry Gréville.*

"GABRIELLE; OR, THE HOUSE OF MAURÈZE," is a very thrilling and touching story most skilfully told, and follows the life of the girl whose title it bears.

'riend; or, L'Ami. A Story of Every-Day Life. *By Henry Gréville.*

 tender and touching picture of French home-life will touch many hearts, as it shows 'ove of a true and good woman will meet with its reward and triumph at last.

CONTENTS.

(19)

THE PRINCESS OGHÉROF.

A RUSSIAN LOVE STORY.

BY HENRY GRÉVILLE.

AUTHOR OF

"SAVELI'S EXPIATION," "THE TRIALS OF RAISSA; OR, LES EPREUVES DE RAISSA,"
"DOSIA," "SONIA," "DOURNOF," "MARRYING OFF A DAUGHTER," "MARKOF,"
"PRETTY LITTLE COUNTESS ZINA," "GABRIELLE," "A FRIEND,"
"BONNE MARIE," "LUCIE RODEY," "PHILOMENE'S MARRIAGES."

CHAPTER I.

THE CHILDREN'S BALL.

THAT evening—Tuesday in Easter week, 1860—all the Quai de la Cour was in a great state of excitement. Madame Avéroef was giving a children's ball.

The house of Madame Avéroef had for a long time been one of the most noticeable among those which each year had the honor of seeing the Imperial family appear at one at least of their magnificently organized fêtes. Everything was in favor of this privilege. The high birth of the hostess, her deep mourning, worn with

(21)

such dignity, in memory of the husband killed at Varna, her salutary influence over the generation that had grown up under her eyes, and, in addition, the charm of her hospitable grace, all caused her invitations to be sought for, and highly valued.

Thus, when at the death of her son General Avéroef, buried in a Caucasian torrent, she closed her dwelling, and gave no more fêtes, it seemed as if there were something lacking in the sunshine of a St. Petersburg winter.

For five or six years the Avéroef Mansion was silent and mournful. Only members of the family and intimate friends crossed the threshold, and were received within the door, formerly thrown so widely open; one day the *noblesse* of the town learned, not without astonishment, that Prascovia Petrovna, in honor of the unexpected restoration to health of her grandson, opened her *salons* once more, and was to give a children's ball.

To her mansion the flower, or rather the buds of the St. Petersburg aristocracy would now flock. The invitations were as eagerly desired by the children, as they had been in former years by the mothers.

Easter Tuesday came this year in the middle of April. The great hall, with its floor of yellow marble, where the children were assembled, was lighted by four enormous windows looking out upon the Néva, the oblique rays of the spring sunshine stole in between the curtains of yellow damask, while the farther extremity of the room, in spite of the tall mirror of the time of the Empire, was already dark and even a trifle gloomy.

The little dancers, most of them, accompanied by their governesses, approached each other and instituted a mutual but timid examination of their toilets; the boys, even more timid, retreated to the windows. Some of the mothers were laughing and talking among themselves.

Suddenly the Master of Ceremonies entered, and like the sun, which at this moment disappeared behind the Bourse, he broke the ice; he placed each little hand in another, and the couples arranged themselves in a long line, nearly lost in the gathering darkness at the other end of the hall.

The band was heard in the next room. The door was thrown open and the Polonaise unrolled its majestic limbs, with measured slowness.

Surrounded by her family, seated or rather throned in a large chair at the end of the crimson *salon*, blazing with light, Prascovia Petrovna, with her white hair rolled up in puffs, her robe of white damask, and wrapped in the folds of a Point de Venice mantella, had rather the air of an Empress of the East, than of a simple mortal. Smiling, and with a most kindly expression, she watched the children coming toward her, led by her grandson Serge in his uniform of a court page.

The boy bowed, and took the white, dimpled hand of

his grandmother, and pressed upon it a most respectful kiss, accompanied by a smiling glance from his handsome, deep gray eyes. His partner, a tall girl of fifteen, blushed deeply, and made a profound reverence to her hostess.

The couples that followed, stopped in their turn before the crimson arm-chair, and even the very smallest children, who could hardly stand on their little, fat legs, did their best to follow the example of their elders.

After having accomplished this duty, the chain broke, a waltz took the place of the Polonaise, and the couples flew about the room, while numerous servants lighted the yellow salon, just now so dark.

Late guests now made their appearance. The mammas now grouped themselves around Madame Avéræf; the tutors had fled to another room, the governesses chatted in low voices, as they sat along the wall, a joyous noise, a rustling of silk, and pattering of little feet had succeeded to the previous quiet.

A quadrille followed the waltz. The smaller and more timid children, began to gallop like young colts, in an adjacent room, and the gayety was its height.

The old roof which dated from Catherine the Great, had seen many fêtes, but none more joyous than this. The eldest of the youths was not more than twenty, no one of the girls was more than seventeen, and all these young creatures moved about without any more care than if every day was to be followed by an Easter Wednesday.

Madame Avéroef, beautiful and young again, seemed to have forgotten all her sorrows, in contemplating the restrained gayety of these young people, whose most expansive joy never caused them to forget their good breeding.

A philosopher, might, perhaps, have regretted this perfect education which leaves nothing to chance — but no philosopher was there!

At half past nine, the oaken doors of the dining-room were thrown open; the dark wood-work had disappeared under the brilliancy of the silver on the high-backed buffets. A blaze of light brought out the deep gold in the hangings of Cordova leather; the three tables formed a glittering mass on the marble flags — with their dazzling linen, and their services of crystal and gold — with their tall candelabra of old silver, buried among bushels of sweet-scented flowers.

The children were too well brought up to say a word, but their mothers uttered a simultaneous cry of admiration. Never had Madame Avéroef succeeded better in the decoration of her dining-room.

"It was my nephew Michel, who arranged it all," replied Prascovia Petrovna, with sincere joy. "He promised to do his best, and I am really glad that he succeeded."

"Where does this conquering hero hide himself?" said a pretty mamma, "he is modest, indeed, if he does not come to enjoy his triumph."

"He dined with his uncle," replied the old lady, "but will bé here presently."

While the children took their places in an orderly manner around the table, and when brooks of tea were running into the Saxe cups, Madame Avéroef said to a pretty brunette of fourteen years, and a little more, who was eating a slice of cake with avidity,

"Where is your sister, Nastia?"

"Over there, Prascovia Petrovna, with the governesses."

An admonitory touch on her dress from a neighbor's hand, brought the color to her face. She recollected herself, and said, gravely:

"With those ladies! That is, Mademoiselle Pauline is with her."

"And why did she not come here with you?"

"She says she is so big that it would be ridiculous."

"Ridiculous!" repeated the old lady with a frown. "Olga," she continued; "go and find Marthe Méla-guire in the blue salon — quick!"

Olga disappeared, and came back in a moment, accompanied by a young girl who was dressed in a simple white robe, while her brown hair was entirely her own.

"What was that you were saying, Marthe? Do you think it ridiculous to come among all these charming children?"

At these words, pronounced in a more than demi-voice, every eye turned upon the delinquent, which by no means, diminished her embarrassment. She succeeded, however, in conquering it, and answered gayly:

"It is I who am ridiculous, Prascovia Petrovna. I do not dare show myself. Just see how tall I am — a head taller than any of these young ladies!"

She was indeed very tall, and looked as if she were at least nineteen. Her bust and shoulders were magnificent, but she was almost too tall, and among the children who surrounded her, seemed like a young poplar grown up by chance in an osiery.

Madame Avérœf smiled; the sweetness of the girl disarmed her.

"As you will have some difficulty in diminishing your stature, you will be obliged to wait until the others grow up to you. It is very good of you to come, my child, when you knew that you could find no pleasure here."

"Do you consider it nothing to see you?" answered Marthe, with a smile.

"Very well, if it pleases you to see an old lady like myself, sit down there, and let us take some tea together."

This was considered a great honor among the little court around the mistress of the house. A guéridon was brought with an especial tray for Madame Avérœf, who never took any tea that she did not herself prepare with her own hands. It was probably no better than the rest, but the distinction was a most flattering one.

The conversation interrupted by this little incident was gradually resumed, and all went gayly in this

most hospitable of dwellings. It was at this moment
that Michel Avércef made his appearance. He was
welcomed by a chorus of flattering exclamations,
enough to turn the head of any gallant young
chevalier. But Michel, it seemed, was accustomed to
this, for he moved on quite undisturbed, distributing
smiles to the right and the left, until he reached his
Aunt, over whose hand he bowed profoundly.

"I am content, Michel," she said.

Unconsciously she spoke like an empress.

"Many thanks, dear Aunt," he replied, once more
kissing her hand.

As he raised his head, his eyes met those of Marthe
Mélaguire, who had not moved since his entrance. It
was he who colored. She returned his bow with an
inclination of the head, which, although polite, was
almost haughty, dropped her eyes, and did not lift
them for a good quarter of an hour.

CHAPTER II.

A BLOW TO THE GOVERNESS.

MICHEL was tall, and his uniform of the Horse Guards showed all the elegance of his figure. Adored by all the young ladies just out of the Institute, and also by many others. He passed through life with the clear conscience of a man who respects himself, and who knows what he is worth. He never trifled with any one; it was whispered behind fans that he had relations with an actress — that he was beloved by a lady in the highest circles — that he was secretly married to a little work-woman in la Gorokhovïa; but this last supposition provoked such peals of laughter, that the person who had concocted it — a woman, of course — young, pretty and spiteful, it is also needless to say — had for a whole week been afraid to utter the name of this redoubtable young man. He was seen driving at certain hours, in a hackney coach, and people asked each other where he was going, and why he did not use his own carriage. It was finally ascertained that when he went to the Military Academy, he thought it bad taste to make parade of his horses, while others, who, in his opinion, were better than himself, went on foot.

Every inquiry had ended just here. The truth was,

that Michel Avéroef had a very great regard for his dignity, that he did not wish to go through existence with that mill-stone about his neck, known as the life of a young man, and—more than anything else—that after his return to his regiment, he loved Marthe Mélaguire with his whole heart and soul.

Just four years earlier, and Michel was just eighteen. When he noticed Marthe for the first time, coming one day to pay Mousieur Mélaguire a visit on the occasion of his first uniform, he had met the young girl, leading her little sister. She was slowly coming down the stairs; the two sisters all in black velvet, stood out against the dark staircase. The face of the elder, and sixteen-year-old sister, had the pensive expression of a young mother, while Nastia's pretty, childish face smiled at this visitor, a Page of the Chamber last Spring, and now in the autumn, a handsome officer in uniform.

Michel drew aside to allow the two young girls to pass, and had eyes only for them. He considerably disturbed the equanimity of Monsieur Mélaguire, by announcing to him a few minutes later that he had met his daughters as they were going out.

"What! Alone?" cried the worthy man.

"I think so; at least they appeared to be alone."

Mélaguire hurried out for information, and returned laughing.

"You did not see the Governess?" he exclaimed. "Upon my word that is very odd, and I shall tell her so."

"And why pray?" said the youth. "I beg of you to say nothing."

"To think that he did not even see Mademoiselle Pauline! And yet she is not small, and by no means ill-looking. At your age, young man, I had better eyes for pretty girls!"

When Pauline returned with her two pupils, Monsieur Mélaguire took a mischievous delight in telling her of Michel Avérœf's blindness. The Governess fixed two piercing black eyes upon her employer, and smiled with an expression obsequious, but keen.

She was accustomed to passing unnoticed, but she had wished Michel to realize her existence, and for four long years after this day, neglected nothing to reach this end.

She looked at herself every night in the small mirror on her toilette table, and said to herself, over and over again, that her beautiful chestnut hair, so long and luxuriant, was worthy of being crowned by the lace cap of a young bride — that the white satin of a wedding dress would fall around her, with as much grace as around twenty others who had grown up with her, and had absurdly married at eighteen, and that it would be a great pity if she should be obliged to accept some clerk in an English house; or some subordinate officer in the army. Any one of those persons, in fact, whom she, in her position, might expect to marry.

She did not wish to take a German; she wanted the

pomp and ceremony of a Russian marriage.   She
dreamed of the Cathedral of Isaac, blazing with candles, lighted for her, of the choir intoning the nuptial
hymn as she entered, and of the husband who would
come to meet her, through the well-dressed crowd.
This husband was always Michel Avérœf.

Why did this ambitious little creature, low born, and
without any exceptional merit—with an education that
was limited to the fact that she had received a diploma
at a boarding school in Livonia—why, I say, did she
cling to the idea of marrying Michel Avérœf, the
admired, and the inaccessible?   Precisely, because he
was admired and inaccessible.   "He is no trifler," she
said to herself, has no aspirations for *bonnes fortunes*,
he is capable of marrying for love alone, and is quite
as likely to love a woman without birth or position as
one who has both.   He will marry any woman whom
he loves, and I mean to be that woman.

Pauline had one point in her favor—a point for
which more than one honest and virtuous dame would
have sold her very soul to the devil.   She was as pretty
as a pink; her little pointed nose did not disfigure
her smiling face.   Pauline was twenty-four, with all
the experience of that age, and the freshness of a girl
of sixteen.

The absence of a mother in the house of Monsieur
Mélaguire simplified the arduous labors imposed
upon her.

It was Mademoiselle Hopfer—"the Mamselle," as the

servants called her—who ordered the dinners and the teas, and who received with her eldest pupil, now a young lady. The education of Nastia, which weighed heavily upon her, she had confided to subordinates, under the pretence that details prevented her from judging of the result. By degrees this cunning girl had usurped Marthe's place. It was she who advised Monsieur Mélaguire in the choice of reception days and of his invited guests, as well as in the arrangement of his dinners. Monsieur Mélaguire had an excellent cook, of whom he was more proud, than a king of the diamonds in his crown. In a moment of effusive gratitude the excellent man had said to Mademoiselle Hopfer that after the death of his wife, he had never dreamed that his house could ever again be well managed. Pauline, in time, might probably have become Madame Mélaguire—that is, after the two daughters were married, for her position would then have been somewhat equivocal in the house of a single man.

But this lookout in the future, was far from pleasing to her.

She wished to enter into her kingdom at once, and then an elderly husband ——!

No—Michel Avéroef was the man of whom she dreamed. She had no reluctance to marry a man two or three years younger than herself. Several precedents within her knowledge reassured her on this point.

"These great Russian lords," she said to herself,

2

"are not apt to worry over trifles. Prince K——, our neighbor, did he not marry a Bohémienne ten years older than himself, whose beauty had altogether vanished? Comte S—— fell in love with a little actress with no attractions whatever, and made her his wife before God and man. Can not I, the virtuous Pauline, hope for similar good luck?"

In consequence of these reflections Pauline arranged her batteries.

Within the depths of her heart she cultivated—like a plant of mignonette in a box—one memorable souvenir.

One day they had been playing games at Monsieur Avérœf's. Three times Michel had chosen her for a partner; three times, too, had he redeemed his forfeit by kissing the hand of some lady, and it was the happy Pauline who had felt the light touch of the young officer's moustache on her white hand. From that moment she never ceased to dream of the hour which should make her Michel's wife.

In the meantime the young officer was at all the dinners, and at all the soireés at the Mélaguire mansion. After the rich dinner, inimitable dishes and exquisite wines, the door of the small salon, with its ivies and growing plants, was thrown open, and he enjoyed its cool freshness, and growing plants, and the sight of the calm, reserved Marthe, who rarely smiled, and never looked at him, but whose vicinity was to him like Paradise.

She poured out his coffee into an old china cup, and

placed it before him. For eighteen months she had not given it to him, as she discovered that her hand trembled, and then reseated herself near her tall ivy. The salon was full of guests coming and going. The clank of spurs, worn by the aid-de-camp, did not drown the music of Marthe's voice, as she kindly addressed some old friend of her father's. Michel could hear nothing else.

Sometimes he spoke to her himself. What did he say? Nothing—or almost nothing—some trivial question — a remark about the weather, or the opera. Marthe would reply almost in monosyllables, and then turn away to speak to some one else, but he lived on these monosyllables until the next dinner.

It was the privileged hour. Mademoiselle Hopfer arranged the silver, which operation took her a good half hour. When it was accomplished, she came to Marthe's side, who at once disappeared to see her little sister before she retired for the night, a duty she had never once omitted, since their mother's death. Michel extended his hand; she touched it as lightly as a bird flutters past a leaf; she lingered a second on the threshold of the door, under the heavy folds of crimson velvet, wherein she seemed almost buried. The train of her dress disappeared, the door closed, and Michel was recalled to earth by the voice of Pauline Vassilscova.

This young woman managed her attack with extraordinary prudence. With no idea of this passion —

a secret from all the world — she yet felt vaguely that there was some mystery she could not fathom. She was tender, and almost confidential in her manner. She asked after the health of Michel's parents; inquired about his friends, his horses, and his pursuits — for everything, in short, wherein he was interested. She liked to talk, also, of her former pupil, now become her friend, she said.

Her friend! Michel in his heart resented this appellation, and knew that it was not true, in the real sense of the word, but he attached little importance to this error of a vulgar nature, which dignifies intimacy with the name of friendship, and forced himself to listen with attention, when Pauline spoke of Marthe.

In winter, on sunny days, he met the two sisters in the *Jardin d'Eté*. He would wander up and down for an hour or two, waiting to catch a glimpse of Marthe's velvet robe and the aigrette in Nastia's fur cap, but he did not dare to meet them, and bow to them very often. If he had seen them the evening before, he went away without being seen, a little ache at his heart, but still comparatively happy.

"I know at least, they are well!" he would say to himself.

Pauline Vassilscova's lynx eye sometimes caught sight of him at the extremity of an alley.

"There goes Michel Avéroef again," she said one day. It absolutely looks as if he were running away from us. He does not wish, apparently, to take the trouble to bow to us. I shall tease him well about it to-morrow."

"By no means," said Marthe, in a tone of contained but intense irritation. "I forbid you to say one word to him about it."

"You forbid me!" replied the ex-governess, in amazement. "You forget yourself, Marthe."

"I consider it in extremely bad taste, to say the least, to attach to the acts of a young man such importance, that he shall see that he has been watched."

Pauline, wounded to the quick, became scarlet.

"But it was a mere jest, dear," she replied, gently.

"So much the better," answered Marthe, with that little bend of the head that closes a discussion; "but at the same time I wish you to understand, that I mean just what I said."

After this day Pauline watched her former pupil closely, to discover just what she thought of Avérœf. The most careful investigations were fruitless. Marthe was as impenetrable as the walls of Oriental mansions.

"Pshaw!" said Pauline to herself; "if she loved him she could not conceal it. She is only eighteen!"

And the companion recalled, not without a heightened color, the advances she had herself made at seventeen, to the eldest son of the rector in her native village. It was her failure there that caused her to dislike her compatriots.

Madame Avérœf's ball had reached that point where the young dancers, eager as they were for amusement, felt their eyes close in spite of themselves. At the end of a quadrille the governesses had approached the ball-room door, and stood together in a group, from which Pauline Vassilscova stood a trifle apart. The youthful cavaliers were scattered in couples up and down the long salon, where the windows had been opened, while the little girls had been hurried to the further end of the room by their mothers, who were afraid of the fresh air on their uncovered shoulders.

"What a beautiful youth!" said an old lady, whose hair had grown white in harness, and having brought up two generations, had earned the right to speak.

The young governesses colored. There were many ambitious hopes in that little circle. At this moment Michel Avéroef, laughing heartily, with his arm under that of his cousin Serge, stopped a few steps from this feminine group.

Pauline Vassilscova looked at him fixedly for a moment. He stood directly under a chandelier, whose light fell on the gold of his elegant uniform, and upon the dark waves of his close-cut, but rebellious hair—on his white teeth, which a fierce black moustache rendered more dazzling. Without intending it, he was almost insolent in appearance, so aggressive was his air of strength, his vital energy and manly beauty. Pauline grew dizzy, and her cheeks flushed. She raised her voice a trifle, and said, with flashing eyes, as if in reply to some exclamation uttered by the old lady:

"Indeed there is no cavalier in the world to be compared to Michel Avœf!"

Michel turned quickly, and looked at her with an air of inexpressible disdain. His lips were tightly compressed, and he dropped his cousin's arm, who, with the love of mischief characteristic of his eighteen years, bowed low before Pauline.

"And I!" he asked in a tone of mock humility.

"You are the worthy cousin of your cousin," said an old lady, laughing—"only he is modest, and you are not."

·Everybody laughed, Michel with the others, and Pauline more than any one else.

The windows were closed; the first measures of a mazourka were heard; the doors were thrown wide open, and the little girls flew about the grand salon like a swarm of butterflies scattered by a high wind. While the governesses beat a retreat to the blue salon, the old lady with white hair turned to Pauline and said in a whisper:

"My dear, you play for too high stakes—nor is it thus that you will captivate Michel Avœf."

Pauline turned quickly, with a stinging retort on her lips, but the old lady was already quietly conversing with a Swiss governess, whose pupil was the most undisciplined child in the world, and who bemoaned her fate in the most audible tones. Pauline therefore did not speak, but her eyes were vailed by a mist—like that which, in malarious coun-

tries, rises at sunset. She still stood leaning in the
door-way. The couples passed before her borne on
the stately movement of the mazourka; the spurs of
the young officers who had come with Michel, resounded
on the shining floor; the tiny boots of the little girls
performed with exquisite precisión the graceful steps of
this dance, which was certainly made for pretty feet
and short skirts. Emboldened by the rhythm, the
boys threw their left arms around their little bright-
eyed partners, and carried them off in triumph.

Serge Avéroef led the dance with Nastia Mélaguire,
and issued his commands with considerable energy,
while all the manœuvres were executed amid much
laughter.

A complicated figure brought a confused group
under the grand chandelier, from which the dancers
again flew off in couples. Michel passed Pauline, holding Marthe's hand, whom Madame Avéroef had
compelled to dance.

Marthe, with rosy cheeks and lowered lids, listened
to the words of the young man, whose triumphant face
looked as if he were ready to conquer the world with
her at his side.

"It is she!" said Pauline to herself, her heart con-
tracting as if in a vice. "He would crawl on the
ground for her — while for me — he has only disdain!"

A bitter smile contracted her thin lips, while she
watched Marthe, as she slowly turned around the room
in the arms of the young man before she returned to
her place.

Suddenly her features lost their contracted look —
her heart swelled. She felt the bliss of Paradise settle
down upon her soul; Michel looked at her — he came
toward her — toward her! "But I cannot dance!"
Must she say that to him?

"Pauline Vassilscova," said the young man, with an
amiable smile; "Marthe has forgotten her fan in the
ladies' dressing-room, will you kindly procure it for
her? I do not dare to profane that holy ground."

"How polite he is!" murmured the Swiss governess,
who agreed with a sign and a flattering murmur.

"Pauline received this blow full in her breast without winking. She turned deadly pale, but that was all.
With her usual smile on her lips she went to the
dressing-room, and returned with the fan in her hand.

"Thanks! Pauline Vassilscova — accept my apolo-
gies," and he rushed off through the crowd.

"A servant," thought Pauline, still standing in the
doorway—"a servant! Her *femme de chambre* — and
he loves her!"

The mazourka continued another hour, and she
remained to the last moment, to see whether the
accidents of the dance, again placed Marthe's hand
in that of Michel.

Mechanically she marked the measure with the
fingers of one hand, while on the wrist of the other,
her eyes followed the capricious windings of this
dance, while a merciless determination and an inexorable hatred strengthened in her soul — like those

gigantic Euphorbias of the Tropics, which grow up in a night, and develop in a few days, their enormous height and their implacable poison.

The weary children were asleep, and the last candles extinguished at Madame Avérœf's, but Pauline Hopfer was still buried in thought, sitting with her chin on her hand in her room on the second floor in the house of Monsieur Mélaguire. She had not yet discovered what kept Marthe and Michel apart, but she was sure of finding out some day.

With this determination she rose from her chair, and something rolled upon the floor from her lap, where it had lain forgotten in her long reverie. In looking for it she crushed it with her foot. It was a locket, which had been her mother's, and on which she set a high value.

Over-excitement and fatigue had strained her nerves excessively. She burst into tears and wept convulsively.

" This, too, I owe to her," she muttered, between her teeth; "she shall pay for all together."

Pauline slept on this noble resolution.

CHAPTER III.

A LESSON IN ETIQUETTE.

MICHEL AVÉRŒF went home, as if he trod on clouds. During the two hours that he had danced with Marthe their conversation, broken by the figures of the dance, were as constantly renewed. She divined his thoughts and finished his sentences, and mutual sympathy caused them to extend their hands eagerly to each other.

Michel had not spoken of love—Marthe had neither flushed nor trembled at any of his words, and yet he was sure—almost sure—of being loved.

His dreams were most extraordinary. He flew across the azure sky with Marthe, seated in a sleigh made of a young moon, and drawn by tiny clouds, vaguely suggestive of white sheep.

He awoke late. A brilliant April sun shone through a narrow opening in the curtains at his window. He rose hastily, hardly taking time to breakfast, and went out on foot, determined to bring a little order into his mind before he called on Monsieur Mélaguire to ask for his daughter's hand.

His thoughts pleased him, for he walked twice the whole length of the Serguievskaï before he decided to enter Marthe's home. But the day was growing old, and the young girl would be out if he did not hasten. He came to a final decision, therefore, and changed his irresolute walk for one of more decision.

The sight of a calèche drawn up before the door, threw him back into the midst of all his perplexities. The irreproachable elegance of the equipage, the magnificent pair of black trotting horses, and the superb coachman, known throughout St. Petersburg by his corpulency as well as by his thick beard, which fell nearly to his waist, proclaimed the name of the king of the *jeunesse doreé* of the city — the Prince Alexander Oghérof.

Two beautiful hounds, with long hair, of a very rare species, white as snow, lay on the cushions, with their delicate muzzles resting on their slender paws. They seemed accustomed to occupying this place in the absence of their master. Their half-closed eyes took little notice of the occasional passer-by.

"I will wait until that great idiot has gone!" said Michel, with some little irritation, and he strolled off again.

Of all his regimental comrades, Alexander Oghérof was certainly the last that he would have chosen as a confidant at this time, not that he had anything particularly against this brilliant young man, but because, as Madame Avércef said, with a laugh:—"He was lacking in consistency." He was always at the head of all the escapades of his regiment; always in search of new inventions, to vary the monotony of the same social pleasures and obligations. He seemed to have at last exhausted all his resources.

He had a hundred times come near being broken for infractions of discipline, but he was so good-natured amid all his follies, and was such a gay, delightful companion, that the most severe faces softened at his approach, and the frankness of his replies changed to laughter, the reproaches on the lips opened to utter them.

He was a thorough child, in spite of his twenty-eight years, whose plays had all the robust vigor of a young Titan. He was not bad in any way, and his proverbial generosity had given him the Mohican surname of The Open Hand—but, as Madame Avéroef said, he was lacking in consistency.

Just as Michel began to grow very impatient, a neighing and prancing of horses, indicated that the Prince had emerged from Monsieur Mélaguire's, and he hastily turned his steps. As he reached the door, Oghérof, who had taken his seat in his calèche, called to him in a loud voice:

"Avéroef, come here!"

Michel in his heart vituperating the Prince, nevertheless obeyed, but his manner was serious, in order to discourage any trifling conversation.

"What a face!" said Oghérof, with a laugh. "You have made a mistake, my friend, Lent is over. Are you going to call at the Mélaguire's?"

"Yes."

"Take my advice and stay away. You have no idea to what you expose yourself. He is in a most ferocious humor—he will tell you his whole history. Come with me; I can tell it to you quite as well as he, and in an infinitely more amusing manner."

"But I wish to see him on business."

"Then you have chosen a most unfortunate time," answered Oghérof, with a shrug of his shoulders, "for he is furious against his niece Sophie, who has forgotten to ask his consent to her marriage."

"To her marriage?"

"Yes, precisely—but come in here—"

"No; there is no room!" said Michel, in a morose tone, as he looked at the hounds.

"This amiable couple will give up their places," answered the Prince, who, with a gesture, made the dogs jump down. "We will take a drive, and I will talk to you—I need some one in my turn, for I have been listening for a full hour."

"If he is furious," said Michel, to himself, "the moment certainly is not propitious," and he took a seat by Oghérof.

"To the *Perspective*, by *le Quai de la Cour*," said the Prince to his coachman.

The calèche rolled off, the dogs bounding in front— the horses going at their long, swinging trot, and the brilliant equipage passed down the almost deserted street, frequented only by the aristocracy at the fashionable hours of the day.

"Well, then," said Oghérof, extending his lazy length, "this is what has happened: Sophie Chére-kof, the daughter of Mélaguire's own sister, was conquered by the fascinations of Constantin Leakhive ——"

"That young idiot," interrupted Michel.

"Sophie pretends that he is idiotic only through timidity, and she undertakes to correct this fault. Both assertions seem to be susceptible of doubt, but this at least is certain, the young couple deemed it prudent to come to an understanding between themselves, before they asked for a blessing from their parents. They "exchanged oaths," after which they informed their respective families of their praiseworthy intentions.

"Old Leakhive, who is as deaf as a post, thought it quite natural that his only and worshipped son should be reluctant to take an ear-trumpet to impart a delicate secret; Monsieur and Madame Chérekof, who are good souls, shed each a tear and blessed their children. But when Monsieur Mélaguire learned of the approaching marriage, and at the same time all these details, he was furiously angry—

"He! Why he is the most gentle of men—"

"Precisely: angry then, as a lamb can ever be, my dear! He declared that it was an absolute perversion of good manners; that the consent of parents should first be asked—that, at least, is due to them. He predicted to Sophie that her own children—those who should be born of this marriage, would fail some day in respect to her; that this union was arranged contrary to all the *convénances*, and finally declared that he should not give his consent."

"But, my uncle, I have not asked for it!" said Sophie, most imprudently.

"The deuce she did!" said Michel.

"You may easily imagine what followed. He called Sophie by all sorts of hard names, and went away vowing that he would never see her again, adding that if one of his own daughters had behaved in the same manner, he would give her his malediction!"

"The deuce he did!" repeated Avérœf, in his heart blessing the man who had prevented him from appearing before Marthe's father, without due caution and the support of his parents' consent.

"What does Sophie Chérekof say?"

"She laughs, like the good - natured soul she is, and declares she will dance the *gavotte* with her uncle on her wedding-day, and she is clever enough to keep her word!"

"All will be happily settled, unqestionably," answered Michel, absently; "but who would ever have imagined Mélaguire to be such a stickler for etiquette."

"An indignant merino, as I told you before! But did you ever see such a pace as these animals keep up! They are well worth the price I paid for them, and I do not regret it."

"How much did you pay?"

"Three thousand, five hundred roubles, and they are well worth it."

"Yes, they go well; but what is your idea of always

taking the same road going and coming? Aren't you tired of this poor *Perspective?* Can't you find another drive as a change?"

"Yes; but don't you know that at this season of the year, and at this hour of the afternoon, my horses would be dishonored if they were seen elsewhere?"

"Is that so? I, for one, have had quite enough of your *Perspective.* Besides, your dogs must be fatigued — they are not accustomed to going on foot. Drop me anywhere."

"Where are you going?"

"Oh! only to take a turn as far as *La Morskaï,* and then to see Flora. Will you go there with me?"

"To see the actress who has the name of a dog and the face of a cat? Not I. Many thanks, but I must go to my rooms—I have some writing to do."

"As you will, my dear fellow."

The calèche drew up, and Michel jumped out. At a sign from Oghérof the hounds took his place. He stood for a moment looking after the superb horses, the white heads of the two dogs, and the indolent, elegant figure of the young man wrapped in his military overcoat.

"Can it be," thought Michel, that a man of sense —. for after all he has some—can live thus, with dogs, horses, and actresses, without asking anything better? However, if he finds his happiness in these, let him have it!" and with some sadness he took the way to his rooms.

3

CHAPTER IV.

MATRIMONIAL PROJECTS.

MICHEL had been seated at his desk with his letter-paper spread out before him, for more than half an hour, but his ideas would not flow freely.

In fact, how could he put on two or three sheets of paper all the graces and the charms of Marthe, as well as the history of his love for her. Then there was also the practical side of the union to be considered; the social position of the Mèlaguires; their wealth and the consideration they enjoyed—things to which he was absolutely indifferent, but in regard to which his father should be informed.

Nothing seemed easier than to write to his father to ask his consent to a marriage, which was certain to be satisfactory in every particular, but it is quite another thing when one tries to write such a letter, and to make it agreeable to the persons who hold your fate in their hands.

General Nicholas Avéroef for at least ten years had not lived in Saint Petersburg, but was elsewhere occupied with the duties of his service. He came every eighteen months to see his son for a brief period, and then departed without having seen other people, except in a whirl of dinners and entertainments.

"When one comes from the country for a fortnight," said the General, gayly; "one certainly does not sit in front of the fire all the time."

Michel, therefore, had to begin at the beginning, so to speak. It was difficult enough to arrange the order of his explanations, but to raise the mysterious vail which had hitherto hidden his love for Marthe—to pronounce that sacred name and take another person into his confidence, even his father, was an unendurable thought.

But it must be done, nevertheless, and he took up his pen and wrote at the top of the page:

"My dear and honored father."

Then he laid down the pen, and threw himself back in his chair, and regarding the whole matter as accomplished, he abandoned himself to sweet dreams of the Future.

Amid his projects a vague recollection of a time comparatively distant, brought a melancholy shadow to his brow. He remembered how ten years before, his brother, then twenty-one, wished to marry, and how he, too, had written a similar letter to their father.

He recalled the eagerly expected response; the joy of his brother, and the terrible shock that had followed this joy, when the young girl from some inexplicable caprice broke the engagement at the end of a week, declaring that she would die sooner than become the wife of Paul Avérœf.

What had happened? Paul always said he did not

know; the young lady had given no explanations, and the family were obliged to yield to her determination—Paul quietly withdrew. For a long time Michel remembered him as morose, and refusing to touch on this sad subject; then by degrees the young man softened — he resumed his usual occupations—his tastes, which had always led him to a quiet life, were now quieter still, and since then he never spoke of marrying.

Michel thought of all this, and regretted sincerely that his brother was away. To his discretion and sympathy he would not have hesitated to confide the fulness of his heart. He was tempted to write to him.

"No," he said to himself, "I will not write him now. After a little we may take our bridal journey, and we will go to Mentone, and spend a month with Paul!"

When Michel had arrived at this conclusion, the clock struck the hour of midnight. He was obliged to be on duty at an early hour. He placed in a drawer with the greatest care the paper which bore the heading, "My dear and honored father," and went to bed enchanted at his evening.

The next day brought him two letters, one of which was from his brother :—

"I am better," Paul wrote, "much better; my neuralgia has almost disappeared. I am going to Biarritz for sea-bathing when summer comes, but the doctor has positively forbidden me to return to Russia, until winter is positively established. He thinks the dampness of autumn will bring back all my sufferings. We have, therefore, seven or eight months of separation before us, which I trust, dear Michel, you will do your best to abridge by writing me often."

Michel smiled as the thought went through his mind, that their separation might not be as long as his brother fancied.

"How he will love Marthe," he said, as he broke the seal of the second letter, which was from his father. "His command was changed, and his duties called him to St. Petersburg on the fifteenth of June, but he was to have a long leave, and should have ample time to enjoy his son's society, as well as the social pleasures which would be afforded by the season of the year."

This letter caused Michel to reflect deeply. It was now the middle of April, only two months before his mother would be with him, and these two months would be occupied by the General in a tour of inspection, and would be in no one place twenty-four hours at a time. Was it advisable to lay before him this matrimonial project, at a time when fatigued and harassed by business and constant travelling, the General tore open his letters and read them hurriedly?

Would he, under these circumstances, find time to appreciate his son's descriptions of Mademoiselle Mélaguire's charms?

It was not, moreover, at all agreeable to Michel that the image of his *fiancée* should be confounded in his father's mind with admonitions to the Quartermasters, and remarks on the soup served to the soldiers.

Everything taken into consideration, Michel decided to wait. He was reluctant, moreover, to break the vague tie which united them almost without their knowledge, and was delighted at having a satisfactory excuse for not allowing their names to become public property for some little time longer. But in deciding not to say anything as yet to Monsieur Mélaguire, he by no means came to the same decision in regard to Marthe.

"I shall certainly allow her to see that I love her, and I mean to compel her to look me in the face some day while I tell her so."

And at the thought that Marthe's deep eyes would read in the depths of his heart the ardent passion he had inspired, he felt his whole being invaded with a delicious ecstacy.

Since the death of his wife Monsieur Mélaguire passed his summers near the city, in a sumptuous villa, which he had leased for two years at Kamenroï Ostron, and this fact singularly favored the young man's plans.

Kept in camp by his duties, he could, nevertheless, during the summer, escape every Sunday, and sometimes during the week, and until then he could walk every evening at the *Isles* and pass the Mélaguire villa by accident, and thus be invited to tea. If the father were busy or vexed, he could walk in the garden with the daughters. In this way he would see Marthe daily. These preliminaries of marriage are so poetic and so sweet, that to many a pair, marriage itself has been far from keeping their promise. Full of these ideas he started forth to pay a visit to Monsieur Mélaguire, that he might thus strengthen their kindly relations. Fearing that in spite of himself, his hopes and wishes might appear on his countenance, he did his best to affect indifference, which imparted a most unnatural air to his whole manner.

It was with this comically serious aspect that he strolled along, when he saw coming toward him the pretty Sophie Chérekof, the victim—or, rather, the instigator of the pacific Mélaguire's anger.

The fresh face of the girl expressed frankness and courage — the joy of loving, and of being beloved — a firm resolution to enjoy all this happiness, as long as she possibly could, and in addition, an unalterable good humor, which had always been one of her greatest charms.

Perceiving Avérœf, she stopped and extended her hand—

"You see," she said, "that I am at last regarded as a woman grown, and allowed to go out alone. Mamma now permits me to go twenty feet without a servant!"

"I congratulate you, Sophie! You are to be married, I hear?"

"Yes; and you?"

Michel colored, and hastily answered with so much energy in the negative, that Sophie looked at him earnestly.

"Your face looks like it, though!" she said, shaking

her finger at him. "Adieu! If mamma should know that I stand and talk with young men in the street, two servants, at least, would be my fate!"

She walked away with a firm step. Michel turned to look at her.

"How happiness changes people," he said to himself. "The other day she was a young girl — like all the others—to-day she has all the *aplomb* of a woman of the world. She looks neither to the right nor to the left—she is entirely at her ease, and has but one aim in life!"

As he sang in his heart this little hymn in praise of marriage, Michel was running lightly up the staircase at the Mélaguires. He was announced, and received in the small salon where Marthe sat at her embroidery with Pauline Hopfer.

"My father will be here presently," said the young lady. "He is occupied just at this moment. Take a chair, will you?"

At the sound of this calm, even voice, Michel's hopes fell prone upon the ground. Pauline's face also was enough to dispirit him. It was she who wished to receive the young man. Marthe thought it best to say simply that her father was engaged, but Pauline gained her point. She had, moreover, an especial purpose in view, she wished to efface the disastrous impression she had made the evening before at the children's ball.

Alas! she took a deal of useless trouble. Michel did not even remember it. Fortunately, Pauline was not aware of this cutting contempt, or she would have been less willing to forgive the rest!

They chatted for a while, of the children and the ball; of the weather and of Prince Oghérof's hounds, and of Sophie Chérekof's marriage.

"I have just met her," said Michel.

"Yes, she has just been here," answered Marthe. "Papa will not see her any more, but she says that is no reason why she and I should not see each other, and she remained an hour or more."

"What does your father say to that?"

"He does not know it," interposed Pauline, slyly.

"But I shall tell him," answered the young lady, calmly. "He, of course, must be informed; besides, his anger never lasts. He loves Sophie very dearly, and is perfectly aware that she prefers him to all her uncles."

"Then," Michel ventured to say without daring however, to look at Marthe: "Then, why is it that he is so vexed at an infraction of ordinary rules, which—"

"Which do not concern him?" finished Marthe, with a faint smile, as she turned her eyes to the young man.

But she dopped them again on meeting a look which hushed the words on her lips. Presently, with a great effort, she continued in a very low tone.

"My father is a great upholder of old customs. He wishes me to address him in the third person, as showing the respect which should exist in a child to a parent, and says he never spoke to his parents in that way."

"Then, why," began the young man, "merely because he felt the necessity of saying something."

"My sister always says *you*. But since my mother's death, he says that I am like her; my voice — "

She colored and became silent.

Pauline looked at the two with a sarcastic smile.

" That is quite a lover-like idea ! " said the Governess.

" You are unfortunate to-day, Mademoiselle," Marthe answered, coldly, using the German language. " You are wanting in respect to my father, after having insinuated that I am deceiving him."

The thrust was a sharp one. Pauline started up, took the keys from a basket before her; and left the room.

Michel rose at the same moment to take leave; the slightest possible movement from Marthe detained him. It was not a look, nor yet a sign, and still less an invitation, and yet he seated himself again.

" Mademoiselle Anastasie is well I trust? " he said, presently.

Marthe drew a breath of relief, she had feared something else, and began to speak of her sister, with feverish haste. The conversation became quite animated, and Pauline, who was listening behind the portière, could not refrain from stamping with anger. When Monsieur Mélaguire entered ten minutes later, he found the young people laughing at the mistakes in one of Nastia's copy-books, forgotten among the albums of the salon.

"That child will never learn orthography," said Monsieur Mélaguire with a sigh. "How are you, Avérœf?"

"Very well, thank you, Sir, and you?"

"I? Oh I have had much to annoy me, lately. An especial annoyance, young man! You will dine with us, I hope?"

Michel refused, much against his will, on the score of regimental duties.

"Papa," said Marthe suddenly, "Sophie was here this morning."

"Here? In my house, do you mean?" asked Monsieur Mélaguire, slowly.

"Yes, papa."

"And you received her?"

"Yes, papa."

"And did you think I would permit it? What did she say?" And Monsieur Mélaguire dropped upon the sofa, which uttered a creak of expostulation.

"She said she loved you with all her heart, that she wanted your benediction, that she hoped to see you at the dinner given in honor of her engagement, which would be the day after to-morrow, and that she should never forgive herself, for having made so much difficulty."

"That proves at all events, that she recognizes the fact that she has been in error. We will see — we will see — I won't say yet — "

"Dear father! say now — this minute, that you will forgive her, and I will send for her instantly."

"No indeed!   Not yet."

"For my sake," said Marthe coaxingly, with her face close to her father's.   He looked at her tenderly for a moment, and then taking her head between both his hands, he kissed her over and over again.

"So be it, then!" he said, as Marthe rang the bell. "I forgive her because you ask it, and because it is she, but, had you done what she did, I would never forgive you."

Michel turned pale; this allusion to Marthe's possible marriage disturbed him strangely.   He looked from the father to the daughter.   Their faces expressed nothing in particular; Marthe colored slightly, as she wrote a few words with a pencil on a card.

"Take this to Sophie Chérekof," she said to the servant, when he appeared.

If Monsieur Mélaguire did not dance the *gavotte* at the wedding of his niece, it was only because she forgot to insist upon it.

CHAPTER VII.

DISCOVERIES AND CHANGES.

TIME slipped away. The May Parade took place in the most magnificent weather. The ice on Lake Ladoga had floated away into the Baltic. St. Petersburg was very warm, and hardly habitable. Michel expected his father in a month. Monsieur Mélaguire talked each day of moving to his villa on the next, and as his circle was daily decreased by people leaving the city, he directed his courtesies more especially to those young men whose duties condemned them to remain in St. Petersburg. Two or three attachés to the various ministrys, some officers of the Guards; among them, Michel and Prince Oghérof, dined with him almost daily.

Marthe and Michel had fallen into a sort of tacit understanding. Their intimacy was not in any degree, noticeable. The young men, who appeared daily, were apparently on the same footing of polite familiarity; but a chair was nearly always vacant at the side of the girl, when the young officer approached; and when visitors left, Michel was always the last to go, and Marthe gave to no other person, the hand he had touched.

One evening, as Avéroef entered the salon, where

all the furniture was draped in white, he saw Marthe coming toward him, in the demi-obscurity. The dining-room next was full of light and noise, and this great, cool, quiet room seemed, by contrast, peopled by phantoms. Marthe, herself in her robe of pale gray, looked like a floating shadow. When she recognized Michel, she advanced with more confidence.

"We are going to-morrow," she said; "the day after, is my birthday, and papa wishes to have a housewarming at Kamenori. You will come?"

"Most assuredly," he answered, as he extended his hand.

They were alone. In the dining-room no one was thinking of them. How many times had Michel longed for this moment of solitude, without being able to obtain it. He held her hand for a moment.

"Marthe Palovna," he said, in a low voice, "I hope —"

A slight noise interrupted him. He looked around, but saw no one.

"I will ask you, and you will tell me —"

"We are watched!" said Marthe, suddenly, loudly enough to be heard in each corner of the room.

This "we" was a confession — at all events, so Marthe seemed to consider it, for she tore her hand from Michel's, and turned away, as if to conceal her face from his eyes.

"Thanks!" he murmured, so softly, that only she, could hear him.

When she reached the door of the dining-room, emboldened by the noise and the lights, she turned, and looked Michel full in the face. Intoxicated with joy the young man read in those soft, velvet eyes that he was beloved.

The evening passed as in a dream. On leaving, he pressed Marthe's hand, no more as a friend, but as one who has a secret to tell, and the girl's slender fingers faintly returned the pressure.

"In twenty-eight days," he said, half aloud, as he laid his head on the pillow; "twenty-eight days — that is not so very long!"

The next day, on awakening, Michel received a letter and a telegram. The telegram was signed Paul Avércef; dated Mentone, and contained only five words:

"Do not lose one minute."

Much startled, Michel opened the letter, which was also from his brother, and dated three days before the telegram.

"MY DEAR BROTHER:" it began,—"your friendship alone can spare me the keenest pain, and the most cruel remorse of my whole life. I, therefore, do not hesitate to ask of you a great service. But let me first explain: Eight years ago — two years after the unhappy rupture of my marriage, I made the acquaintance of a young girl, who was all that I could desire as a wife. One thing only was against her, and that was her birth. She was the illegitimate daughter of a Prince K——, who, however, had educated her in the most careful manner. I had not courage to brave public opinion, and marry her. Perhaps the rupture of my marriage counted for something in this repugnance, for I did not wish people to see in this a *pis-aller*. Condemn me if you will, you are in the right; but spare me your reproaches, for I am well punished. She was irreproachable in her conduct toward me; while, as a mother,—for she bore me a little girl, three years ago—she was no less perfect. She was, I say, for I have just learned of her death, last month, by the rupture of an aneurism. The people with whom she lodged took care not to send me this information—they appropriated every thing that she possessed, and I learned it by accident. My poor little girl is in absolute destitution, badly-fed, hardly-clothed, and beaten, Michel. This child of my flesh and blood, is beaten, through my fault, and I am a wretch, unworthy of being a father!

"I shall not dwell on the grief I feel, at the death of the woman whom I would now, at the price of all I hold most dear, call my wife. I will speak only of the child, as the mother is beyond all pain. As soon as this letter reaches you, apply for leave; say that I am very ill—dying if you will—and you will not speak falsely, for so much sorrow has brought me very low.

Go to Rue——. No.——; take the child, whose name is Marie—our dead mother's name—engage a Governess, who will bring the child at once to Mentone; but do you not leave her yourself, but come with her, and bring me all that is left of my past happiness. If any misfortune overtakes the child, I shall feel that I am rightly punished by High Heaven, and I shall die, devoured by remorse!"

A check to a large amount accompanied this letter - "that all obstacles might be removed," added Paul Avéroef.

As Michel read this letter, it seemed to him that he must be dreaming. Was it possible that his brother, so steady, so grave, could have a daughter three years old, and that he, Michel, a Lieutenant of the Horse Guards, was commanded to take this child to her father—to engage a Governess, and buy clothes for a child that was nearly naked. His head grew dizzy; he heard the whistle of a locomotive, and the leave—the passport, and the Governess, must be procured in twenty-four hours, and Marthe was expecting him the next day.

He dropped into a chair, utterly discouraged; but started up again presently—went to see his Colonel, to ask for leave, for this, of course, was the first step.

The leave was obtained without difficulty, for Michel was the best officer in his regiment. That portion of his mission, which concerned the child, was less easy to fulfill. The people who had taken her since her

4

mother's death, made many difficulties, when they saw this brilliant officer. Michel was driven to threats, and talked of the police. This settled the affair. He lifted the child all in tears, and placed her in a carriage, which he found with difficulty. He drove then to a succession of shops, where the child was dressed from head to foot. This took a great deal of time. It was four in the afternoon, when Michel realized that he had no governess for the little niece, which Heaven had sent him so inopportunely.

A bright idea came to him. He could, in going to take leave of Marthe, ask her for some *protégée*, some maid who would take care of the child on the journey. Marthe, in fact, was one of the Lady Patronesses of an establishment for young girls, who were without means.

He hurried to Monsieur Mélaguire. The steps and sidewalk were covered with straw and paper. He rushed up the stairs without seeing a human being, but coming down again, in despair, he found himself face to face with Pauline Hopfer.

"Ah!" he cried in a tone of heartfelt joy, "I have found you, then! Where is Monsieur Mélaguire."

"Monsieur Mélaguire and his daughters, left two hours ago for their country house. But you knew this, Monsieur Michel, and you dine with us, to-morrow, if I am not mistaken."

"No," answered Michel, piteously; "I cannot, I am about to take a long journey."

"A long journey?" repeated Pauline, in consternation, "and shall you be gone any length of time?"

"No, I shall be back in a fortnight. And they are gone?" he repeated.

"Yes, and I am to follow at once. The carriage is to be sent back for me," answered Pauline, coldly; "is it not at the door now?"

"No," said Michel, absently. Then, all at once, he added:

"Do you know of a governess?"

"A governess," she repeated, more and more astonished. She wondered vaguely, if Michel were in his right mind.

"Yes, a governess or a nurse; it is the same thing," said Michel, innocently.

"It is the same thing," repeated the irascible young lady to herself. "You shall pay for that, young man! No sir, I know of neither governess nor nurse. What is the nurse to do?"

"Take care of a little girl," said Michel.

He felt all at once that appearances were against him, and that this child in his guardianship was certainly very singular. He knew, moreover, that Pauline's discretion could not be relied on like Marthe's.

"An orphan," he added, slowly.

"Wait a moment; yes I do know some one," exclaimed Pauline, struck in her turn by a bright thought. "What do you give as salary?"

"I don't know, I am sure," answered poor Michel, taken aback. "What is usual under such circumstances?"

"Four hundred roubles, and travelling expenses back, if not content.   Where to go?"

"To the neighborhood of Nice."

"A charming place.   How old is the child?"

"Three years," answered Michel, with some reluctance.   He felt as if he were walking into a trap with his eyes open.

Wait a moment for me, here," continued Pauline, "and I will see if I can persuade the person who, I think, will be exactly suited for you."

Michel seated himself despairingly, in the deserted salon, where the image of Marthe refused to come to him.

The state in which he had found the child, the expression of the coachman's face, when he placed her in all her rags in the carriage; the interchange of looks between his servants, when they saw her appear with him; the question of his old nurse, who officiated as cook, "Good Lord! where did you get her?" all these details haunted him with most unpleasant persistency.

In his feverish haste, and with too much natural honesty to think of the wrong side of things, he had not dreamed of surrounding his movements with any secrecy.   He might have hidden the child — or, at all events, he might have refrained from speaking of her, particularly to this German woman, whom he vaguely distrusted.   But the evil was done.

But, after all, it might be as well.   Pauline kept him waiting nearly an hour, and then, accompanied by a middle-aged woman with a sulky air, who was presented as "Mamselle ——," and "capable of bringing up, more than one child."

"Very well," said Michel, struck by this phrase. "Never mind the rest. Are you ready to leave to-morrow?"

"If you can take me on your passport, sir," was the reply.

"Then that is settled," said Michel, enchanted at seeing this last difficulty disappear. "We will start to-morrow."

"Very well, sir; am I to sleep in your house?"

"Well, no," answered Michel. "I have no place for you. You must be there at eight o'clock, however." Then turning to Pauline, he said: "Will you kindly say to Mademoiselle—to Monsieur Mélaguire, I would say—But no, you need say nothing; I will go to-night, after dinner, and make my own excuses for my hurried departure. I thank you with all my heart, for the trouble you have taken on my account. I really hardly know how to express my gratitude."

"You must come and thank me on your return," said Pauline, graciously, as he left her. Then returning to the woman who stood in the centre of the salon:

"Listen to me, Marguerite," she said. "You, of course, understand, that I have not taken you from your kitchen, and obtained for you four hundred roubles per annum, instead of the hundred and twenty you have hitherto had, merely for the pleasure of doing you a service. You will write me just what takes place."

"I do not know how to spell very well," said the ex-cook, just promoted to a superior grade.

" Write as well, spell as well, as you can, and do not economize on postage. Wait, I will give you some envelopes already directed, that your writing may not attract attention from those — well! from those whose business it is not."

" You think then, that the little girl is this young gentleman's child, do you, Mademoiselle Pauline?"

" No, I think nothing at all, and that least of all. If she were his child, he would not be so stupid!" murmured Pauline, with irreverence toward her former idol.

"And now, what must I do?" said Marguerite.

" You must dine somewhere, and keep your tongue between your teeth," answered her protectress, giving her a rouble.

CHAPTER VI.

S U S P E N S E.

WHEN he returned to his rooms for dinner, Michel found the child seated on the floor in the corner, with her hands hanging loosely, and in a state bordering on imbecility. It was easy to see that she had not been spoiled by over-indulgence since her mother's death.

"She has been just like that ever since you left," said the old servant when he questioned her. "Is she going to remain here?" she added.

"No, indeed," said Michel, with a long sigh of satisfaction. "We are going far away to-morrow."

"Far away? Holy Virgin! And you, too? But your linen is not ready. Why did you not tell me?"

"I shall go without linen," answered Michel, with some impatience. "Let us have dinner."

The child ate little. Her heart was very full, and her eyes heavy with sleep.

"But, where am I to put her!" said the old servant, utterly demoralized. "There is no place."

"Let her sleep with you," answered Michel, equally disturbed.

"With me, in the kitchen! What are you thinking of sir? She is a gentleman's child," and she looked at Michel, interrogatively.

"Well, then! put her on the sofa in the salon."

"But, she will roll off."

"Heavens and earth! put a chair in front of her, twelve chairs, if you choose, only let me alone!" answered the young man, impatiently.

When he had finished dressing to go to Kamenroï Ostron, he left his room; the salon was lighted by a single candle, held by the old woman standing at the foot of the divan, where the child was sleeping. Her brown hair and long lashes, gave her an older look than her years. The mouth and chin, betrayed her paternal origin clearly and distinctly.

"She is pretty," said Michel, looking at her with compassion; "poor little thing!"

"She is an Avérœf," answered the old woman, in a low voice. "She is your very picture at your age."

Michel drew back in horror.

"What!" he said; "do you think——"

"No, sir; I do not think that she belongs to you. Paul Nicolaïtch is her father, I am sure. I always thought there was something; and then his old coachman, the one that he sent away four years ago, talked about a young woman——"

"She is dead," interrupted Michel, in a low voice.

The servant did not speak for a moment. The child was asleep, but her sleep was as sad and agitated as had been her waking hours. She had wept silently while they thought her soundly sleeping, and the trace of a shining tear was on her cheek.

"Poor little soul!" murmured the old woman, her maternal instinct deeply aroused. "To think that at her age she should know what trouble is. Sleep! poor child, we will not make you shed a tear!"

She pushed the chairs close to the edge of the sofa, arranged the coverings, and as Michel went out, she made the sign of the Cross over the child, whose mother was not there to bless her.

The road seemed very long to Michel. There was a great deal of dust and many carriages. His horse, fatigued by his long excursions in the morning, would not move very rapidly. He became frightfully impatient. These fifteen days would be interminable. How would Marthe regard his absence? What would she think of during this long interval?

"I shall have time for a brief word of explanation, and she will have confidence in me, for the rest," he said, by way of consolation.

As he approached the villa, Michel saw three or four carriages at the door. No time had been lost by the neighbors, in coming to pay their respects cordially.

As he entered, Michel heard a gay laugh, followed in quick succession by others.

Nastia's shrill tones and the monotonous bass of Monsieur Mélaguire, mingled with the general uproar.

Seeing no one to announce him, Michel decided to enter, and found himself opposite a large bay horse!

Oghérof had arrived ten minutes previously, and had been very anxious to show his mount to Marthe, who had refused to come out on the balcony, alleging that her dress was tumbled and dusty.

"Nevertheless you shall see him!" cried Oghérof, dashing down the stairs again.

Five minutes later he was back again, holding by the bridle his horse, which without difficulty had mounted the four or five steps from the garden to the balcony.

The noble animal, although a little frightened by the lights and the voices, made a very dignified appearance.

"Bow to the company!" cried Oghérof, just as Michel appeared upon the scene, and the horse lifted the right foot and inclined his beautiful slender head several times.

Michel reached toward the master of the house, who was purple from laughing. Everybody was amused, for the dignified countenances of the town had yielded to the *lesser alles* of the country. Of course Oghérof would never have been guilty of such an escapade in a St. Petersburg salon, but at *The Isles* it was altogether different.

"Now," said a young officer, "you have got him up, the next thing is to get him down."

"For," added Marthe, still laughing; "handsome as he is, he can't spend his days here," and as she spoke she smoothed the animal's head, he looking at her with friendly, intelligent eyes.

"You will see," answered Ogherof. "Mademoiselle Marthe, have you a bit of sugar?"

As the young girl turned, she found herself face to face with Michel, whom she had not before seen. She stifled an exclamation of surprise.

"You here, Monsieur Michel!" she said, with a slight blush.

"Yes, Mademoiselle; I have many things to say to you. I shall not be able to come to-morrow."

"How is that?" asked the girl, coldly. "I thought you accepted the invitation."

"I certainly did—but listen to me a moment. Marthe Parlovna, a matter of serious importance—"

The horse reared a little.

"Marthe," cried Monsieur Mélaguire; "pray bring the sugar, unless you wish this creature to eat us."

"In one moment," Marthe replied, and then added, as she turned away: "I will be back in a few moments, Monsieur Michel, and you will continue your explanations," and she disappeared.

"Ladies and gentlemen, my horse is more intelligent than a human being: he will not eat this sugar except from the whitest, and most delicate hand in this assembly. Watch him, and see if he does not show his wisdom."

Amid the laughter of all the spectators, he ordered the sugar to be offered the animal, first by a young officer, by Nastia, by Mademoiselle Pauline, by Monsieur Mélaguire, and finally by Mademoiselle Marthe, from whom the horse accepted that which he had refused to all others.

The applause was deafening. Monsieur Mélaguire fairly rolled on the sofa in paroxysms of laughter.

"And now, my good fellow, it is time for you to go," said Oghérof to his horse, who was pawing the floor with impatience. "Mademoiselle Marthe, which way shall he depart—through the door or the window?"

"Whichever you please, Prince, provided there is no danger," answered Marthe, a little gravely.

She was unaccustomed to such public homage, and was ignorant, let us here say, of the fact that the poor animal was accustomed to this exercise, and had often performed the same feat for one or the other of the actresses whom the Prince affected.

"Danger!" repeated Oghérof; "Oh! there is no danger. You prefer the door?"

"Yes, certainly," answered Marthe, a little confused.

"All right!" said Oghérof, gaily, and he leaped upon his horse.

Marthe could not restrain a light cry, on seeing the handsome creature curvet over the waxed floor, urged and excited by his rider. They both passed through the door, which was scarce high enough; crossed the ante-room, and reached the balcony, where Oghérof drew up his steed at the first step.

"Attention!" he said to the animal, patting his neck kindly as he spoke; "look at what you are doing, and be careful."

Then gathering his reins together, he made a little salutation to Marthe, who was anxiously watching him.

"Wish me good luck, Mademoiselle," he said, half in jest and half in earnest.

"You are not going to jump," cried the girl, in terror.

."You desired it, Mademoiselle. Anything for the ladies. Hurra!" he cried, raising his horse.

A general outcry followed this movement.

Marthe pressed her hands upon her eyes. When she took them down Alexander Oghérof was trotting quietly over the greensward, and answering with smiles, the congratulations he received.

Michel could not exchange a word with Marthe all the evening. Oghérof's escapade had imparted a certain feverish excitement to the atmosphere. Never had such constant or such loud laughter been heard in the villa.

The clock struck eleven. Michel knew that his trunk was yet unpacked; that he had nothing ready for his journey of the next day, and also that he had yet to go to the banker's and cash his brother's check, but he could not make up his mind to beat a retreat without giving to Marthe some plausible reason for his departure. But how was he to speak seriously among all these simpletons? He would have preferred also to see Oghérof fairly off, for the Prince had shown considerable devotion to Marthe, and contrived to absorb her attention. Michel saw that he must, however, abandon his intention, and he determined to address Monsieur Mélaguire:

"I came to offer my excuses," he said to his host; "for I shall not be able to drive with you to-morrow."

"But to-morrow is Marthe's birth-day," cried the good man. "Oghérof has promised us some fireworks."

"I am compelled to leave for Italy at once," said the young man, very gravely. "My brother is very ill and has telegraphed for me. I shall be back in a fortnight."

"Your brother is worse, then? It is very sad," and Mélaguire became serious at once. "Is there any danger?"

"No," Michel hastened to reply; "there is no danger, but Paul is very anxious to see me. "He wishes to see me on business," he added, with some embarrassment.

"Go, then, my young friend, only before you leave let me advise you to make your peace with my daughter. She never likes any one to break an engagement."

"With your permission," stammered the young man, enchanted at finding so good an excuse for speaking to Marthe in private. He went in search of the young girl, whom he found in the dining-room. The servants were preparing an improvised supper.

"Mademoiselle," he said.

She turned and looked him full in the face.

"Mademoiselle," he repeated, "believe me, I pray you, when I tell you that it is not for my own pleasure that I go away to-morrow—"

"Then you are going?" she answered, with a persistency of which she vaguely felt the injustice.

"I must leave for Italy to-morrow. I am summoned by my brother, who needs me on a matter of business. He has had a relapse, also," he added, after a second's hesitation.

"Is he dangerously ill?"

"No," said Michel, with a vague regret that he could not answer yes.

"Wait until the next day——"

"I cannot."

"Not even when I ask you?" said Marthe, involuntarily extending her hand, as if to lay it on the young man's arm.

She was in a strange state of mind. She was tempted to urge him, while at the same time she was deeply wounded by the obstinacy of his refusal on, as it seemed to her, such insufficient motives. Michel was silent, but his eyes spoke volumes.

"You are going alone," she resumed. "You have no travelling companion?"

"No; but——"

"Well, then, you can, I am sure——"

"Forgive me, I entreat you. In a fortnight I will explain."

"I have no right either to ask, or to accept explanations," answered Marthe, with some haughtiness, annoyed, probably, at having asked so much.

"If you knew——"

"I know that I have urged you to remain twenty-four hours to assist at my fête, and that you have refused, although your brother's health does not demand such haste.

"Marthe Parlovna!" cried the young man, in despair, "to please you! I would give my very life. I would do far more valiant deeds than this mad Oghérof, but I cannot stay. I will tell you all——"

Marthe turned slowly away. Pauline had entered the room. Her eyes of hate took in Marthe's offended air, and the suppliant look of the young man.

"Go, Monsieur Michel, I will make your peace," she said in a low voice. "I have not yet had time to tell your friends of your visit of this afternoon, but I will explain to-morrow."

The young man felt a sense of relief. He thanked Pauline, and pressed her hand cordially, and then rushed off in pursuit of Marthe, whom he reached just as she was about to enter the salon.

"I leave at one o'clock to-morrow," he said, "and at ten, with your permission, I will be here to offer my congratulations."

In Marthe's eyes shone a light soft and gentle as the stars, but she did not speak.

"*Au revoir!*" he said, as he extended his hand.

She placed hers slowly within it.

"Marthe," he murmured in her ear, at the risk of being heard, "I shall come back to tell you, that I love you."

She withdrew her hand hastily, and turned away her head.

"*Au revoir*, Monsieur Mélaguire," said Michel, aloud. "I leave to-morrow, but I shall come in the morning to present my congratulations."

"Very well, my young friend — very well. I am always glad to see you. My regards to your brother, if I do not see you again."

It was half past two in the morning, when Michel threw himself on his bed after having packed his trunk. He had, before retiring, been to look at the little girl on the sofa, in the salon. In her sleep, she had pushed away the chairs, and rolled upon the carpet where she slept as well as on a feather-bed. Michel raised her carefully, without eliciting from her more than a long sigh, and placing her on the couch, kissed her, covered her, and left her.

"Thank Heaven he said to himself; "this will soon be over, for were it to last another week, I should simply go mad!"

The next day, Michel awoke with a start, and with the sensation well known to most travellers, that he had missed a train. He hurried from the bed, and looked at his watch; he had not missed the train, but it was half past ten.

"Why did you not wake me?" he exclaimed angrily, as his servant entered the room.

"You gave no directions sir," the man replied, "and as you went to bed so late, and the train did not leave

5

until one o'clock, I supposed it was not necessary. Tea is ready, and the cook has prepared an excellent breakfast."

Cursing the affection of his servants which had caused them to respect his slumbers, the young man dressed hastily, and discovered that he had forgotten a dozen indispensable articles. The governess had arrived—he gave the child into her charge, and went out. He hurried to a florist's and ordered the most beautiful bouquet that had ever left the man's hands, and wrote Monsieur Mélaguire's address on one of his cards, to which he added:

"Unavoidable delay; impossible to call in person; explanations two weeks from to-day; respects and congratulations."

He took every care that this card, and the bouquet, should reach their destination, and then, hastened back to his rooms.

An hour later, he reached the train, only just in time to hurry into a compartment, with the strange society wherein Heaven had so inopportunely thrown him.

CHAPTER VII.

ORANGE BLOSSOMS.

MARTHE had slept but little. As early as seven, to Nastia's great amazement, she had risen. The child shared the room of the elder sister, and declared that it made her ill to rise early on a fête day, when she could remain in bed. Having made her little speech, Nastia turned over and was soon sound asleep again.

Marthe, glad to be alone, made a most careful toilette, her pretty morning costume, white and floating, suited her, marvellously. After looking at herself in the mirror with a smile, she went down to the garden with a book that she did not read.

Eight o'clock, nine, and ten, struck, and then the half hour. She became a little nervous, and paced the broad walk with some little impatience. For the last hours her imagination had depicted Michel as he would appear in the wide turning Avenue, on the shore of the Néva. She had seen him recognize her afar off, and hasten his steps toward her. It was time that her dream should become a reality.

The young man's last words had moved her to the very depths of her soul. She reproached herself for her own looks and words, which had elicited these from him. She was ashamed, and colored at the recollection that it was the expression of her eyes, which had unsealed young Avéroef's lips; it seemed to her that she had been lacking in womanly dignity, and reserve.

In her eyes it was a degradation to accord aught that had not been formally solicited, but her *amour-propre* made her anxious to have the advantage all on her own side, but a lack of reticence was to her the same as a lack of modesty.

She had not intended to urge him to come that day, but she was not quite mistress of herself upon this point, for she had for some little time attached to the presence of this young man, an importance that was almost superstitious. It seemed to her that his coming brought her happiness, and she regarded as unlucky all those days, when she had no reason to expect him.

Consequently, when he volunteered the morning's visit instead of that of the evening, all her indignation fled, and it was then, that she turned her gentle eyes full on the youth; it was this glance that she now regretted as she paced the sunny avenue. The Néva was blue and lovely, the *Isles* were bowers of green; their white tents and tender May verdure were reflected in the water. The morning breeze played with the ribbons, and caressed the cheek as velvety as a rose leaf.

She was both happy and troubled. She had the consciousness that this day would decide her whole future life, and that happiness was coming—was coming to her through the shadow of those trees. Marthe leaned over the palisade, and looked down upon the road below. The evening before, she would have condered this an act of indecorum, but now, she examined every carriage, and interrogated every distant cavalier.

The clock struck eleven, Marthe left the palisade, and entered a summer house, where she threw herself on a seat, and burst into tears.

Tears were rare with her. She regarded them as an evidence of weakness; but this morning, she felt overcome by a sense of complete desolation, a feeling of absolute abandonment.

In vain did she say to herself that Michel had been detained by some commonplace obstacle. She even divined the exact truth,—that he would be gone a fortnight, and that she would probably receive a note and an explanation; but her heart, enfeebled by suspense and expectation, would not accept this consolation, but she dried her eyes, and tried to recover her tranquillity, in order that she might present herself before her father.

Pauline, who was watching from her window, saw the messenger arrive, sent by Avéroef with the bouquet. She met him on the steps, and told him she would deliver his message. A half dozen bouquets were already in the ante-chamber, of course it was not worth while to add this one.

Taking advantage of a time when no one could see her, she fled to her own quarters, bearing her precious

burthen.   From her post of observation, she could see
Marthe's white dress, in the summer house.

Pauline read the card over and over again, and then
tore it methodically into small bits, which she tossed
into a glass of water; then, she seated herself, and
contemplated her petty larceny.

It was a lover's bouquet, or rather, the bouquet of a
fiancée.   The gardener had divined the state of things
possibly, for his flowers were a poem.   Jasmines,
tuberoses, camelias and lilacs, not a color about the
bouquet, while a cluster of orange blossoms in the
centre, were half hidden in a whirl of fern leaves.
Intoxicated, probably, by the powerful combination of
perfumes, Pauline tore out the orange blossoms at the
risk of destroying the harmony of this odorous hymn.
She held them tightly in her hand for a few moments,
intending to tear them to bits, then, with a sarcastic
laugh, she placed them hastily in her hair, and looked
in the mirror.

She was wonderfully pretty, certainly.   The subtle
fire in her black eyes, offered an extraordinary and
piquante contrast to the traditional ideas that these
bridal flowers are apt to awaken.   She smiled with a
satisfied air, as she murmured,

"They will suit me as well as they will her, for I am
quite as beautiful!"

Then, she separated the bouquet, placing the flowers
one by one carelessly in a vase.   Suddenly she had an
idea, and laughing maliciously, she turned the bits of

card already wet, and floating in water, into the vase which held the flowers.

"All together!" she said aloud, "that is best!" She threw the débris of the bouquet into the chimney, and with a glance of approval at the result of her labors, went down to the dining-room.

Marthe had joined her father at the table, and tried to be cheerful; but as an explanation of her reddened eyes, gave a bad headache.

"All because you rose so early!" Nastia exclaimed, and then, in her penitence, rushed to her sister to kiss her.

"Your dress is wet, you have been crying," she said, patting Marthe's sleeve.

"It is the dew," said the elder sister, with an effort.

Alas! was she, who prided herself on speaking the truth, now to condescend to dissimulate, and utter falsehoods?

Monsieur Mélaguire had bought for his daughter, a magnificent pearl necklace.

"They say that pearls bring misfortunes to brides," he said, as he placed it around her throat; "so I determined to give it to you, before there was any talk of your marriage, and in that way get rid of the omen."

Each word uttered by sister and father, seemed to drive the arrow deeper into the heart of the young girl, and she burst into tears.

"Bless my soul," exclaimed Monsieur de Mélaguire, "what have I said? Does the word marriage produce an effect like this?"

"I do not wish ever to leave you," stammered Marthe, as she buried her face on her father's breast.

Monsieur de Mélaguire pressed her closely in his arms then with a sigh he said:

"Let us be happy, while we are together!"

Pauline presented her little gift, embroidered by her own hand, and kissed Marthe with effusion.

Bouquets with their cards attached, were now brought in; Marthe hoping to the last, that one would come from Michel, but her expectations were disappointed; and she relapsed into silence.

"Avérœf has not come," said her father, "and I am not surprised, for when one is starting on a journey, there is always more to be done on the last day, than one supposes. But, dear child, you are not like yourself; you enter your twenties sadly enough."

"I got frightfully tired yesterday," answered Marthe; "and then we retired very late, you remember."

"You must try and sleep this afternoon," said Monsieur Mélaguire, "for sleep is a universal panacea; you know we have people here to-night, and a dance. Rest now until dinner, and I will receive any guests who come."

Only too glad to escape the necessity of talking, and of making herself agreeable, Marthe returned to her chamber after breakfast.

She lay on her bed for an hour, buried in thought. She was thoroughly humiliated at having attached so much value to the presence of this young man; humiliated at having allowed him to see this, and also deeply wounded, that he had not found time to send her a word of congratulation, a card or a note. She was worn out with emotion, and filled with self-contempt, when all at once some one knocked gently at the door.

"Can I come in?" said a flute-like voice, and without waiting for a reply, Pauline entered, and closed the door cautiously behind her.

"What do you want?" said Marthe, turning her face away.

"May I talk to you a little?" asked Pauline, in a caressing voice.

"If you choose, only I think I should prefer just now, to be alone."

"But I have something to tell you," said the companion, taking a seat by the side of the bed.

She had stormed the fortress, and was determined with or without Marthe's consent, to tell the tale she had prepared. Marthe uttered a long sigh, to which Pauline paid no attention; but settled herself comfortably in her arm-chair, and looked pityingly at her young lady, who, with half closed eyes, feigned excessive sleepiness, in order to rid herself of the unwelcome companion.

"Monsieur Michel had left for Italy," said Mademoiselle Hopfer, in her most suave tones.

Marthe opened her eyes, and looked her companion full in the face.

"Indeed!" she said quietly.

"I knew I would make you speak," said Pauline to herself. "But he has not gone, alone," she added, emphasizing the last word.

Marthe rose on her elbow, and interrogated Pauline with indignant eyes which plainly said: "what do you mean?"

"No; Monsieur Michel has not gone alone; he took with him ——"

Marthe asked no question, and Pauline was obliged to continue.

—"A child," she added, slowly.

"I see nothing so extraordinary in that," said Marthe, dropping down among her pillows again, "any body may take a child."

"A child that resembled him to a wonderful degree!" added Pauline.

The governess had not thrown her time away; her maid had remained in St. Petersburg, the night before, and had found time to make Avérœf's coachman talk. The next morning, she came to report the whole to her mistress, whose genius she admired, without being able to penetrate its depths.

Marthe closed her eyes, but the whiteness of her face told Pauline, that the blow had struck home.

"A child three years old; a little girl very like him. He came to me yesterday, to ask me to recommend a governess—of course under the seal of secrecy, you understand."

"And you succeeded in procuring one for him?" asked Marthe, with some dignity.

"I thought it best——"

A flash in the young girl's eyes proved to Pauline that she had made a mistake, and the companion added, in a moment:

"You know, Mademoiselle, that poor girls without any position are much to be pitied. It so happened that one had just come to ask for assistance from me, and I recommended her to Monsieur Michel."

A long silence followed.

"He took her and the child to Italy," Pauline added.

"What is that to me?" asked Marthe, starting up. "Why do you tell me all this?"

"But, Mademoiselle," answered Pauline, who had reserved her last blow, "in a house where there is no mother, young girls must be careful who are received by their father, and when a great scandal makes itself known, they must be informed, that they may take proper precautions."

"A great scandal," repeated Marthe, and covered her eyes, as if to shut out a shameful spectacle. "What do you mean?" she asked, after a moment's silence.

Then Pauline narrated the little romance she had invented. Michel had had an affair in St. Petersburg with a married woman—this little girl was hers. In the early autumn they had quarreled, and she had gone to Italy, but Michel wished to keep the child. Finally, there was a reconciliation by letter, for Michel was passionately attached to the mother of the child, and they agreed to seal their reconciliation in Italy.

Michel had received a letter and a telegram together — he at once asked for leave, and took the child to the mother.

"This, Mademoiselle, is evidently the reason why he has been so much at our house this winter—he did not know where to pass his evenings. He said he should return in a fortnight. This is not so. He intends to remain there—or, if he comes back, it will be with her. It is said, indeed, that she is to be divorced, and that he will marry her."

Pauline had so adroitly mingled real facts with false suppositions, that the whole had an air of probability. The sudden departure of the young man, moreover, left the field clear to conjecture.

"Who told you all this?" asked Marthe, suddenly.

"Oh! everybody is talking about it."

"But you—who told you? The servants?"

This last question, uttered in a tone of intense contempt, struck Pauline to the heart, hardened as she was.

"I felt it my duty to inform myself, Mademoiselle, for the honor of this house, as well as on your account. Monsieur Michel comes here very often — you are young—he is handsome——"

"Enough!" said Marthe, in a choked voice, which was always with her an indication of excessive indignation. "It is to my father that you should say such things. It is not for me to hear them!"

"Mademoiselle——"

"Enough! You insult me!"

"I intend to repeat them to Monsieur Mélaguire, but have you no gratitude for the poor governess who has watched over and loved you like a mother?"

She was quite touching, with her subdued, tearful voice, and Marthe reproached herself for her severity. She allowed Pauline to kiss her, and then dismissed her, saying that she disliked all such gossip; and that she must think twice, before she brought any more tales of the kind to her.

Pauline was sweetly submissive, and went away on tiptoe, feeling certain that she had achieved her end.

She meant to be very cautious in what she said to Monsieur Mélaguire, who would certainly have taken immediate steps to discover the truth, which, without absolutely destroying the romance built by the pretty and ambitious governess, would certainly have considerably shattered the edifice.

She knew, beside, that Marthe would never speak to her father of what she had heard. She knew, also, that Monsieur Mélaguire never made the most distant allusion in the presence of his children to the scandals of society; and, proud of the result of her diplomacy, she went to her room to make herself beautiful for dinner.

CHAPTER VIII.

A SUDDEN DETERMINATION.

AS soon as Pauline had gone, Marthe locked her door and threw open her window. The air seemed absolutely tainted. She looked at the leafy path, and at the green turf, bathed by the Néva.

The sun had sunk behind the trees, the river was blue, and almost cold in appearance. All was changed since the morning—the light, the sparkle, and the festal air had vanished—only the cold and chilling reality remained.

Marthe was seated by the chimney. She wept no more; the springs in her heart were suddenly dried; years passed before she regained the gift of tears. Her ideas were not very distinct. "I am twenty, to-day," she said to herself, every few moments, and this thought, which was in no way connected with any of her present impressions, had for her an inexplicable bitterness. She remembered those long talks in her pretty salon, among her flowers.

"He deceived me, then!" she said. Her honest nature rejected this supposition as impossible.

"But he is gone," she repeated. "He did not come this morning—he sent no message."

"He has deceived me ever since I knew him," she

exclaimed aloud. " This child is three years old. He must have just entered his regiment, and I—I loved this man while he loved another! I gave him that for which he did not ask, and it was because he saw this that he pretended to love me—out of pity, perhaps? Ah! me; this is too much!"

Crushed by shame, it seemed to Marthe that there was no longer a place on the earth for her. She felt that she would rather die than see him again. But at twenty, one thinks twice of dying, especially when one is beautiful and rich.

" Anything!" she said aloud; "anything!—no matter what, rather than see him again. We will travel, if need be!"

With feverish cheeks and sparkling eyes Marthe made her toilet. Never had she been so lovely, and there was not the faintest suggestion of a deserted woman about her. Certain words uttered by Pauline had made her fear that Michel's assiduities had attracted attention, and she determined to prove to the world, that the departure of the young man did not affect her in the smallest degree.

She entered the dining-room at the hour of dinner, pearls on her white neck, roses in her hair, and rose-colored ribbons scattered over her dress—the very incarnation of beauty, of triumphant youth and pride. Her appearance elicited a cry of admiration, even from the women—her relatives and friends, who were there assembled.

"You are a very fairy!" said Sophie Cherekof's father. Sophie was now Madame Leakhive. "You only need a wand."

"Mademoiselle Marthe has a wand!" cried Oghérof, who was very busy at a side table, and turned around hastily with a glass of Kummel in one hand, and a sandwich in the other. "She hides her wand now, but it is only after we are all changed into beasts for love of her."

The laugh that this speech elicited, was so contagious that Oghérof laughed also. During the whole of the dinner, at which she presided with the air of a young sovereign, Oghérof's homage never ceased, and, strange to say, she that day seemed to enjoy it.

After having seen herself disdained, it was with intense satisfaction, that she heard men say, she was beautiful and worthy of inspiring love. Others than the Prince, encouraged by her new manner, showed her frankly the admiration inspired in them, by her triumphant beauty. She, smiling and jesting, discouraged no one. She was utterly transformed.

Her father watched her in astonishment. He had never seen her so pretty nor so coquettish.

Oghérof disappeared just after dinner. He came in after the expiration of an hour, and invited every one to go into the garden to see the fire-works.

"It will be just as good on the balcony," answered the host, always indolent after dinner.

"No! papa, the garden! the garden!" cried Nastia,

skipping about him. "Serge will bring out an arm-chair for you!"

Serge Avérœf had not left her since dinner, and she made use of him, as of a young dog, who can fetch and carry.

The party went down into the garden, where the ladies found chairs prepared. The Prince had taken a great deal of trouble; the soldiers who had charge of his great fire-works were not especially skillful, how-ever, but the spectators were amiably disposed, and the universal gayety covered a multitude of mistakes.

"Prince!" cried Monsieur Mélaguire, "why do you not come and enjoy the result of your labors?"

The Prince, who was very busy giving certain last directions, turned at these words, and leaping the flower-bed with a bound, stationed himself behind Marthe.

"Go on," he cried to his assistants.

The bouquet spread into the air, amid the wildest applause of the young people. But while vari-colored stars fell like rain from the pale blue sky, a whizzing rocket broke, a piece came in a zigzag direction, and lodged among the folds of Marthe's dress. She started up; the light muslin instantly caught fire and the flames ran up to her waist.

Before Marthe had time to scream, Oghérof snatched her in his arms and bore her to the house—the others followed in some disorder. The first to arrive, found Marthe in the salon, somewhat pale, but smiling,

6

wrapped in the folds of a great woolen table-cover,
and lying among a pile of broken porcelain. Oghérof,
on his knees, was still pressing the heavy folds which
had extinguished the fire.

"There is no harm done," said Marthe, in a
trembling voice, as she saw her father's haggard face
appear at the door. "Do not be afraid; I assure you
that I am not in the least hurt." She threw aside the
cover, and took one step forward, but she tottered, for
she had been fearfully frightened.

A dozen hands were extended; Oghérof was the
nearest, and caught her. She disengaged herself with
a deep blush, and her father drew her arm through his.

"Prince!" said Mélaguire, in a low, hoarse voice, "I
owe the life of my daughter to you."

"You might have owed me something else," muttered the Prince, testily. "I am a great simpleton—I
know that. If ever I meddle with fire-works again,
may I know it, that is all!"

"You have saved me from a frightful death," said
Marthe, almost tenderly, as she extended her hand.

"Kiss it, Oghérof—she owes you that privilege,"
said Monsieur Mélaguire, still agitated, and looked
around mechanically, as if he wished to find something
to give as an indication of gratitude, to the man who
had saved his daughter's life.

Oghérof did not require to be urged.

"You are looking for your treasures?" he said to his
host. "Well, don't trouble yourself; the pieces are all

on the floor. I pulled off the table-cover to throw around Mademoiselle Marthe, without paying much attention, I assure you, to what was upon it!"

It was but slowly that the little party recovered from this alarm. The mammas talked of going away, but this the host opposed. Marthe retired to put on another robe, and they began to dance. Nastia, who in her fright had sobbed uncontrollably, recovered her spirits, and gayly danced a quadrille.

Marthe could not dance, for every few moments she was seized with a little nervous trembling. She reclined upon a sofa, and looked at the dancers, and all that had passed in the morning seemed like a dream. Even the recollection of Michel was not altogether clear. When she thought of him, it was as if a sharp arrow passed through her heart, and she thrust it hastily aside.

Oghérof hovered about her, and was much graver than usual—in fact, he was very grave, for he was really deeply in love. Marthe's pearly shoulders, veiled by transparent muslin; the light curls which fell over her girlish, timid form, as he had carried her in his arms, had awakened in him a sensation that was as new as unexpected, and most intoxicating.

It was not a woman familiar with life, whom he had pressed to his breast; it was a young girl, whose innocent lips no man had ever touched, and the recollection of this novel impression, so brief that it was like a dream, gave him a mad desire to renew it.

"I am quite capable of marrying her," he said, suddenly—he who had never thought of marriage, since he left his military school.

In fact he must marry her, since there was no other way of obtaining her.

For Oghérof, a thing he wanted, was a thing that was absolutely necessary to him. He reflected five whole minutes, and then went to Monsieur Mélaguire, who had not cared to play, and who, under an appearance of great dignity, occupied a vast fauteuil, and took a gentle siesta.

"My dear sir," said Oghérof.

The sleeper started.

"What is it?" he stammered. "Ah! Prince, it is you, is it? I did not see you. What can I do for you?"

"I love Mademoiselle Marthe, and I have come to ask permission to say so to her."

"How well he says it," thought Monsieur Mélaguire, with a vague recollection of the easy manner in which his niece had managed things.

"Have you spoken to your relatives of this project?" he asked, still thinking of his niece.

"I have no near relatives," answered the young man. "I have no one to consult but myself. My happiness is in your hands."

"And I have every regard for you," replied Monsieur Mélaguire, completely roused by this time, "but this is my daughter's affair."

"You give your consent, then?" cried Oghérof, eagerly.

"I have no plausible reason for refusing it, but giving it, you understand, is a vastly different matter. My daughter must decide for herself."

"I prefer to accept her decision," said Oghérof, with dignity.

He was in a whirl of new ideas, and was both interested and amused. It was like witnessing a play, in which, however, he was actor as well as spectator. It was all very odd—very original—and Marthe was perfectly adorable, and would make an incomparable Princess Oghérof.

He went toward Marthe, but she was not alone. Fretting at his bit — for patience was not his forte—he seated himself at some little distance, and contemplated the future Princess; that royal brow, crowned by brown hair; that tall, slender figure, so well fitted to wear sweeping velvet trains; those aristocratic hands, that air of hauteur, which she knew well how to adopt; the grace of her smile and her manners, all this exterior, of which alone he was qualified to judge, made Marthe a most charming mistress of a mansion.

"This marriage will compel me to take a new position in society!" he said to himself. He vainly waited another hour for a favorable moment; people were going, and he had not yet opened his lips. He determined to outstay the others, but he was surrounded by several friends and carried off by force.

Besides, Marthe was evidently fatigued, and was

probably ill-disposed to listen to a proposition of marriage, and then, too, would it not look as if he were asking payment for the service he had rendered?

He returned to his rooms more serious than was his custom. As he passed the Dessaux restaurant he thought of going in for supper — not that he was hungry, but from mere force of habit.

"No," he said to himself, "it would not, under the circumstances, be at all proper." And, quite proud of this sacrifice to Hymen, he retired and soon fell asleep.

CHAPTER IX.

TELLS WHAT PAPA THOUGHT.

MARTHE also slept soundly that night. The rapid succession of impressions had dulled her senses, and everything seemed veiled in a light fog.

When she awoke, she perceived the dress she had worn the previous evening thrown over a chair—the skirt was all burned and tumbled. She recalled with horror the moment when the flames had enveloped her and she had fallen. She had no recollection of being carried to the salon, and, in short, remembered nothing until the heavy table-cover was wrapped around her by Oghérof. The impression of this mass of stuff weighing her down, was as vivid as anything. A sudden idea occurred to her, and a most disagreeable one.

"This man held me in his arms," she said to herself, and she colored furiously.

It was true that but for this, she would have perished in the most horrible manner. But in spite of this conviction, she could not become accustomed to the thought that this man had held her in his arms, and that he would remember it each time he saw her.

She drove away this importunate idea, only to give place to another. Michel was *en route* with his child, rolling toward Italy, where a woman he loved was waiting for him.

"He is very impatient, probably!" she said to herself, and a cruel jealousy tore her heart. She was not wicked, but if she had held in her hands this woman whom Michel loved, and to whom he was joyously flying, she would not have made her suffer, but she would perhaps have killed her.

She rose slowly, with that weary languor which follows a great crisis. When she went down to breakfast, she found her father anxiously awaiting her at the foot of the stairs.

"I was just going up," he said. "I was afraid you were ill; you are very pale."

"Only very tired," she answered. "I shall be all right soon."

After breakfast Mélaguire induced his daughter to go to his cabinet, and there seat herself on the divan. Full of solicitude, he threw a shawl over her shoulders, which he went in search of himself.

She smiled half sadly. She was happy in being so cared for. In her distress and loneliness she was grateful for any mark of affection and sympathy.

When Monsieur Mélaguire had established his daughter comfortably, he dropped into his arm-chair, drew a long breath, looked at Marthe, and then at his finger-nails, two or three times before he spoke, and then asked, abruptly—

"Did Oghérof say nothing to you yesterday?"

"No, dear father!" answered Marthe, lifting her astonished eyes.

"Yesterday, at eleven o'clock, he came to ask for your hand."

Marthe hastily threw aside the shawl about her shoulders, and sat with her eyes fixed in profound reflection.

"He asked my hand?" she said, slowly.

"Yes."

"And at what hour last evening?"

"At eleven."

Marthe's questions were incomprehensible to her father. He watched her in silent surprise.

"What did you say?"

"I said that it was for you to reply."

Marthe rose, and throwing her arms around his neck, kissed him tenderly.

"And what am I to say?" asked Monsieur Mélaguire, astonished at her manner.

"Say just what you please," answered Marthe, in her gentle voice.

Her father, more and more amazed, could not refrain from saying:

"But have you no feeling, one way or the other?"

"Never mind that now; at present I only desire to know your wishes."

"Oghérof has never been looked upon as a marrying man. His habits, perhaps — but after all he is a good fellow; a little wild, but not bad in any way. He has no near relatives; his position is excellent; no one speaks ill of him, and he is very amusing and good-natured."

Marthe listened, not without a secret bitterness.

"Why does he wish to marry me?" she said, after a little hesitation.

"Because he is in love with you, of course! What a very strange question," her father replied.

Marthe did not answer.

"Well! What have you to say?" he asked, with some little impatience.

"I don't know yet. I must speak to him first. You would be pleased at this marriage, then?"

"Of course; the Princess Oghérof will have as high a position as any woman in St. Petersburg, and the Prince will make a charming son-in-law."

"I will take the proposition into consideration," said Marthe, as she rose to leave the room, after kissing her father once more.

She left him, however, in a state of uncertainty that was almost droll.

CHAPTER X.

THE PRINCE AS A SUITOR.

PRINCE OGHÉROF was not long in making his appearance in the faultless costume, not only of a man who is madly in love, but also of a man of the world, who wishes to carry the citadel.

Marthe forewarned, was in the salon, and received him in the attitude of a hero, ready to conquer or to die.

Pauline, who was on her way to join her, was intercepted by Monsieur Mélaguire, who was watching for her, and led by him into his cabinet, where the carefully prepared *menu* of a dinner was laid before her, and discussed with the most minute care. Monsieur Mélaguire, although the least shrewd of mortals, preferred, nevertheless, that Pauline should know nothing of this proposed marriage until everything was settled. He sometimes thought Pauline's nose too pointed — at least that was what he said one day to Madame Cherékof, his sister.

Marthe seated herself, and signed to the Prince to take a chair. He might be absurd, but he was never ridiculous. His natural distinction of manner and his excellent breeding elevated him above any such possibility. It was therefore with simple dignity, and with excellent taste that he expressed his sentiments, and made the offer of his hand.

Marthe was quite at her ease with this simple and natural manner of treating things. She had dreaded enthusiasm, and an expression of sentiments which she could not share. Her liking and her sympathy for this gay young fellow, who had saved her life the night before, were suddenly revived, and it was with a smile that she said to him:

"It is a most singular idea, Prince, for you, such a favorite in society, to ask a young lady so serious and quiet as myself, to marry him."

"Ah! Marthe Parlovna, I love you with all my heart!" cried Oghérof, suddenly restored to his wonted vivacity. "If you were to tell me to crawl on all fours for seven years I would submit."

"Seven years," said Marthe, with a sigh; "that is very long. But I do not love you, Prince, and I ought to tell you so.'

"A virtuous woman always loves her husband," said the young man, with an air of conviction; "and every-one knows that Marthe Parlovna is the model of all virtues, consequently, if I am fortunate to be —— Ah! Mademoiselle Marthe, will you not take pity on an unfortunate soldier, who is dying at your feet?"

"But you are not in earnest, Prince," said Marthe, who, with difficulty refrained from laughter, so droll did the whole affair seem to her.

"Not in earnest! What can I do, what can I say to

prove to you the sincerity of my sentiments? I am ready for anything. Give your orders."

"Wait for my reply for a fortnight, then," answered the young girl, as she rose from her chair.

"A fortnight!" cried Oghérof, in consternation; "two weeks! But, Mademoiselle, if you intend to refuse me, it would be best to tell me so at once."

"What would you do in that case?" said Marthe, suddenly, turning and facing him.

The gleam of passion in the young man's eyes, was as sincere as the tone in which he replied,

"I would go and be killed at Caucasus."

And he would have done it, if the ball of the enemy had struck him before he had time for reflection, for he was really in love.

It was a fire of straw which Marthe's coldness, like a north wind, made flame all the more fiercely.

"He loves me, that is certain," said Marthe, struck by his voice and look.

She did not ask herself if this love were pure gold, or only shining dross.

"All I can say is, to bid you wait for a fortnight," she repeated, her eyes drooping under his earnest gaze, and pale with the struggle that was going on within herself.

Oghérof snatched her hands, and covered them with kisses. Marthe's first impulse, was to withdraw them indignantly. "I have no right," she said to herself, and crushed by this thought, she stood like a lamb led to the sacrifice, meekly submissive.

"Well, Prince?" said Monsieur Mélaguire, attracted by the clank of the young man's spurs, as the two passed into the garden.

"Mademoiselle Marthe sends me away for a fortnight. Is not that rather cruel, sir?"

"It is very sensible," answered Mélaguire suddenly, realizing that in two weeks more, perhaps, he must begin to think seriously of a separation from his daughter.

But Oghérof was not of the same opinion. At last, however, he was induced to listen to reason. He made the condition, however, that he could come every day—twice each day — to assure himself of the progress he was making in the good opinion of the young girl.

She became accustomed to most things, and at the end of four or five days, Marthe had formed the habit of seeing Alexander Oghérof enter the salon, like a whirlwind, snatch her hand and kiss it, then, drop into a chair at her side, and narrate to Monsieur Mélaguire who laughed until tears filled his eyes, a series of the most impossible adventures and preposterous *bon mots;* the whole seasoned by original remarks, at which, Marthe, too, was forced to laugh.

But this love bore little resemblance, after all, to what she had hithero called love. She felt very sure that the Prince was quite ready to run away with her, to lift her upon his gentle steed, and gallop to the ends of the world with her. His abrupt movements, the restraint he placed upon himself in her presence, the expression of his eyes and his broken words, all proved to her that she had touched the heart of this handsome young officer.

"He certainly loves me," she said to herself, and his very submission, and his silence, touched her far more than words could have done.

In the habits of the young man, moreover, what a change had taken place! Oghérof, no longer went to the theatre at the *Eaux Minérales;* he no longer supped at the fashionable restaurant; his calèche was no more seen on the road from Kamenroï Ostron; his white hounds lay in the sunshine on Monsieur Méla-guire's door steps, having forgotten the way to the *Bois de la Perspective,* and Marthe's hand, which occasionally gave them sugar, had become familiar to them.

Marthe, in the meantime, had by no means decided to give her hand. Bitter as was the recollection of Michel, she was forced to dwell upon it. She did not wish to feel that her marriage was a sudden impulse, the result of a disappointment as sudden, and had, therefore, fixed this date, two weeks hence, to give Michel time to return.

Nine days had elapsed since the young man's departure. She waited, determined if he did not return at the appointed time, and offer adequate explanations, to announce her engagement.

"It is terrible weakness on my part," she said to herself; "but, still, in spite of all the evidence against him, he may be innocent!"

Pauline mentally rubbed her hands with delight, at seeing the impending success of her plans. At first, the delay imposed by the young girl, had annoyed her; then she made her little calculation; she had considerable arithmetical talent, and said to herself that the chances were very much against her, if she could not find some means of holding Michel in cheek. She knew Marthe was too proud to retract a promise once given, even if it were to cost her the happiness of her whole life.

"After all," she said, half aloud, "he who risks nothing, wins nothing!"

The morning of the eleventh day, after Avérœf's departure, Pauline was the first, as usual, to come down stairs, and look at the tray on a table in the anteroom, which was filled with letters and papers.

For a long time, this inspection had been her first labor of the day. She liked, she said, to hunt for her letters through this pile. The truth was, that she troubled herself less about her letters, than about those of other people, and her careful inspection of the various postmarks had long since given her a very clear idea of the business connections of Monsieur Mélaguire. On this day of which we write, she turned the papers over, with a more eager and feverish hand than usual, for she expected a letter from her *protégé*, whose laziness in writing, had more than once elicited a reproof. In the midst of advertisements, prospectuses and journals, a foreign letter appeared, addressed to

Monsieur Mélaguire, and bearing the Mentone post-
mark. She recognized the writing as Michel's.

Pauline looked at it a moment, then slipped it into
her pocket.

A moment later, she found another, addessed to herself. The one she was expecting, and this too, she
placed in her pocket, and hastened back to her chamber
with a beating heart.

"What was she to learn from the two?" she asked
herself. She bolted her door, and broke the seal of her
own letter, which was to this effect:

MOST RESPECTED MADEMOISELLE PAULINE: "We
have arrived at Mentone. The young gentleman who
brought us is with his brother, who is not young, and
is very ill. This gentleman is the little girl's papa.
Young Monsieur Michel wished to leave at once, but
his brother is so very sick, that he will be compelled to
stay here, at least, another month. He has written
to-day to St. Peterburg, to ask that his leave may be
prolonged. We are very comfortable; the little girl is
very good, but I fancy that good Monsieur Avéroef is
not pleased with me."

"Who cares!" muttered Pauline hastily, runing her
eyes down the rest of the letter; "he is not coming
back yet, that is all I care to know. But what on earth
can he be writing to Monsieur Mélaguire about?"

With the air of a willful child—Pauline, sometimes,

when by herself, enacted these little comedies, and laughed when she met her own eyes in the mirror, her sole confidante — she opened the confiscated letter, and read it from beginning to end.

Michel touched upon his journey, in a few words begged Monsieur Mélaguire to excuse his sudden departure, made an allusion to the bouquet, the stolen flowers which had made so good, through brief, appearance on Pauline's head, and ended by saying to Monsieur Mélaguire that he expected on his return, now deferred for another month, to call with his father, to ask a favor at his hands, on which his whole happiness depended.

"I did well to put this in my pocket," said Pauline, as she folded the letter carefully. "In a month there will be many changes."

CHAPTER XI.

DISAPPOINTMENT.

AS Oghérof entered that day, Pauline asked if his fellow-officer, Avércef, would not soon return.

"No;" replied the Prince, "he has just sent for his leave to be extended."

"And got the extension?" asked Pauline, watching Marthe from the corner of her eye.

"Certainly; his brother is very ill. It is very sad," added the Prince.

The conversation now turned on the misery of delicate health. A little incredulous smile was on Marthe's lips.

Pauline never turned her eyes away, and thought with malicious delight of the letter hidden up-stairs in a little quilted jewel box, with the withered orange-blossoms from the famous bouquet. She was enchanted by the success of her manœuvres. How "stupid" did these people, who served her unconsciously, appear to her. And this Prince, was he not a mere tool in her hands?

And good Monsieur Mélaguire, who wished to be so cautious, and who had politely taken her away, lest she should hear Oghérof's application to his daughter — was he not hopelessly dull to think she had not detected his too evident subterfuges?

Then, there was Michel who had thrust his head into the snare, by asking her for a governess — her, whom he had so humiliated, and who expected her to reconcile him with Marthe after his departure. Here, she laughed aloud.

And Marthe, poor simpleton! who had treated her like a servant—who had overwhelmed her with disdain, and whom she should herself marry as she pleased.

"I do things well!" she said, glorifying herself. "I make her a princess, and give her three millions! Ungrateful little puss!"

Her hands trembled.

"What on earth is the matter with you, Pauline Vassilscova?" said Nastia, suddenly. "You are putting tea in the saucers, and there is no sugar in the glasses."

Pauline laughed, and began to jest with the little girl.

That night Marthe could not sleep. Until this last minute, she had indulged in a faint hope of seeing Michel come home and exculpate himself. She did not realise the strength of this hope, until she found that it, like all others, had crumbled away.

"I love him still," she said in pain and anger. "I love, notwithstanding his unworthiness, this man who does not care for me."

All her pride suddenly revolted. She wished that this importunate love—this love that had outlived insult and neglect, were a living, palpitating thing, which she could crush in her hand, and trample under her feet. The struggle was long. She desired to fly —to take refuge in a convent; to become a Sister of Charity; a teacher under a feigned name—to do anything, in short, so that she might never again see this odious man who had deserted her in this cowardly manner, without a word, after having trifled with her affections as he had.

"And my father!" said Marthe, suddenly; "he would die; my poor father!"

The thought that she had a father to love her — a father for whom it was her duty to feign happiness, finally decided Marthe's future.

"To-day it will be settled!" she said aloud, as the morning sun streamed into her room through the wide open window, and found her sore at heart, but firm and determined.

Oghérof found her that day less unapproachable than usual, and was emboldened to say:

"Mademoiselle Marthe, abridge my martyrdom! Remember that we can't be married at once—it will take at least eight days to make all the arrangements, and you have made me wait twelve already. What can three more matter to you?"

Marthe could not refrain from a smile at this melancholy wail, uttered in a tone calculated to soften the hardest heart. Her father and the Prince followed her example and laughed also.

"Such a gay house—such a gay house!" said a voice

from the road, suddenly. "People are laughing there all day long. Each time I pass, I hear them laugh, while we poor devils live such a hard life!"

The windows were wide open, and the little circle rose to see the orator. He was a poor devil, indeed! His miserable clothes were not those of a peasant; his aspect suggested, in some degree, a divinity student, grown old without a parish—or an employé, dismissed without a pension. With his head lifted toward the *rez de chaussé*, he extended his long bony neck like a hungry bird imploring food.

The folds of his loose coat fell about an emaciated form, and buttoned to the throat, indicated the absence of all linen, while his ragged boots revealed the want of stockings beneath.

"Poor devil! he has not had a mouthful, I dare say, for a week," said good Monsieur Mélaguire, involuntarily.

"Fool that I am!" cried Oghérof, looking through his pockets. "I never have any money about me. Here, my friend, take this, and don't be cheated in the weight when you sell it." As he said this, he held out his repeater, at the end of a heavy chain.

The old fanatic clutched at the princely gift, and uttered a profusion of thanks. The party at the window turned away, while the old man took his way to town as fast as his long legs, emaciated by fasting, would take him.

"Prince," said Marthe, "with my father's blessing I grant you my hand."

Oghérof had acted on the impulse of the moment, and shown a goodness of heart that was simply superficial, though sincere as far as it went, but the young girl allowed it to weigh down the scales which were then trembling.

Oghérof, happy and agitated, pressed his lips on the arm and hand which his fiancée yielded to him.

"I make one condition only," said Marthe; "which is, that on the day of our marriage, we leave St. Petersburg, in the English fashion."

"All right!" cried the Prince, beside himself with joy. "I am going to order a travelling carriage at once."

And he snatched his cap, while Monsieur Mélaguire had the greatest difficulty in making him understand that this order could be given quite as well a few hours later—the next morning, in fact.

CHAPTER XII.

CAUTIOUS.

THIS decisive step once taken, Marthe went resolutely to the end. The time that separated her from her marriage was very brief, the Prince being impatient, and she herself was very anxious to be gone before Michel's return.

These three weeks passed with a rapidity that left her no time to think. The summer season, which scatters to the four winds of Heaven the society of St. Petersburg, relieved her of the necessity of making many visits. There was, however, sufficient fatigue and annoyance in regard to the trousseau and other arrangements, to make her regard the day of departure as an absolute relief.

From time to time her thoughts flew back to the past, led there by some slight event. One day especially, she paid a farewell visit to old Madame Avéroef, who lived at Ksarskoë - Sélo during summer. The lady received the young pair with the kind grace that distinguished and characterized every act of her life, and at the close of a collation, she took Marthe into her sleeping-room, "to talk with her," she said.

Madame Avéroef made Marthe take a seat in the large room darkened by green curtains; the trees in the garden seemed anxious to peer in at the windows; the dark hangings, the huge bed, covered with dark green damask — the carpets and antique furniture, blackened by time, gave to the apartment a mysterious aspect. At the back of the room the lamp burned before a carved armoire full of gold and silver images, enriched by precious stones.

Marthe seated herself in a huge arm-chair, while the old lady searched through her drawers with a bunch of rattling keys. It was very cool in this asylum where the sun never penetrated; a vague odor of incense—of faded roses — of all things sweet, exhaled from this venerable furniture, and seemed to bring with it the peace of sleeping souvenirs. Marthe, in the silence, felt her heart swell with emotion. A great portrait of General Avérœf—the first General Avérœf; the one who had been killed at Varna, faced the bed, where the eyes of his wife, who had been thirty-two years a widow, greeted it each morning when she awoke. Marthe looked at it a moment, and without knowing why, felt the tears rise to her eyes.

Madame Avérœf, who had found that for which she was looking, examined the girl with penetrating eyes.

"My child," she said, "when you were but sixteen I put this aside for you," and she laid a jewel case on the young girl's knee. "I have the same thing, only in sapphires, for Michel's future wife."

Marthe lifted her eyes, and looked Madame Avérœf full in the face, but the old lady's countenance w̄ s undecipherable. She glanced at the jewels, and uttered a few words of gracious thanks.

"And here," resumed the old lady, "is a locket that I gave your mother on her marriage. After your father lost her, he gave it back to me in memory of her—this souvenir is yours—you have a right to it. Her portrait is in it now."

Marthe, deeply moved, opened the diamond locket, and recognized her mother, whose majestic beauty she had inherited in all the radiance of her eighteen years.

Her gratitude, touchingly expressed, showed her aged friend that she had re-opened the heart which the name of Michel had so imprudently closed.

"May you be as happy as she was, but I trust your happiness will be of longer duration than hers — or mine," she added, as she followed the eyes of the young girl as they turned toward the great portrait.

"Yes," she continued; "I was a widow very early in my life, but when we are beloved, èven death does not completely sever — and I loved my husband very dearly."

Marthe turned her eyes away uneasily.

"Will you love yours?"

"Certainly," said Marthe, in a low voice, without daring to look up.

"I had different projects for you; old women, you know, like to make plans, my child. I hoped that you would one day belong to me."

Marthe rose with flashing eyes, in which, quickly

veiled as they were, however, Madame Avœrœf read some mystery, the explanation of which she determined to discover from Michel.

"An old woman's dreams, dear!" she said, as she took Marthe in her arms. "Receive, nevertheless, my dear child, the benediction of one who will love the Princess Oghérof as dearly as she has cherished Marthe Mélaguire."

The embrace was so cordial, the tone so sympathetic, that Marthe returned the caress as warmly as it was given. But she was troubled all that day, and in the evening she showed her new jewels to her sister.

"Did you see Serge?" asked the little girl, who seized every occasion to speak of her best friend.

"No; he was at the camp."

"And Michel? Have they heard from him?"

"No."

This "no" was as sharp and decisive as a pistol shot.

"Do you know, Marthe," said Nastia, approaching her sister with open arms in a coaxing way — "do you know that I like Prince Oghérof? He makes me such beautiful presents!—but for a brother-in-law I prefer Michel."

"And why?" asked Marthe, embarrassed by the eyes of the tall girl.

"Because he is an Avœrœf," murmured Nastia, devouring her sister with kisses.

Marthe did not understand then. She shrugged her

shoulders, and it was not until long after this, that she understood her sister's meaning.

Marthe had another attack, more difficult still, to parry. This assailant was Sophie Leakhive, her cousin, whose marriage had been an admirable success. The awkward being whose manner had been so often taken for impertinence, she had in two or three months transformed into a man of the world — witty, and full of grace and ease.

She had often said that "Leakhive was foolish from timidity, and now that the timidity had vanished, he became to every one just what he had always been to her, who had set him at his ease on their first acquaintance by the frankness of her manner."

"Send me the bears from your forest," she had said one day to Oghérof, who was teasing the young couple in a friendly sort of way; "I will teach them to dance without beating them."

When Sophie learned of her cousin's approaching marriage she went to see her, and scrutinized her carefully, but said nothing; the visit was returned by the newly-engaged couple, but still without anything but common-places being exchanged. One day, however, Marthe having gone alone to see her, Sophie stood in front of her, and looked her full in the face.

"Why are you going to marry Oghérof?" she asked abruptly.

"Probably because it pleases me to do so," answered Marthe, really displeased.

"Now please descend from your high horse, my dear! You know very well that I never quarrel with you. Can you tell me why Michel Avéroef went off to Italy?"

"No!" answered Marthe, with a smile of cruel contempt.

"Did he quarrel with you?"

"By no means!" said the young fiancée, with a sarcastic smile.

"He offered himself to you, and you refused him?"

"No, indeed; but it seems to me that this is a cross-examination, admirably fitted for a court of justice," said Marthe, haughtily.

Sophie reflected a moment, and then seized Marthe by the arm as she was going away, and compelled her to come back.

"You are to be married in a week?" she said.

"Yes."

"Well! try not to repent afterward, for it will then be too late!"

"I never repent of what I do," said Marthe, proudly.

She spoke the truth; she never repented. As soon as a thing was a fixed fact, she accepted it as one accepts hail or rain. But this resignation did not preclude many a secret pang.

CHAPTER XVIII.

THE WEDDING DAY.

THE marriage day arrived, Marthe wished the ceremony to take place, contrary to custom, at noon,
and at the pretty little church by the road side.

All went off well; at one o'clock the newly-married
pair had returned to Monsieur Melaguire's, where
breakfast awaited them in the English style. When
the repast was over, Marthe exchanged her sumptuous
white toilette, for a travelling dress of gray silk. The
travelling carriage, lined with white satin, as for an
empress, and drawn by six white horses with white
rosettes at their ears, drew up before the steps. The
bride tore herself from her father's and sister's arms in
the recognized style, they weeping like two fountains.

"We shall look for you in a week," she said, by way
of consolation.

While Nastia rubbed her swollen eyes with her little
handkerchief rolled up in a ball, damped with tears,
and a little sticky with sugar plums, the eminently
proper Pauline shed a few tears — such tears as are
wiped away with a lace-bordered handkerchief — and
murmured in German a series of congratulations to
the epauletted shoulder of Prince Oghérof, who, however, paid little attention to her words. Once, indeed,

bewildered by this flow of monotonous words, he felt
in his pocket mechanically to find a sou; then, perceiving his mistake, he stammered a few unintelligible
words, accompanied by a vague smile of condolence.

"We must go," he said, to Monsieur Mélaguire,
"and forgive me for carrying off your daughter so
abruptly; but if we delay, we shall not arrive before
night."

He extended his hand; Marthe laid hers within it,
and seated herself in the carriage. As she sank into
the white cushions, a vision passed before her eyes.
She beheld Michel sick, dying, dead, on a bed in an
inn, with his eyes closed, and his face rigid.

"I am married," she said. "All is over," and her
heart contracted, and became as stone under her silken
corsage.

A few words of tenderness to those she left; a last
kiss to Nastia, who climbed into the carrriage as agile
as a young kitten, and then the Prince seated himself
at her side. The door was closed with a bang, and the
horses started off, she leaning from the carriage, for one
more look at those who were dear to her.

"Farewell, dear home!" murmured Marthe, with a
quickly-stifled sigh.

The Prince took her hand gently in his.

"You are mine, now," he murmured; "and I adore
you!"

Marthe did not reply. An inexpressible sadness
overwhelmed her, like a wave, and threatened to sub-

merge her.   The Prince talked on, then came a long silence.

The sun was setting, and the shadows of tall trees fell along the road.   Their destination was a country house, which Oghérof owned on the shores of Lake Ladoga.   Five hours in the carriage, and they were there.   The oblique rays of the sun entered through one of the windows, and threw silvery reflections on the folds of the satin in the carriage.

Marthe did not allow herself to think; as we have said, she never repented, and the thing was done.

The road was deserted; the horses trotted with an even, rapid step.   The Prince suddenly seized his young wife in his arms, and pressing his lips to hers, said:

" You love me, dear ? "

" I shall love my husband ! " answered Marthe, pale with anguish, but resolved to keep her bridal vow.

At this same hour, Michel was entering Geneva by the afternoon train, swearing at all Swiss railroads, on which trains travel only by day.   Thus condemned to lose twelve hours, he climbed the Grand-Sacconex, in order to occupy himself, and looked at Mont Blanc, illuminated by the setting sun.

The triple summits of snow fascinated him.   Two or three times he turned to go down, but each time went back, to once more contemplate this immaculate whiteness, over which played a soft and rosy flush.   He could not turn away his eyes; his thoughts flew over hills and valleys. He longed to embrace these snowy summits, so white and inaccessible.

"They are like Marthe!" he suddenly exclaimed. "She is as inaccessible as these snowy Alpine heights, and her face sometimes flushes also."

He did not conclude his parallel. He dwelt on the absent beloved one, long after Mont Blanc was no more than a phantom against the dark, blue, starlit sky.

8

CHAPTER XIV.

TOO LATE!

THE next morning, at eight o'clock, the Princess Oghérof was wandering in the garden of her new domain.

She paid little attention to its beauties. She walked rapidly along an avenue, by the side of the lake, which was shaded by tall lindens. She moved as if by machinery, and, as soon as she reached the end of the walk, turned back again. Once or twice she caught her laces on the branches of the bush, on a root protruding from the ground. She continued her walk, leaving the frail tissue floating in the wind, until some bird carried it off to its nest.

The lake glittered before her. She looked at it without being blinded; then her eyes turned upon the sand of the path, which seemed to her as if strewn with black spots.

She walked thus for nearly an hour, then stopped, tired to death. Leaning against the trunk of an old linden tree, she folded her hands and allowed them to drop helplessly before her, as she bowed her head sadly.

"Insulted! Insulted!"

This word she repeated over and again, although her lips were dumb.

For an hour she had read this word written on the shining surface of the lake, on the gravel of the walk, on the turf of the lawn. A new world had opened before her since the previous day. The Prince, always a gentleman, with irreproachable manners, had revealed to her something of his past life. She had heard him address words of tenderness to her, which were not the spontaneous outburst from a husband's heart.

"Insulted!" repeated Marthe; "and I, who was so proud!"

Her pride was great, and she smiled when she joined her husband in the breakfast-room.

He, like the rest of the world, would never know that this woman regarded his tenderness as an insult, that she had dreamed of a heart which should beat only for her, of lips which had never murmured any other name than hers. She had accepted everything, rather than see Michel after his desertion of her. And now she saw before her a life of mortified pride, of secret and unavowable suffering; but, at all events, when Michel came back, he would find her married. And, contrary to what she hoped, this thought only buried the dagger deeper in her soul. The tea urn smoked between them; the Prince breakfasted with a good appetite, their conversation was that of two well-bred persons, who were to pass their lives together. The old silver, the Saxe porcelain, the ancient tapestry, all breathed of luxury—the luxury of an old and wealthy house. The glass in the conservatories sparkled in the sun, while through the open window came the sweet odors from the flower-beds. Marthe's heart swelled.

"It is all mine," she said to herself; "and yet nothing pleases me, nor interests me. I had much better have become a governess in some country family, where I, at least, should have had freedom!"

The Prince, at this moment, kissed the hand which extended his glass toward him. Marthe smiled, and looked him full in the face. It was necessary to become accustomed to this existence!

The first eight days were interminable. Alexander Oghérof was a charming fellow but as hollow as a red balloon.

Without his saddle horses, and his dogs — without his sumptuous sail-boat, and his hot-houses, fragrant with orange blossoms — without, in short, all that luxury which placed some new plaything in his hand with every fleeting hour, the life of the Princess would have been more than she could have borne. Fortunately, her husband filled up his daily life and hers, with so much active exercise, that fatigue prevented her from thinking, until the day of the arrival of her family.

The first face she saw, when the berline drove up, was that of Pauline Hopfer — Pauline and her pointed nose.

Devoured by the natural desire to contemplate her work, that lady had had this same nose at the window for some time. She wished to be the first to embrace the dear princess: but, nothwithstanding these good intentions, Nastia fairly walked over her with the reckless determination of a young animal, and she leaped into her sister's arms, laughing, and crying at the same time, and making such a commotion that the Prince was obliged to ask his father-in-law three times, where the luggage was.

Monsieur Mélaguire had grown strangely old during this week. He began to think, almost unconsciously, that they had all been a little too quick. His first look about his daughter's home, threw his paternal soul into that ocean of placid felicity wherein he usually resided.

Marthe was beautiful, superbly beautiful. Her smiles were those of absolute content and happiness. She was, for the moment, very happy in having near her once again the two precious beings, who were in her heart, more than ever before.

Marthe had not grown thin; Marthe was fresh and rosy. Monsieur Mélaguire was delighted. One would have supposed that, in coming to see his daughter, he expected to find her bones sewed up in red velvet, after being gnawed by the wolf.

Pauline Hopfer was not pleased. She had vaguely shared Monsieur Mélaguire's ideas, in relation to the wolf, and here she was in the sheepfold, where peace reigned, where the song of birds replaced the classic flute, and not a cloud darkened the horizon.

"Things are altogether too smooth," said this amiable

personage, with that perspicacity with which Providence, in default of other gifts, had so largely endowed her; "there is something wrong!"

Marthe was, however, fully determined that Pauline should discover nothing. The husband was astonished at the vivacity with which she conversed,—at the excessive courtesy with which she treated him, and equally so, by the excessive fatigue and prostration which, in the evening, succeeded these·well days, so filled.

"She is exercising too great a strain on herself," he thought; "but she can rest by and by, when we are all quiet."

What he called being quiet was putting the house upside down, from ten o'clock in the morning until midnight.

But he was destined to see this especial form of enjoyment postponed, for Marthe went back with her father to his villa.

About three weeks later, the Prince was alone in St. Petersburg, preparing a home worthy of Marthe. He went constantly, of course, to the country but it was not the life of which he had dreamed, he said to his colonel, with a sigh, one day when he met him.

"But it will come soon!" answered the Colonel, who was a man of considerable cleverness.

"Oh! certainly," answered the Prince, with some energy.

That evening he did not leave the rooms, in which

workmen were at work until five o'clock, too late to go to the villa, for his arrival there, in the middle of the night, would have terrified every one.

After dining at the restaurant, he went to take a little bath. The weather was superb—the evening almost warm. A brother officer passed him, driving alone.

"Ah! Domanoff," cried the Prince; "where are you going?"

"To the Isles," answered the Cornet, bidding his coachman stop.

"Ah!" said the Prince, a little disconcerted; "that is a good horse you have there."

"An Orlof trotter, my dear fellow."

"And you are going where?"

"To the Isles, I tell you; there is a new singer, who makes her first appearance to-night. Will you come?"

"No—" answered the Prince, irresolutely, after a moment's hesitation; "you have no room for me."

"No room, my dear fellow!—this sort of vehicle does just as well for two as one. Each keeps the other in. Come on; I want to show you how my horse trots; we shall not be fifteen minutes on the way."

"Not fifteen minutes?"

"No, indeed! Come on! I tell you."

Oghérof jumped into the tiny vehicle, and took his seat half on his companion's knees. The drojki at once started.

It seemed as if the very Evil One had meddled in

the matter, for Oghérof met that day a charming blonde, whom he had courted six months before, and who had suddenly taken her departure for parts unknown. He renewed his attentions, and the Prince did not return in his friend's drojki, but drove into town in the carriage of the cantatrice. He was indeed quite right, when he complained of being unlucky.

CHAPTER XV.

AN UNEXPECTED BLOW.

MICHEL had come to St. Petersburg four days after Marthe's marriage, and on entering his rooms, weary and travel-stained, he found a letter from his Aunt Avéroef, which had been waiting for him for several days.

"Come quickly," wrote the old lady; "do not delay a moment. I need you instantly!"

Michel's watch said six o'clock, and the young man took only time to change his travelling dress, and, rushing to the station, took the train, and at seven arrived.

At the sound of his spurs in the ante-room, Madame Avéroef did what she was in the habit of doing only for her Sovereign: she rose and went to meet her guest. Surprised at this unusual concession, Michel looked his Aunt earnestly in the face: she was paler than usual, and seemed fatigued.

"I have been expecting you several days," she said, after the first compliments. "When did you arrive?"

"Just now—in the five o'clock train."

"Then you have not dined?"

"I found your summons, Aunt, and could not delay."

The old lady was touched by this deference, and said they would dine together. ·

They took their seats, but Madame Avéroef ate little. She watched with maternal eyes the young man as he appeased his hunger, and her aged hand — delicate and white — laid more than one dainty morsel on Michel's plate.

He, in the meantime, was too well bred to ask his Aunt why she had sent for him. He waited until she was quite ready to explain herself.

When dinner was over—when the hot and fragrant coffee had disappeared from the tiny Sevres cup, Madame Avéroef rose and led her nephew into her sleeping room. The setting sun tinged the tops of the Linden trees with gold; the old garden was filled with brooding quiet; all was fresh and cool within. She placed herself in her chair, and signed to Michel to take one near her.

He obeyed, and waited in an agony of suspense until it pleased his Aunt to speak.

"Have you seen any one since your return?" she said.

"No, my dear Aunt; no one."

"Your servants, of course?"

"My old housekeeper only—for about five minutes."

"Did she tell you nothing?"

"Absolutely nothing."

Michel grew more and more uneasy. His Aunt's face, usually so smiling, had a strange expression, and yet his respect for her years was so great that he dared not ask a question, or evince impatience.

"Michel," she said, kindly; "why did you go away so suddenly, without letting me know?"

"My brother was ill, and telegraphed me to come."

"You did not go alone, Michel," continued the old lady, in a compassionate tone, which touched the heart of the young man.

"You heard that?" he answered, in some embarrassment.

"Yes; some gossip of the servants, came, I assure you, to my ears accidentally."

Michel did not reply.

"You had a child with you?" she resumed.

"Since you know all about it, my dear Aunt, I need not deny it."

"And it was said to be your child," continued Madame Avérœf, sadly.

"And you believed it?" cried Michel.

She calmed him with a gesture.

"No, Michel; I did not believe it. This child, I am quite sure, was not yours. You have too much respect for yourself!"

With a dignified gesture, she extended her hand to the young man, who kissed it with tender deference.

"Why were you not open with me?" she asked. "I could have protected your name from all gossip."

"I had no right, Aunt. Silence was enjoined upon me, as it is now."

"Then you did right, my child," said Madame Avérœf, quietly.

She relapsed into silence. Day was fading in the
garden, while within, the room was nearly black.
Madame Avérœf's white face and whiter hair stood
out against the dark curtains.

Michel felt a vague foreboding; the unwonted tenderness of his Aunt—the mystery of this interrogation,
which seemed to have no especial aim—all this caused
him an anxiety that was momentarily increasing.

"Dear Aunt," he said, in a low voice, "if any
danger threatens me, tell me so at once. I prefer to
know the worst."

"Whatever it may be?" asked the old lady.

"Yes; I have courage for anything."

She was silent for a moment, and then leaning
toward him, she laid her hand on Michel's arm—

"My child," she said; "you love——"

"Yes, dear Aunt," interrupted Michel; "I love with
all my heart and all my soul!" and the young man
threw back his head, all aglow at being able to confess
his secret for the first time.

"And she whom you love?'

"Is Marthe Mélaguire," and Michel uttered the
words like a defiance to the whole world.

"Does she love you?"

"I don't know," answered Michel, honestly, although
in the depths of his heart a voice cried out—"It is
false; you know very well that she loves you!"

"You quarreled with her?"

"No, indeed—why?"

"She is married," said Madame Avéroef, almost in a whisper.

"Married!" cried Michel, starting up impetuously, ready to crush to the earth him who had robbed him of his treasure.

"God sees you, Michel!" said Madame Avéroef, who rose at the same time, and then sank back in her arm-chair. "God sees you; guard your words!"

The young man fell on his knees before her. She placed her hand on his bowed head.

"Michel, I love you, with the same love I feel toward my grandson. I did not wish a stranger to bring you this news. I thought that a relative—almost a mother —would deal the blow, and staunch the wound with a more compassionate hand than a stranger. If I was wrong, blame your old Aunt, but forgive her."

Michel, without answering, buried his face in the trembling hand which caressed him, and softly smoothed his cheeks and his hair. She saw that she had done wisely, and had read Michel aright.

"Married!" repeated the young man, after a long silence.

He rose and seated himself opposite his Aunt.

"Tell me all you know," he said, sternly.

Madame Avéroef began her recital at Marthe's birth-day. She described things as they took place simply, and as they occurred, without comment of any kind. She gave utterance to no suspicions, whatever she may have had, feeling that she had no right to excite those of Michel.

Nor did she make any allusion to the conversation she had had with Marthe, seated in that same fauteuil. What was the good, now that Marthe was married? Was it not wiser, too, on her part, to make the separation between these two hearts, which had failed to understand each other, wider and more complete?

Was it not best that hatred and contempt should succeed to love in Michel's heart, rather than run any risk which could stain the honor of two families? If these victims should meet and understand each other, what then? She brought no accusations against Marthe, however. She neither would nor could blame "the dear Princess," as she called her to herself. She knew very well that Marthe had believed what was said of Michel as soon as he had left. The young woman might be weak and credulous, but as soon as she admitted the reality of these suppositions, her conduct was perfectly natural. "All for honor," said Madame Avéroef, and Marthe's device was the same.

When she ceased speaking, Michel sat in silence for a full minute, and then rose to depart.

"I thank you, from my very heart, dear Aunt," he said, quietly. "I shall never forget your goodness to me. I trust that I may some day have it in my power to prove the truth of my words."

"Where are you going?" said Madame Avéroef, in some astonishment at his composure.

"I am going home and to bed," was his reply. "I have been travelling the last three nights, you must remember."

" And then what do you intend to do?"

" Fulfill all my duties to the best of my ability. My father is here, I believe?"

"Yes; he is here."

"Then to-morrow morning I shall go to see him. My poor father! Had he come two months sooner, none of this would have happened. But what is done is done. Good night, dear Aunt."

"But you are not going——"

"To kill Oghérof? Poor fellow!—it is not his fault if he found her among his fire-works. It was all fore-ordained, I suppose."

He left the room with haggard eyes and a burning face. The cool fresh night air calmed him, and he went home and to bed, but he buried his face in his pillow to stifle his sobs, and bit it in his agony before sleep came to him.

CHAPTER XVI.

THE MEETING.

THREE or four days after the evening at The Isles, Oghérof was returning from the country, where he had been to see his wife, and to carry her the expression of his secret repentance, in the double form of a wonderful bracelet and a tiny dog—two things which were, as the men who sold them said, unique in style. As he turned into the Place d'Isaac he found himself face to face with Michel, who, having looked forward to this encounter ever since his return, was able to assume an impassive countenance. Oghérof was enchanted to see his comrade, whose existence, however, he had absolutely forgotten in the past four months, and now greeted him with great warmth—spoke of his horses and his new dwelling—"for you know that I am married," he said, parenthetically.

"So I heard," answered Michel, calmly. "You married Mademoiselle Mélaguire, I believe."

"Yes, my dear fellow; and is she not beautiful? You, too, if I do not mistake, was one of her adorers?"

"Most assuredly," answered Michel, very gravely.

"Very well; you may continue to make love to her if you choose. Come home and dine with me, won't you?"

" Many thanks ! but I have a thousand things to do. When shall you bring your "— he hesitated —"your family back to town?"

"Not until the 1st of October. The Mélaguires are with us at our country house now; you knew it, I suppose."

"No; I had not heard of it. Good-bye."

"You will come and see my wife after the 1st of October?"

"Most certainly," answered Avérœf, as he strode away.

This meeting, and the borders to the new carpets which could not be found to match the furniture, dissipated from Oghérof's mind the shadow of remorse he had brought back from the country — remorse that had grown sharper, when he found his wife so serene and unsuspicious of his misdoings.

Nor did his remorse prevent him from going to The Isles, alone, and often; and by degrees, his visits became essential to the little blonde, who, she herself told him, found those days a blank that she did not see him.

On the first of October, Marthe returned to town ; but Michel did not see fit to present himself. At this remissness she was not astonished, for, after all, why should he wish to see her again? She told herself that they must meet sooner or later; in the street, at the house of a friend — any where; but sufficient for the day is the evil thereof, and Marthe deliberately drove

9

all thoughts of Michel from her mind, and thought so little of him, that his name was forgotten as soon as she heard it spoken.

Nevertheless, the hour so dreaded by Michel, and anticipated by the Princess Oghérof, was near at hand. One evening, as Marthe entered her father's house, to preside at one of his elegant dinners, which were never satisfactory to him, unless his dear daughter were there, Monsieur Mélaguire said, abruptly :

"By the way, I met Michel Avéroef to-day, and invited him !"

"Here, this evening?" asked Marthe, startled at the abyss opening before her.

"Yes, this evening. You seem to be astonished !"

"By no means !" and Marthe's voice was calm; "but after his abrupt departure, without a word of explanation, it seems to me —"

"But he sent a bouquet; are you sure that you never received it?"

"Perfectly sure !"

"Then the fellow that brought it cheated him, and sold it on his way to our house. He wrote also from Italy, but the letter never reached us."

"There are some people who are proverbially unlucky," said the Princess, coldly, as she arranged a curl before the mirror.

Michel was the last to arrive of all the guests. Twenty times he had said to himself, that he would not go to this dinner, and then ended by going, thinking that it was a mere question of to-day or to-morrow.

The salon was brilliantly lighted. Marthe had laid aside all her old habits, and instead of the shaded lamp, which formerly lighted her little nook, there was now a candelabra, this was not enough in her eyes, and she added a host of candles, whenever her father received. She, who once avoided noise, now shrank from silence. Her thoughts were too exacting when the external world was not tumultuous enough to drown them.

The assembly were standing ready to go into the dining-room as Michel entered. The Princess was the centre of a group. Her violet velvet dress was close in the throat, and the pearls in her ears shimmered in the light. Never was she so lovely; her beauty too, had assumed new characteristics, and was far more imposing than of yore. At the sound of the spurs worn by Michel, she turned, and looked him in the face for a moment. The young man bowed before her, as she uttered the simple words, "Good evening, sir," in a cold, grave voice. This was all. Michel answered her with equal stateliness, and they all moved toward the dining-room.

Michel sat nearly opposite Marthe. He could see her every movement, every fleeting change of expression, and it was with the greatest difficulty that he could believe that Marthe had really become the Princess Oghérof, though the fact was thus presented to his eyes. The whole affair was a mystery to him, which he determined to solve.

The Princess was apparently in the best of spirits.

She, whose taciturnity had formerly amounted in society to a fault, now talked constantly, laughed often, catching as it flew, some detached phrase in the general conversation, and sending back a reply, like the shuttlecock from the battledore, and then, resuming her graceful chat with those next her, without losing its thread for a moment. Her cheeks were flushed, and her eyes were very brilliant. At the end of dinner, she took up the *carafe* to pour out a glass of water, and broke it.

"That brings good luck," said her father, pleasantly.

Marthe glanced furtively at Avérœf. His eyes were fixed upon her, dark with passionate reproach.

Marthe could not contain herself. With a rapid movement, she pushed back her chair, and rose impetuously, thus throwing into piteous disarray the elderly persons at the table, who had counted on a few minutes grace to tip their *Vin de Hongroie.*

In the salon, Michel, at the risk of attracting attention, at once approached Marthe, and was about to address her, when she spoke.

"You had an agreeable journey, I think?" and her voice was stormy.

"Thanks, Princess. I was happy enough to leave my brother much better," he answered, with his habitual calm.

"I am delighted to hear it. How long is it since you returned?"

"Four days after your marriage. I did my best to return earlier, but it was impossible."

"And why, pray; a sojourn in Italy is by no means disagreeable, and you were wise to extend your leave to its extreme limit, particularly as there was nothing to call you home."

Michel looked at Marthe with such assurance, and such honest indignation in his eyes, that she fairly shivered with anger.

"Hypocrite!" she thought, and abruptly turned her back upon him, to address a short-winded old general, who had struggled through the furniture which, as he said, "was dreadfully in the way now-a-days."

Pauline Hopfer had suffered untold anguish during this brief conversation between Michel and the Princess. She was detained by Monsieur Mélaguire, who was giving her some especial direction in regard to the liqueurs, and the centenary curaçoa, which must be brought in its little basket with the greatest care.

"It must not be shaken," repeated Monsieur Mélaguire, catching her by the dress, as she tried to escape.

At last she was free, just in time to see the light of indignation in Marthe's eyes, which comforted her, as it proved that as yet no explanation had taken place.

"But it is a great risk to run again! I must find some way of preventing them from talking to each other!" she said to herself as she went to get the wine.

Toward midnight, Marthe went up to kiss her sleeping sister before she went away, such being her usual custom. Finding Pauline in the room, she lingered to talk a little.

"Monsieur Michel has returned," said the girl, with averted eyes.

"Well?" answered Marthe, more gently than she had recently spoken, when this wound was touched.

"I do not believe he will go away again very soon."

"And why, pray?"

"Because there is no longer any necessity for him to take such a long journey to find the person he wishes to see," murmured this officious young person.

Marthe did not reply. She held her handkerchief in her tightly clenched hand, and the handkerchief was in slits when she opened it.

"The child is left in Italy, and the governess has written to her relatives that she shall spend the winter there."

"And the mother has returned?" said Marthe, with a nervous laugh; "that is certainly much more convenient."

A movement of Nastia made her look round; the young girl half-opened her eyes, recognized Marthe, stretched out her arms to her with an incoherent word or two, and fell asleep again.

The Princess was ashamed of her temper, and of listening to this unworthy gossip in the room of her innocent sleeping sister. She leaned over her, and pressed upon her lips a kiss almost maternal in its tenderness. She felt a sudden softening of her heart.

"Good night, Pauline," she murmured, and hurriedly

left the room, for she felt the necessity of being alone. She leaned from her carriage window for some time, looking out into the mist and drizzle of this sad October night, at the wet streets, at the occasional foot-passengers, and she envied the very beggars, whom Destiny condemned to pass the night out of doors, without the shelter of a roof, and who would find under some doorway, with a cold stone for a pillow, the heavy sleep which comes when poor Humanity is worn out by physical fatigue.

Marthe and Michel after this, met continually.

It could hardly be otherwise. Avérœf came two or three times to the Mondays of the Princess, always, however, at an hour when the salon was likely to be full. Oghérof invited him to dine, over and over again, but the young man was always provided with a good excuse for refusing these invitations. Marthe said to herself, with some bitterness, that he did not wish to take the time from another place, where he preferred to go.

Oghérof's life was very similar to what it had been before his marriage. His labors were not very arduous, though they kept him much from his wife. They consisted mainly in procuring boxes at the theatre, and providing "certain ladies" with amusements.

The Princess passed most of her time with her young sister, either in her own house, or at that of her father, so that Monsieur Mélaguire often forgot that his eldest daughter was married.

CHAPTER XVII.

EMANCIPATION.

THE sun, on the 19th of February, rose in a clear sky, and shone upon placards affixed to all the walls and fences, from the humblest planks to the most solid blocks of granite, around the palatial dwellings. Before it was fairly light, people gathered before these placards, and those who were able, read to the others the decree by which a body of slaves was transformed to a nation of men.

"Is it printed?" said those who could not read; "are those words really printed there?"

"Read for yourself, if you don't believe me," answered the orator.

The ignorant ones shook their heads, and went away in a doubtful state of mind, divided between a desire to believe and the distrust and suspicion natural to those who are not free.

On this day, which was Sunday, the Princess Oghérof started to drive to the *Eglise de la Poste*, but, seized by a sudden caprice, she left her carriage, and, alone and unattended, went, on foot, through the snow, toward the *Eglise d'Isaac*.

To enter it, seemed impossible, so great was the crowd upon the pavement; but the rich raiment of the lady produced its usual effect, and, by degrees, the Princess pushed her way into the cathedral.

Within reigned a profound silence; every face was turned toward the centre, where the blue incense was slowly mounting to the vaulted done, and whence came a voice that, after a few words, became suddenly silent. The thrilled assembly, with one impulse, bowed every head, as if a storm wind swept over them, and the word " *Glory to God on High* " went up to Heaven — the voice of an emancipated nation! The lines just read was the Act of Emancipation of the Serfs. Regenerated Russia, before thanking him who had given them liberty, thanked the Most High, who had sent the blessed thought to the Ruler.

Psalms of praise floated through the cathedral. Many wept; others looked stunned, as if weighed down by strong emotion. Some, with rigid faces, and compressed lips, seemed to dwell on the Past, and contemplate reprisals in the Future; but the countenances of the masses were calm and thoughtful.

"I heard people say yesterday," thought the Princess, "that the people did not know what Liberty meant; but they were mistaken. These men comprehend very clearly, that they are free."

She left the church with the crowd, and crossed the square. Everywhere she encountered these same steadfast, earnest faces, elevated by a light from within. On the *Place du Grand-Marché* the church was too small for the multitude, who wished to pour out their thanks there; and the peasants of the most humble class were kneeling far out in the snow before the door.

"You heard it?" they said to those who emerged from the portal.

And, on their reply in the affirmative, they touched the earth with their foreheads, and blessed God and the Emperor, their Father. They had doubted the testimony of those who read the Proclamation; but they accepted without question, the assurance of those who heard. A tall old man, with hair and long beard entirely white, stood upright, and recited the canticle of Simeon.

"And now, O Lord, let thy servant depart in peace!"

Marthe felt the generous blood of her twenty years mount to her head. It seemed to her that she, too, must sob and cry with those about her. She emptied her purse into the hands of those who were nearest.

"Good!" cried the old man, "give it all, little Lady; it will be spent in candles!"

Marthe walked on, where she hardly knew, but came out on *La Place du Palais*. The snow lay white on every roof; the cold was fierce, but the square was black with people. Wherever two feet could find standing room, a peasant's form was planted. Every face was turned toward the balcony of the Palace. The window opened, and the Emperor appeared.

Those who heard the shout that went up from every broad breast, will never forget it, even did he live to be so old that he forgets his own name. And Marthe—the reserved and calm Marthe—wept like a child, and fled, covering her face with her handkerchief. She waited impatiently for the return of her husband, who was on duty at the Palace. Then, at last, he came in at night, she greeted him with an eager

"Well! How did it go off?"

"I have had a vile day of it," he answered, with a yawn. "The heat in the Palace was intense, and so much bread and salt has taken away my appetite. But, Heavens and earth! Marthe, what is the matter with you; you look as if you were in a high fever!"

"I went out on foot to-day," answered the Princess, evasively.

"On foot! In this cold! What an idea! And such a crowd, too, as there was in the street to-day—a crowd of dirty peasants!"

"But it was the peasants whom I wished to see," said Marthe. "It was a great event that took place to-day!"

"A great event, yes; and a great hole in our purse. We have lost at least twenty thousands roubles."

"Prince," said Marthe, "there are some points on which we shall never understand each other."

Oghérof looked at his wife with some surprise, then mentally shrugged his shoulders.

He was charmed by his marriage; the Princess was just the mistress of his house that he desired. Her manners were perfect and dignified; but, he said to himself, Marthe had certainly the strangest whims in the world. Having thus disposed of the question, he turned away.

That day, had the Princess received from the Royal Palace a mandate, bidding her leap from the window, she would have obeyed with joy, so great was her loyalty; and that night she fell asleep with a prayer for the Czar on her lips.

CHAPTER XVIII.

SINGULAR IDEAS.

THE next day Marthe met Michel at the house of Madame Avérœf. Fortunately, other people were there. The conversation, as may be supposed, fell on the event of the previous day—an event looked forward to with doubts and fear, for so long, but now being a thing of the past, it seemed very simple, as do all things when once accomplished.

"Now then, Prascovia Petrovna," said Marthe, with an air of triumph, "it is done, and you see they have eaten no one!"

This "they" referred to the twenty-two millions liberated the previous day. For more than a year this significant "they" had been used to designate the serfs; and nothing further was necessary.

"Yes, it passed off quietly enough," answered the old lady; "but" she added, after a short pause, "it is not yet finished."

"But the danger is past," said Michel; "it was only the intoxication of their triumph that we feared. But as they knew, even in their hour of intoxication, how to remain within the boundaries of moderation, surely there is nothing more to fear."

"Their triumph?" repeated Marthe, in a disdainful

tone; "a fine triumph indeed! Their pleasures, it seems to me, are all negative. They will not be beaten nor treated like dogs! They must have strong heads, indeed, to resist such intoxications!"

"It is none the less liberty to the imprisoned, light to the blind," said Michel gravely.

Marthe looked at him without a word. A light of the old days shone momentarily in his brave eyes, but it faded away. This man was not the Michel whom our readers first knew. What did it matter, nowadays, what he thought or said!

"You are right, my dear nephew," resumed Madame Avéroef, "and yet I would gladly have given many years of my life to advance the hour of emancipation. I did not wish to see it. We old people have lived too long; and you, General?" she added, turning to an old white-haired man, who, sitting in the corner, listened to this conversation with attentive interest.

"I am of your opinion, Madame," he answered, quietly.

"Oh! my dear Aunt!" cried Michel.

"Yes, my friend; we were brought up with the idea that we were superior to the race that served us. This idea is most unjust, I admit, but all we heard, and all we saw, tended to make of us, the absolute masters of our estates, and of all that multiplied and grew there.

"And now, I am seventy-one, my dear nephew, and I must make for myself new rules and new habits of thought! I do not speak of the peasants, they will now be property holders, to which I make no objection. May the blessing of God rest upon them! But, the servants who have been with me for twenty years, whom I have seen born and grow up under my roof — young girls, whom I have taught, who have embroidered my gowns — boys whom I have transformed, and some of them with no little difficulty, into adroit coachmen, well-mannered, clever servants, and skilled mechanics — all this generation brought up at my expense, and by my care, can leave me to-morrow, if the whim seizes them, leave me to die, surrounded by unknown faces and mercenary cares. No, my dear nephew, I cannot grasp the idea. Emancipation is a great thing; I know that; but I should have preferred to close my eyes before it was accomplished.

A long silence followed, broken by the old General in a most unexpected manner.

"Well said, Prascovia Petrovna," he exclaimed, in his shrill voice; "but for me — living on my estates as I do — it is a vastly different thing. My peasants, or I ought rather to say, my ex-peasants, have fallen into the habit of catching their fish in my waters, on the pretext, that there were so many more there, than in the river. I have allowed this for, well, I can hardly say for how long, ever since I had the honor of being named page to her majesty, the Empress Catherine. Well, now, suppose that to-morrow—no, not to-morrow, as the season is hardly favorable for fishing, but next summer, were I to send my people to fish in the river that runs through their farms, you would see them bring a suit against me without a moment's delay —"

"But, General," interrupted Michel.

"They would do just that I tell you! And you will see, moreover, that they will insist on my paying the fine! So in the same way have I fed their cattle in the hard years. Now let one of my cows, the cows of their former lord and master, so much as put out its tongue in their meadows, and you will see that they will pounce upon my poor animal. I shall be obliged to go and take it from the pound, and interview the — what is the name of their official?"

"But, General," said Michel, laughing; "that official may be either you or me, you know. It is precisely as we choose."

"Thank you," answered the old gentleman; "at my age, one does not care to assume such responsibilities, and go scouring the country in a *tarantass*. No, no, you are right, Prascovia Petrovna, we have lived too long. But let them look out! If I find even one of their hens in my fields —"

"You will bring a suit against it?" asked Michel, gravely.

"No, I will have it plucked and boiled," replied the old General, morosely, as he buried himself in the corner of the sofa.

Madame Avéroef could not preserve her gravity during this tirade.

"You will have many difficulties to contend with,

my dear General," she said. "I see that very clearly.
I, however, am resigned to every thing; I am only
grieved at witnessing the ingratitude about me. My
maid, whom, I myself, held at the baptismal font, asked
me this very morning, how much I intended to increase
her wages."

She turned away as she spoke, for tears were in her
eyes — pride prevented them however, from falling.
Michel leaned over her hand and kissed it.

"Dear Aunt," he said, "bondage did not prevent
ingratitude; it promoted its growth under another
form, that is all. What does the ingratitude of these
people matter, if your friends and your children love
you? It is in their arms, that you will breathe your
last, it is they, who will close your eyes, for you shall
not be left to mercenary cares."

The old lady kissed Michel's curly head. Marthe,
stiff and stately, was turning over the leaves of an
album. Madame Avérœf glanced at her, and the tears
that she had until then restrained, dropped on her
nephew's hair.

"You are a dear, good boy," she said; "with the
kindest possible heart; and you are right!"

"You will see dear Aunt, that before long you will
be proud of having lived to see this great event."

"May your words be true!" she said, sadly, shaking
her head. "May every one else be pleased, too!"

"Not I, at all events," grumbled the General, "and
you, Princess?"

10

" Yesterday was the most beautiful day of my life," replied Marthe, as she rose.

Her voice rang like a bugle on the battle field. With her head erect, and haughty, steady eyes, she seemed to set at defiance, all the prejudices of the old aristocracy. Michel's eyes, full of enthusiasm and youthful ardor, answered to hers. She turned away quickly, and became very pale.

There was no need of words between them; so well did they understand each other.

Marthe could bear no more and quickly withdrew, bowing to Michel with an air of indifference rather than disdain, but she dared not meet again those honest eyes, which pierced her heart like sharp arrows.

CHAPTER XIX.

SUSPICIONS.

SOME days later, Michel met Sophie in the salon of a mutual friend. She was always attracted by this grave and sympathetic young man, who was as reserved as she was expansive; but whom she knew to be as frank, and loyal as herself. The little circle was discussing emancipation as was the case everywhere.

"And you, Sophie, what do you think of it?" asked Michel.

"Oh! I am enchanted," she answered, "my husband is nominated as arbiter, and I shall buy his insignia to-morrow. We shall spend a year in the country, which will be an excellent thing for my health. My Uncle Mélaguire is furious, which is good for him."

"Furious, is he?"

"Most assuredly, but mildly so; for you know he is as good as gold, after all, and a little anger assists digestion. He sleeps now after dinner, having abused the peasants, emancipation and right of redemption. He has wanted occupation since Marthe's marriage, he has it now!"

As she rattled on with apparent carelessness, Sophie watched the young man. She saw something, which gave her courage to continue.

"You have no enemies, Monsieur Michel?" she asked, suddenly.

"None that I am aware of," he answered, in some surprise; not as much, however, as he would have felt at the same question a year before.

"You see," she continued, "that I cherish the fixed belief, that you have some hidden enemy. Mysterious and implacable," she added, half smiling, as if to soften her words. "Have you ever killed any one?"

"Not even in a dream," answered the young man, gayly.

"Have you ever carried away some fair creature, from a less favored rival?"

"Still less."

"Then have you disdained the love of some woman?" continued Sophie, lowering her voice, and speaking very seriously; "such enemies never forgive."

Michel looked so earnestly at the lady, that she felt compelled to speak more clearly.

"You see," she continued, "various circumstances have compelled me to the belief that you have some active enemy, some enemy who hates you. Now, this enemy has employed such perfidious arms, that I am convinced that it can only be a woman, and not an ordinary woman, either. Now think well of what I have said, and see if you can find no reason to believe in the truth of my words."

"If I am mistaken, if nothing in your life demonstrates to you the possibility of this secret enmity, then all is — I am utterly blind. My uncle Mélaguire has always said so. One thing is certain, however, I am meddling with matters that are none of my business, and I really beg your pardon. But I see my husband looking daggers at me. He has been talking for five minutes with his Chef, and expects me to go up and pay my respects, otherwise, we shall have no promotion at Easter."

She disappeared, leaving Michel a little moved and much perplexed. Several times he had asked himself since his return, how it was that Marthe had so quickly changed her opinion in regard to him, and why neither his bouquet nor his letter, had reached their destination, and Sophie's question, "Have you no enemies," had more than once occurred to him.

But Michel had too honest a nature, to believe in enemies, and the question remained without a reply. Sophie's statement that the enemy must be a woman, opened to his research, new horizons, but poured no further light upon them. The result of these reflections was that, if any one could give him any information on these points it must be Pauline Hopfer, and he resolved to question her on the first occasion.

My readers may be inclined to ask how it was that Michel, intelligent as he was, had never suspected Pauline's admiration, or the hatred that had replaced it. The truth was, that Michel had little vanity — he thought it an insult to a woman, to suppose that he, without courting her, could have won her favor, and the idea had never entered his head.

And then, too, Pauline was not a woman to him. She was the governess—the housekeeper, a neuter being with whom one might chat a little, but who belonged in no sense to the world, where he could love or marry. Poor Pauline! Fortunately, she did not know the extent of her abasement.

Since the marriage of the Princess, a new set of ideas had replaced the old ones in Pauline's brain. She fully realized now, that Michel would never marry her; the rarity of his visits, his polite indifference, proved as clear as day, that the affair was hopeless. Since the children's ball, she had indulged no hope whatever; having then fully realized that Michel was hardly aware of her existence.

Since then, this man, whom she had so skilfully bejuggled from Marthe's grasp, counted for nothing in her eyes. She had disposed of her old passion as easily as one gets rid of the lemon, when the oysters are finished, to make ready for the soup.

Michel had been a most desirable speculation, and one in which she was by no means disposed that any other than herself should embark—least of all, her ex-pupil; but when he ceased to be a possible husband for Marthe, he lost the charm of being contested for—a charm which doubled his value.

Pauline, like a practical creature as she was, had more than one string to her bow. She looked forward to Nastia's marriage, before many years, and to Monsieur Mélaguire's being left alone in sad old age.

It was then, that she would decide on her destiny. It would be impossible for her to remain alone in the house of this unmarrried man — her reputation and regard for her honor, would compel her to quit her benefactor with a half broken heart, after so many happy years. She arranged her little speech, and decided that the name of Madame Mélaguire would smooth over every thing.

But that was long to look forward to, and then if the marriage and the position were so desirable, the man was not! And Pauline reproached herself vehemently, as having allowed Marthe to marry the Prince, for she mentally claimed to have made the match.

It was with a feeling of bitter anger against herself that she said, had she not been so blind — and so absorbed in her mad passion for Michel, that she might have married the Prince herself, instead of making him marry Marthe.

Princess Oghérof! This name which she heard over and over again all day long, filled her with a sullen rage. Two sentiments, distinct, and like twins, stood out among the somewhat confused ideas of this young lady. A profound hatred against Michel, who was the sole cause of all this difficulty — and a thorough aversion to Marthe, who had never received her into her confidence and friendship, and who had by her haughtiness, erected between them a line of insurmountable separation.

She promised herself some day in the future, to

make these two insolent creatures pay for the error of
which she had been guilty, in allowing the Prince to
slip through her fingers; and the day that Michel, who
had been for some time, seeking an opportunity of
having some especial conversation with her, met her on
the piazza, she, at once, hailed the rencontre, as the
most desirable thing in the world, and the first occasion
for the reprisals, she meditated. She was, however,
slightly mistaken. Michel had merely a few questions
to ask, the replies to which she had held on the end of
her tongue, for the last six months.

"I beg your pardon, Pauline," said the young officer,
"but I am extremely desirous of addressing to you a
very simple question; but one that is to me of very
great importance."

"Go on, Monsieur Michel," said Pauline in her most
honied tones; "I am always at your service."

"The day after my departure to Italy was, unless I
greatly mistake — Mademoiselle Marthe's birthday. I
should say, the Princess Oghérof's birthday."

"I think you are right," answered Pauline, pricking
up her ears like a war horse at the call of the bugle.

"I sent a bouquet. Do you know if it was received."

"How can I tell you — since it was not intended for
me?" answered Pauline, with her sweetest smile.

"Monsieur Mélaguire knows nothing about it either.
It is not a matter of much importance, and yet —"

"You might ask the florist if he sent it," interrupted
Pauline.

Mademoiselle Hopfer made this remark with the air of a young mother, anxious in regard to the health of her new born infant. She awaited the reply with a nervous contraction of the throat.

"The Florist assures me that it was sent, and even showed me his books; but the boy whom he sent to deliver it, has left his employment, and I cannot trace him."

The companion drew a long breath of relief.

"He probably sold it on the way," she answered, in the most persuasive tones; "these things are done daily; we are so badly served, nowadays!"

Michel did not speak for a moment; then, he added, slowly.

"I wrote to Monsieur Mélagnire from Mentone. He never received my letter."

"Ah! You went to Mentone, then?"

"Yes. Do you think this letter was lost in the mail, or have you any reason to suspect any of your people of negligence?"

"As I said before," she answered, "servants are so wretched, nowadays—they are capable of anything! But as regards the correspondence of the household, this is the first difficulty of which I have heard. I always get all my letters — which, to be sure, are very few," she added, with a sudden change of voice, and a melancholy smile, which spoke only too clearly of her desolation and loneliness in this vale of tears. "And *apropos* of Mentone," she continued, "what did you do with the governess, whom I entrusted to you?"

"Has she not written you?" asked Michel, suddenly realizing that his brother's secret was in great danger.

Pauline was unprepared for this especial question, but she was made for a statesman. Foreseeing that Michel might ask who had put in circulation all the rumors to his discredit, she resolved, at once, to strike a great blow, and thus protect herself for the rest of her days, against any indiscreet suppositions.

"She has written to me certainly, Monsieur Michel," she answered, looking her interlocutor directly in his eyes, "she is an excellent woman, simple-minded and warm-hearted. You need never regret having given her your confidence."

Michel was utterly dumbfounded.

"She is very prudent, and not in the least communicative," added Pauline, with a shrewd glance; "and will be a precious acquisition to those who awaken her attachment."

"So much the better," said the young officer, abruptly; "but that is none of my business. Excuse me, Mademoiselle, but I have still another question."

"Hasten please," interrupted the young lady, "for I am wanted down stairs."

"Has any one spoken disparagingly of me, to you?" said Michel, burning his vessels, "or to "—he hesitated —"to Monsieur Mélaguire?"

"Oh! Monsieur Michel! No, indeed; never! A young man like you, so well brought up—so well educated! No, indeed! Who would have dared—I give you my word that no human being has ever said a word against you, either to Monsieur Mélaguire or myself. Of course, Monsieur Mélaguire would never have permitted it."

"Thank you, Mademoiselle," said Michel, without effusion, however, for he felt a vague distrust; "these questions must have seemed very singular to you; perhaps, even somewhat indiscreet."

"No, Monsieur Michel; I understand you."

Avéroef looked up quickly.

"I regretted all that happened," she continued, "more than I can tell you. I even ventured to say this to Mademoiselle Marthe—to the Princess I should say; and this it is that has turned her against me. Young girls, you know, are subject to caprices."

"Thank you, Mademoiselle," interrupted Michel, whose very lips were white; "You are very good; I ask your pardon for having disturbed you. *Au revoir!*"

And he turned away.

"Try again! Try again!" muttered Pauline, between her teeth, with sardonic joy. "You are but a poor hound!"

And she entered the house with an air of triumph.

CHAPTER XX.

MONT BLANC.

THIS winter was a dreary one for every body. Court mourning prevented any balls. Concerts and parties alone remained, which are not especially agreeable distractions, taken in large doses.

Marthe barricaded herself in her pride — her health visibly declined. Michel tried to forget her, and the Prince was out of spirits and anxious.

His anxiety was of a peculiar nature. A horse jockey with whom he had had more than one affair, found himself suddenly in great need of money; the sale of a superb stud was announced, and this same horse jockey, wishing to turn an honest penny, applied to the Prince.

"Lend me ten thousand roubles, your Highness," he had said.

At this request, Oghérof, who was always willing to give, but, never inclined to lend, assumed so severe an aspect that the horse jockey hastily added:

"Listen to me, one moment. If your Highness will listen patiently, you will see what I mean. I have six race horses, for which I have had many offers; but I did not propose to part with them to the first applicants. Take these as security, they are worth twice as much as the amount I ask. Come and look at them! You can keep them in your stable; you can run them if you choose, you can do with them precisely what you wish, until I return, which will be in two months, with a two-year-old foal as interest for you."

"I have plenty of horses, what do I want of yours?" answered Oghérof, somewhat thrown off his equilibrium.

"Sell your own. I will furnish you with infinitely better animals. Come and see mine, and if you don't approve, consider my words unsaid. Comte Garantine wants them, but I prefer to give them to you, because you are a connoisseur."

The Prince went to see the animals, and found them really superb; whereupon, after bargaining a little, eight thousand roubles left his portfolio at the same time that the six horses were installed in his stables. But all was not absolutely advantageous in this bargain. The oldest of the six horses was not four years old. The first time that the pair of trotters were put in harness, they dashed so violently through the *porte cochère*, that the pole entered a carriage, peacefully bearing an old Senator toward his curule chair. The carriage was damaged — so was the Senator; and Oghérof, after having had the carriage repaired at his expense, was obliged to make, at least, a dozen visits to the invalid, who never received him once without a reproach for his unmanageable horses. The second time these turbulent animals went out, they took the bit between their teeth, and smashed a lamp post on the *Place d'Isaac*. The calêche was so damaged that the Prince thought it better economy to buy another, than to have this one repaired. These two adventures were followed by so many others, that Marthe told her husband that she preferred to go on foot, rather than make use of these admirable animals. Oghérof was therefore obliged to purchase for his wife a pair of old, steady creatures. The four other horses were no better as investments; one, a saddle horse, went lame without any apparent reason. The fourth reared and kicked in such a way, that the stable men positively refused to touch him; while the other two would not consent to go together.

"And if you only knew how they eat!" said Oghérof to Michel, meeting him one day on the drive. "I never dreamed of horses eating as they do. They are growing absolutely ferocious from want of exercise, and I have now engaged two grooms, whose sole duty will be to go out with them."

"And your horse jockey?"

"He went off five months ago, and I have not heard a word of or from him. I fear I have made a bad thing of it," continued the Prince, meditatively, "for I have no right to sell; and the cost of keeping them, is something fearful. It is a bad piece of business!"

"It certainly looks so to me," said Michel, trying not to smile.

"But I am not astonished," continued the Prince, "for I never had the least luck."

The evening before, when Oghérof, at his usual hour entered the salon of the handsome brunette,—the Diva, who was for the time the recipient of his homage—he found there, an unknown diplomatist, who, instead of taking leave at once, was detained by the Diva, while Oghérof was treated with coldness; whereupon ensued a quarrel and a rupture."

"Come and dine with us," he said to Michel, entreatingly, without however, dwelling on his last misfortune, for it was not to Michel, that he revealed such things, for Michel never understood them!

"No, thanks!" answered Avéroef, "I dine at my Aunt's."

"But that is what you always say, whenever I ask you!"

"Is that so?" said Michel, laughing in spite of himself. "But you know, my poor friend, as you have often said, you never have any luck."

And most assuredly that year, Oghérof's winter was a very dull one. Spring came at last, however, after long, sad months of winter. Marthe, however, did not feel her wonted pleasure, in seeing the leaves appear on the dry, black branches; she had lost much of her love of Nature.

Seeing her so white and silent, some persons thought her consumptive, and charitably gave advice, which struck death to the soul of Monsieur Mélaguire, who consulted three physicians, exhausted their patience each in turn, and finally told Marthe that he would never leave her until she was completely restored to health.

A journey was planned therefore, and every detail arranged for a departure within a few days.

Oghérof allowed his wife to depart with a greatness of soul, which completely concealed the pain of the sacrifice. But in reality he did not need Marthe during the summer, because he was then in camp, occupied with military manœuvres, and with the Russian company engaged at the theatre of Karskoé-Sélo.

The only person who rebelled, was Nastia; this journey to foreign lands, of which the girl had heard constant talk ever since her childhood, affected her now like a nightmare; all her good humor vanished; she grumbled at the trunks, at the hotels, the railroads, and at every thing in short—all before she saw them, as if she knew by an experience of twenty years, all the discomforts of travelling.

"It would be so much better to remain at the *Isles*, or at Karskoé-Sélo," she said, one day.

Pauline looked at her and smiled sagaciously.

"What an idea," murmured Marthe, passive and indolent, as she had been for some time.

"I declare, Nastia," cried Monsieur Mélaguire, entirely out of patience — his lamblike amiability vanishing; "one would think you cared nothing for your sister! How can you regret a journey which will cure her entirely? What on earth is so attractive in the environs of St. Petersburg, that you prefer them to all these new scenes?"

Nastia threw herself into her sister's arms, and wept with so much vehemence, that it was almost impossible to soothe her.

Before her departure, however, she was shrewd enough to manage to be invited to spend a Sunday at Karskoé-Sélo with Madame Avœrf, who was becoming more and more fond of her. This tall fifteen-year-old girl amused her; her chatter and her constant jesting quarrels with Serge Avérœf, enlivened the silent old house. On returning home that night, she was un-usually silent and grave, but her eyes glittered like diamonds, while she stood waiting on the platform at the station for the train.

Monsieur Mélaguire who had come for her, was talk-ing with Michel in the twilight. Nastia slipped her arm through that of Serge, who had accompanied them.

"Four months," she murmured, "that is a long time!"

"Pshaw!" he answered; "the incessant drills, my uniform, and all that, will take up the time, for you know, Mademoiselle, that I shall be an officer when you return."

She looked at him with a smile, her eyes sparkling with joy and pride.

"And you, in your turn," he said, "will have the Tyrol, Chamois, Swiss embroideries, and little watches!"

"You ought to be ashamed of yourself," she answered lightly, striking his arm with the handle of her um-brella.

11

The train whizzed into the station.

"Adieu," said Serge to Monsieur Mélaguire; "*bon voyage!* and a happy return, Anastasia Palovna," he added with a ceremonious bow to Nastia, who bowed in return, and said not one word all the way to St. Petersburg.

The four travellers—for Pauline Hopfer was of the party—fulfilled their duties as sight-seers and travellers for the four summer months. Marthe swallowed any amount of mineral water, took long walks, but was still pale and inert, until they went to Switzerland, there the fresh mountain air brought the color to her cheeks. She remained at Geneva for a month. She was carried away by Mont Blanc, and spent hours gazing at its whiteness.

She wished to go to Chamounix; her wishes were orders. When she was there, and saw Mont Blanc so near, she was frightened—filled with terror at the enormous white mass. The mere thought of the glaciers made her dizzy, and she hurried back to Geneva where she could see the giant afar off, without that overwhelming terror that had assailed her at Chamounix.

She contemplated it in its serene calm, glittering in the moonlight, blue in the fresh morning air, yellow at noonday, dazzling in the rays which pierced the storm clouds, murky and severe before the tempest, and flushed at sunset with a deep, rosy light, as it was when Michel saw it. She looked at it as Michel had done, and one day when she heard that human footsteps had violated the snow upon the summits, the tears rushed to her eyes as if she had been robbed of a last illusion. She wept, and with these tears, life returned to her dry and withered heart. From this day, the tears which had for a long time ceased to flow, fell abundantly at times, and the roses returned to her cheeks, and strength to her body. Marthe was saved.

Autumn approached, and they returned to St. Petersburg.

CHAPTER XXI.

PAUL'S RETURN.

ONE October night, about eight o'clock, Michel was seated at his desk, revising the accounts of his regiment. The figures fell accurately from his pen, but his thoughts were elsewhere. During the summer, Michel had lost his father. He also could say, "it is the first sorrow he ever caused me." Never had a cloud obscured their reciprocal affection, tender if a trifle superficial, on the father's side, more devoted and more profound, on that of the son. General Avérœf went rarely to St. Petersburg, his death consequently created no void in the daily habits and pursuits of the young officer; but Michel loved this absent father, and wrote him constantly, receiving in his turn enormously thick letters, written in huge characters with lines far apart, letters which amounted to little, except as evidences of paternal affection.

Never had Michel felt so lonely — his brother was still in a foreign land—and a foreign land is almost another world. The frontier which separates the traveller from those who remain behind, is not an imaginary line or one traced by a pencil on a map; it is a rupture with customs, dress, and with the sweet native tongues, familiar to the ear, and which, when

heard in Paris or Rome, rivets
behind two men whom he do
whom, very likely, he would l
hands, but whom he follows i
they turn away, because they s
tongue.

Michel thought of his dead fatl
—he thought of Marthe only a
passed before him during the day
weary, unable to cope with the c
before him. During her illness,
suspense, awaiting the mortal blo
him at the same time as the Prin

Then he saw her cured, no long
and youth as she had been eighte
transfigured by suffering, almos
world, and yet, still a Queen in sc
air of high breeding, her *savoir*
beauty refined in the crucible of
self what was the secret sorrow fi
whom he loved, now suffered.
simple one. From her husbai
desertion! He, therefore, found
in keeping up any air of friendli

The Prince saw nothing of this
jockey had returned, paid back
and taken his horses; and the l
resumed its former current in the
blonde wigs, priceless equipage, a
and flourish!

Michel was deep in his additions, and his melancholy, when a sudden pull at the bell startled him. A hurried step in the ante-room — the door opened quickly, and by the shaded light of the lamp on his desk, he beheld his brother Paul, who came to him with open arms.

The relief was so great and so unexpected, that Michel felt tears choke him.

"Brother, dear Paul!" he said over and over again.

At last, regaining his self-possession, he seated himself by his brother's side on the sofa, and plied him with questions.

"Yes," said Paul, when the conversation grew calmer. "Yes, I have come back for good, I am perfectly well now, and do you know who is my physician?"

"No; who is he?"

"My physician is my daughter. The caresses of her tender little hands, her smiles and her tears, her eyes — so like her mother's — have done, what a host of doctors and a southern climate have failed to do. The child occupies my entire life, I myself instruct her entirely, and to see this mind develop, is a pleasure of which you can form no idea. Even her faults are interesting to me, because, well managed, they may be transformed into virtue. I am telling you things which it is impossible for you to understand, until you are a father yourself. In short, my dear Michel, I have come back to reside at St. Petersburg, and I am happy and well— two great cures you see!"

"And your daughter, what will you do with her?"

"Keep her with me. The governess you brought to Italy is no governess at all, she is a cook. Paul builded better than he knew — she makes patés to perfection, and is a most excellent woman, sincerely attached to the child, and takes the best of care of her, inculcates no bad principles, and what more can I ask?"

"But you can't hide the child, if she lives with you. People must see her and know that she is there."

"Precisely, that is just what I wish. I am, at this moment, filing a petition that she may take my name. What harm can that do me? Prevent me from marrying, you say? Not so — and if it did, I should not care, for I have no intention of marrying."

"Then you intend to acknowledge her openly, while awaiting legal permission to give her your name?"

"Exactly."

"All right!" said Michel, "I am content."

Paul pressed his brother's hand affectionately.

"When I think it is to you that I am indebted for this angel, I am overwhelmed with gratitude to you. Without your devotion," continued Paul; "I should still be a stranger to the joy of being loved by my daughter — my own, dear daughter, who has no one to love her in this world but me, and who loves no one but me! I am very selfish, am I not? I admit it!" he continued with a frank laugh, such as Michel had not heard from his lips for ten years. "By the way, it was a most singular commission, I thrust upon you to find a governess, and bring me a child! At that time, however, I was so very ill, and so eager to see the child in my house, and at my side; I was in short, so disturbed and upset, that I did not once think that your abrupt departure must naturally have awakened much gossip. I trust that nothing disagreeable took place? If it did, I shall never forgive myself."

"No, indeed," answered Michel, full of the joy of self sacrifice. "Nothing disagreeable happened."

As he spoke, however, a host of sad memories rose before him.

"No one then spoke to you on the subject?"

"Yes, Aunt Avéroef did."

"What did you tell her?"

"Simply that I could say nothing."

"She thought the child was yours, then?"

"No, she did think so, but my word was sufficient to undeceive her."

"You are on good terms with her?"

"I love her as if she were my mother."

"Do you think she will welcome my daughter?" Michel hesitated.

"I cannot tell," he said, at last, "once I should have said, — no, certainly not. Now, however, I know her better, or perhaps she has changed, but I feel that it is impossible for me to judge what she will do in these circumstances."

"I will go and see her, and find out for myself. She is a severe angel, but an angel all the same, like those, Michel, which guard the gates of Paradise!"

He laughed so gayly that Michel joined him. They were like two boys as they chatted side by side.

"I am going! I will see you to-morrow," said Paul, starting up.

"Going? why, it is not half past nine."

"I must put my child to bed," answered Paul, smiling; "she would not sleep if any one but myself put her head on her pillow. Ah! I spoil her — I know it; but she is worth it, and it does her no real harm!"

He departed with a quick, youthful tread. Paternity had given him a new lease of life. Michel went back to his desk, but his eyes were fixed on vacancy for some minutes. A bitter, but most intense joy filled his heart to overflowing.

"My labors have not been in vain," he said at last; "I have lost Marthe, but my brother is preserved, as is his child. I am content," and Michel thanked Fate, while tears filled his weary eyes.

"It is extraordinary," he thought, "how figures hurt one's sight. I have done enough for to-night, I think."

He pushed aside his accounts and continued to dream. His reverie was sweet and sleep profound, that night.

CHAPTER XXII.

A PROPOSAL.

ONE fine morning, Monsieur Mélaguire, with his brow leaning against the window of the library, and his arm around Nastia, was watching the steady down-pour of the rain,—a real autumnal rain, heavy and regular, when he saw approaching a most respectable looking carriage —the carriage of an old lady, drawn by two fine horses, altogether too fat, as the horses of elderly people are apt to be. He looked intently, and great was his surprise, to discover Madame Avérœf's footman at the back of the carriage. The man saluted him and jumped down.

"It is impossible," cried Monsieur Mélaguire, thinking he had lost his senses. "Prascovia Petrovna never leaves her house except to go to her villa in the spring, and to return to St. Petersburg in the autumn. No, it is impossible!"

"Madame Avérœf wishes to know, sir, if you will receive her," said a footman, opening the door.

"Receive her! receive her!" cried the worthy man. "Pauline! Nastia!"

Nastia had disappeared like a mouse in its hole. Her father wished to have all his family and servants assemble to do honor to his guest. Then the idea occurred to him, that he might do better, were he to go and meet her. He, therefore, dashed to the stairs, red and out of breath, at the moment when the old lady, assisted by her two servants, reached the upper step.

"What happy chance has procured me this honor," stammered Monsieur Mélaguire, when they were all comfortably established in the salon.

"Ah! Paul Nicolaïtch, it is not a chance," answered Madame Avéroef, shrugging her shoulders, lightly; "if you only knew! You will say I am quite crazy, and I give you my word that ever since last evening, I have been asking myself if it were true! Where is Nastia?"

"I don't know, she was here when we saw your carriage driving up, and disappeared; she went possibly to make some little change in her dress."

"You need not be troubled; you will not see her until I ask for her."

"I don't understand," said Monsieur Mélaguire, a little troubled; he was indeed considerably bewildered.

"But why all this preamble?" resumed Madame Avéroef, "let us get on. I have come to ask, in the name of my son Serge, for the hand of your daughter, Anastasia."

Monsieur Mélaguire, in spite of his weight, bounded like an India rubber ball, under which his chair creaked painfully.

"Yes," repeated Madame Avéroef, nodding affirmatively. "You have rightly understood, and I am not crazy. Serge wishes to marry Anastasia."

"Upon my life," murmured the old gentleman, "if you and I are in our senses, it must be he who is mad. Serge asks Anastasia's hand! Was that what you said?"

"Precisely, and I don't deny that he is mad, but he seems to be in his right mind, and quite serious."

"Serious! But how old is he?"

"Nineteen and four months."

Monsieur Mélaguire at this reply laughed so heartily, that Madame Avérœf lost her gravity. When they had ceased laughing, Monsieur Mélaguire said:

. "He is making fun of us. He must have a taste of the birch, and be sent back to school."

"They won't have him, he has got through all his studies there," answered Madame Avérœf, gayly; "I assure you that he is quite in earnest. How old is Nastia?"

"I don't know — fourteen, I think; no, fifteen, I believe. Wait, I can tell you in a moment."

"It is not worth while," interrupted Madame Avérœf; "Nastia will be sixteen in the summer. Count for yourself, you will see that I am right."

"Yes, you are right," said Monsieur Mélaguire, after a little calculation, and considerably upset, by this revelation; "but, how could you know?"

"I knew, because Serge told me. Of course, you know that they are acting in concert."

"In concert? The little scamps! Nastia!"

He rolled toward the door, and angrily called his daughter.

Madame Avérœf entreated him to return to her side.

"Listen a moment," she said, "these children love each other, and after all, they are not so very much to blame. You see, I came myself," she emphasized these words, "which proves that I, at least, see no harm in the plan. They are young, to be sure, and marriage is a singular lottery; those matches which seem to unite every possible condition of happiness, often turn out very badly. What would you have? they love each other, therefore, let them marry, while we are here to watch over them, and teach them how to live."

"There are no more children!" cried the good man, piteously. "They will soon marry, while they are in the nursery. Nastia still wears short dresses, and you want—no, no, it is too absurd!"

"Yes, it is absurd; but she can put on long dresses at once, and we will let them marry—when?"

"But I don't wish them to marry, cried Monsieur Mélaguire, in a spasm of indignation. "The Princess was not married until she was twenty, and then, to a man of thirty, and now this child, this mere infant, wants to marry a mere boy. It is preposterous I tell you!"

He walked up and down the room two or three times, and then sank into an arm-chair.

"Tell me in what terms this goose told you this," he asked presently, half angry, and half laughing. "It must have been very funny!"

"No, it was not funny," answered Madame Avérœf, "and it is for that reason I came at once to make my application in person. Serge came into my bed-room, last evening; I, thinking that it was to say good night, raised my hand to bless him, when, instead of leaning toward me as usual, he fell on his knees before me. I looked at him in some surprise, and saw that his eyes were unusually bright, and his whole face animated. I thought he was ill, and began to feel very anxious, when he suddenly said:

"'Grandmother, you have brought me up, you have been every thing to me, an orphan. Bestow on me now, the crowning blessing of my life, in giving me the only woman for a wife, whom I will ever consent to marry!'

"I must admit to you, Paul Nicolaïtch, that I was utterly dumbfounded at this address; for a moment, I was terrified, lest he had got into some trouble. You know a handsome young fellow can easily do that—for there are creatures who have no shame whatever. So I said to him in a severe tone:

"'Who is the woman whom you wish to marry?' 'Nastia Mélaguire,' he answered. 'Oh, grandmother, I love her like a madman. She loves me, too; we have known each other always, and we shall be so happy. Grandmother, let me marry her, and implore Monsieur Mélaguire not to refuse, for it would kill me.'"

Let us here say that Madame Avéroef had, involuntarily, of course, uttered a falsehood, and thus stained her immaculate conscience. Her grandson had never mentioned the name of Monsieur Mélaguire, for the reason that it had never entered his mind, that Monsieur

Mélaguire could have a will or wish of his own. This pious falsehood was not thrown away, for the excellent man was quite touched, and murmured in a low voice,

"Serge is a good boy; he respects our family at least, and what did you say, Prascovia Petrovna?"

"I made all the objections you have just made, and more beside. But he found an argument which left me without strength, and—"

The old lady's voice trembled, as she ceased speaking, and raised her handkerchief to her lips.

"Well! what did he say?" inquired Mélaguire, anxiously.

"These are his very words: 'I am a soldier, grandmother: the career that I have embraced, according to the wishes of my honored father as well as my own, is that which best suits an Avéroef. I should be glad to die, as did my grandfather, upon the battle field, in defence of my country; but if I am to die young, like my father and my grandfather, at least, let us feel—Nastia and I—that we have been happy early in our lives, for afterwards, it may be too late.'"

"I admit to you, Paul Nicolaïtch," said Madame Avéroef, no longer restraining her tears, "that I had nothing to say in reply. My married life was brief. My season of happiness, short; I hope that the good God will give to the child the long life he denied to my son and my husband, but if it must be otherwise, I should never forgive myself for having placed the smallest obstacle to the joys which Serge might have had in this world!"

Monsieur Mélaguire, much moved, uttered a few consolatory words.

"Pshaw!" he said, "there is not much fighting now-adays, and people do not all die on a battle field. He is right, however, it is never too early to be happy. But Nastia, poor child, knows nothing of the management of a house."

"Let her alone for learning all necessary, in a wink. Ah! she is a cunning creature," exclaimed Madame Avéroef, smiling as she recalled some occurrence in the past. "They have been a long time arranging this. I have noticed all her little courtesies, her eagerness to gratify me, and I have said to myself, what a kind little heart the child has. Was she not cunning, to lay siege to the old grandmother. Where is she? I wish to pull her ears a little."

Monsieur Mélaguire went into the hall, and shouted at the top of his lungs.

"Anastasia Palovna! Anastasia, I say!"

He then returned and took his seat. Anastasia Palovna, suddenly promoted to the rank of a marriage-able young lady, entered the room timidly, moving very slowly, with downcast eyes, like a young culprit who feels that she is to be mercifully treated, and who is striving to deserve it.

"The little witch!" murmured Madame Avéroef in her father's ears, while the two elderly people watched the slow approach of the girl. "She has lengthened her skirts!"

"It was true, the robe of the delinquent swept the

ground. She approached Madame Avéroef, kissed her hand with a submissive air, then, full of conpunction, awaited the lecture she anticipated."

"How is it Mademoiselle," said Monsieur Mélaguire in a voice of thunder, "that you venture without your father's consent, to form any projects of marriage. Instead of occupying yourself with your studies as befits your age, you are thinking, it seems, of marrying, and of leaving the paternal mansion.

Monsieur Mélaguire's voice failed, he burst into tears, and folded his daughter to his breast as he murmured:

"And you would leave me! leave me to die all alone and deserted, in my old age."

"No, no, papa!" cried Nastia with a sob, "we do not wish to leave you — you must come and live with us; we have settled all that, Serge and I."

Madame Avéroef could not stand this, and she burst into a hearty laugh; kissing the girl, she said:

"You little scamp! we consent if you behave well until the day you are married; if you do not, we will put you—you and your Serge, each in a corner with your faces turned to the wall."

Thus it was, that Nastia dropped her short skirts.

After Madame Avéroef's departure, the youthful *fiancée* went in haste to carry the news of her engagement to her sister. Marthe was strangely impressed by it, and saddened at the thought, that her little sister, who was almost like her own child, could have learned to love, had kept the secret from her, and had

12

never come to her with all the fears and hopes which the child should have poured into the heart of her, who had been as a mother to her. She said this without anger, but with some feeling. Nastia, in some confusion, listened with a bowed head, and then exclaimed impetuously:

"But Marthe, you are a little to blame, yourself. Do you remember the day I told you that I preferred Michel Avéroef for a brother, rather than the Prince?"

"Yes, I remember," said Marthe, turning her head away.

"You asked me why?"

"Yes, I remember," repeated Marthe.

"I told you, because he was an Avéroef; you did not say a word, then. I was ready to tell you everything, but, I thought, that for some reason or another, you had taken a dislike to the Avéroefs, and determined never to mention them to you again."

"I never took any dislike to the Avéroefs," said Marthe, in a faint voice. "I have always been on excellent terms with Madame Avéroef."

"Yes, but you detest Michel, oh! you need not deny it, it is perfectly easy to see," continued Nastia, with cool determination, born of her new dignities, "and it makes me very unhappy, for he is a cousin of the man I am to marry. Besides, he is altogether charming."

"I promise not to detest Serge, at all events," answered Marthe, trying to smile, "You know I love him with all my heart; talk to me about him."

And peace was made between the two sisters.

CHAPTER XXIII.

CHANGES AND DIPLOMACY.

WHEN the question of the date of the marriage came under discussion, there was considerable difference of opinion.

"Next autumn!" said Monsieur Mélaguire.

"After Lent," said the more indulgent grandmother.

"No, that won't do! Say, at once," exclaimed the young man, "or I will run away with her."

Finally, the middle of January was fixed upon.

Paul Avéroef, who had not delayed presenting himself before his aged relative, had not yet found a propitious moment for speaking of his daughter. He finally decided, in talking with Michel, that it were best to wait, until all the confusion created by this unexpected marriage, was over.

The two brothers were very happy together; Michel had found an object at last, upon whom he could lavish the long hoarded up tenderness of his heart. He adored his niece, Marie. This child, precocious as children are made by early suffering, was quaint and original, and astonished her uncle every hour in the day; her childish grace, and her affectionate caresses, gladdened his very soul, and he readily understood how his brother had found joy and health in those tender arms, wreathed about his neck.

Michel had another reason still, for loving Marie, who was the innocent cause of his misfortune; it seemed to him that the least harshness shown toward her, would have been like avenging his misfortune upon the child.   On certain days, when he was sadder than usual, he tried to forget himself by a frolic with her, and peace soon entered his soul.   Marie often said to him, "you are sad, uncle, wait and I will tell you a story."

Lulled by the dreams of this fresh imagination, the young man's wounded heart rapidly healed, and he laughed with all the gayety of his boyhood.

Autumn passed away, and Monsieur Mélaguire was considerably astonished one evening, when at Madame Avéroef's, his little Nastia told him that her marriage day was only forty-eight hours off.   The poor father had seen all the preparations going on, and had admired the freshly decorated apartments intended for the young couple.   Nastia had not spared him the sight of a single dress or knot of ribbon.   He had excited all his ingenuity in perfecting the thousand and one trifles about the happy girl, but, notwithstanding all this, he had not yet fully realized the situation.

"What! in two days?" he cried.   "Do you mean that in two days, I shall be left all alone?"

"No, papa, you know very well that you are coming here with us.   Wait only until we return from our wedding journey, and we will settle ourselves together."

"A wedding journey! In January!" sighed Monsieur Mélaguire, with a shiver.

"We shall not go very far," exclaimed Nastia; a sign from her *fiancé* closed her lips, but the youthful pair exchanged a rapturous glance.

Monsieur Mélaguire had seen nothing.

"And Pauline," he said, with a start. "What is to be done with Pauline?"

The two young people looked at each other, with terror in their eyes. Madame Avérœf looked up in some astonishment, and said to Monsieur Mélaguire:

"Why! I thought you had dismissed her."

"Yes," answered the unfortunate man. "I did attempt to dismiss her, but when I spoke to her about it, she declared that she meant to live and die among us, that she wished to educate the children of my children"—and he nodded toward the *fiancés*—"as she had mine, and then—"

"You promised to keep her," concluded Madame Avérœf, "I am not surprised, but, what will you do with her when you move? There is no place for her in the *rez-de-chaussée* which you will inhabit. I do not want her on the next floor, and these children certainly will not have her on the one above, which is theirs."

"Do you mean then that you do not want her?" stammered Monsieur Mélaguire, considerably discomfited.

"No, indeed," answered Serge.

"No indeed!" repeated Nastia, very gently, but shaking her head deliberately as she spoke.

Monsieur Mélaguire put his two hands on his two knees, and looked about him with the expression of a shipwrecked man, who has just seen his last plank go down in the tempest.

"But what is to be done about it?" he said with abject terror.

Everybody looked at him, but no one spoke.

"If Marthe would only take her," he cried with a sudden glimmer of hope.

Marthe was in the dining-room making tea. He called to her:

"Marthe, will you take Pauline as housekeeper?"

The Princess regarded her father with an expression of unmistakable repugnance, but poor Mélaguire saw nothing but his own distress.

"Come now, Marthe, be good and sweet, we don't know what to do with her."

"Give her a pension, and let her go back to her family," said the Princess, coldly.

"But she says that she has no family but ourselves. She regards herself as belonging to us. She knows that ingratitude is not a fault of the Mélaguires, and she is so warmly attached to us that she would die of grief, were she to part from us now."

"Ah! my poor dear Mélaguire," said Madame Avércef, who had kept silent, "you need our help now. There is only one thing for you to do, but it will demand time and caution. Will you all follow my advice?"

"Most assuredly," cried the circle, as with one voice.

"Marthe, my child, you will take Pauline into your house as soon as your father moves, for it is not at all proper that she should reside in the bachelor apartments arranged for Monsieur Mélaguire. We will tell her that our young people will want her in the autumn, to keep house for them. I say in the autumn for my house is not large, and these young people —"

"Oh! grandma, we don't take much room," cried Nastia.

"Only one small one in the attic, if you will," said Serge, coaxingly.

"Precisely," answered Madame Avéroef, smiling, "but for Pauline, my house is too small. I should have to put on too many locks, and stuff too many keyholes, it is not worth while! You, my child," she said to Marthe, "will always have a room in my house, and will occupy it whenever you wish to be with your sister, and you will confide the care of your country house to Pauline for the summer. You understand, on the first of October, that person will come here with these young people, and I will then take her in hand. I assure you it will not be more than six weeks, before I find a way of packing her off without beat of drums, or flourish of trumpets. If I do not, I am less adroit than I think myself, and she will be thankful to have got off so well."

"Pauline!" cried Monsieur Mélaguire, in horror. "Pauline, sent off!"

"Yes, Pauline, sent off!" repeated Madame Avéroef, elevating her voice a little, without knowing it; "you are an excellent man, and any woman who knows how to weep, can melt your heart, because she is a woman, and because she weeps; but your Pauline is not worth the rope by which she will certainly be hung one of these days. I tell you this in all seriousness, but mark my words, for I am not often deceived!"

"But, what have you heard?" stammered the wretched Mélaguire, "who has been talking to you?"

"No one; I have been watching her ever since, — well, for a long time, and I know what I am saying."

"But, what has she done," murmured Mélaguire, prostrated by the tone of conviction, with which the lady spoke.

"She — "

Madame Avéroef, hesitated, and glancing at Marthe, who, with her large eyes widely opened, and head erect, listened intently, as if she felt that she herself, was interested in the coming disclosure. The old lady checked herself, and then, with a glance at Monsieur Mélaguire, said in a calm, steady voice:

"She wishes to marry you."

Serge and Nastia threw themselves back among the cushions of the divan, choking with laughter, so ridiculous did this notion of Madame Avéroef's strike them. Mélaguire himself, was absolutely stunned, and looked at Madame Avéroef as if to assure himself that she was in possession of all her reason, and then, said slowly:

"Wishes to marry me?"

"Yes," repeated the old lady, imperturbably; "and will gain her end if I don't come to the rescue."

"Gain her end?" repeated Mélaguire, with considerable energy, "Oh! no!"

"Oh! yes," replied Madame Avéroef, "notwithstanding all your struggles, she will succeed if I do not prevent her. You must see that you do not know how to stand against her, she is of the kind who throws out deep roots, wherever she plants herself. It is said that a root of grass with its subterranean forces can dislodge stones, and cause temples to fall to the earth."

"Must I keep her until we move," said Mélaguire suddenly becoming very uneasy.

"Yes, it would be better," answered Madame Avéroef, regaining her good humor, "but nothing need prevent your beginning to move, the day after the wedding."

"Good!" said the brave man, with a sigh of relief; "and you will take her then, Marthe," he added, turning to his eldest daughter.

"Yes, if I must," she replied, shrugging her shoulders.

When one remembers that at this moment Pauline was in imagination, ordering her wedding costume at the first dress-maker's in St. Petersburg, one is tempted to compassionate her. When Monsieur Mélaguire laid his plans before her however, she did not flinch.

"The fools!" she said, with the easy judgment she passed on all things, "they give me a good part to play. That old simpleton will not have been alone one week, when he will come in search of me himself, and take me from the house of his dear Princess!"

The name of Madame Mélaguire will not look so badly, on my visiting cards!"

CHAPTER XXIV.

ANOTHER WEDDING.

THE marriage took place on the appointed day, at
six o'clock in the evening.   Of course, it was,
like most marriages, very brilliant; a great crowd
congratulated the young people, and showered upon
them every evidence of affection and sympathy.

The most sumptuous tea was served at Madame
Avéroef's, and at nine o'clock, Marthe's travelling
carriage, borrowed for the occasion, drew up before the
steps.   Serge wanted six horses and many bells.   He
seated his young wife and jumped in after her, and
they drove off to parts unknown.

He had told no one where he intended to spend his
two weeks' leave.   The most curious had failed to find
a clue, and even his grandmother's direct questions
elicited no reply; he evaded them with a laugh, and
the clearest reply he would make, was this:

"I am going to the house which I prepared for her,
in case we eloped, as we certainly should have done,
had they not allowed us to marry!"

The family were obliged to rest content with this
somewhat vague information.

Monsieur Mélaguire began to move at once, as he
had said he would do.   Pauline, who now inspired him

with insurmountable fear, seemed to environ him with her presence. He left her at Serguievskaï, and he met her face to face on the Quai de la Cour. He thought he had left her packing the sweetmeat jars and behold! she came to meet him in his new dwelling with a clock in her arms.

This ubiquity inspired him with positive fear, and on the third day he determined to sleep in his new rooms, with his valet across the door. The worthy man had arrived at such a pitch that it seemed to him he should behold Pauline standing at his bedside, smilingly offering him a pair of slippers. At this idea, a thrill of horror ran up and down his spine.

Mademoiselle Hopfer inhabited the old house as long as she could. She adored those large, airy rooms, the vast and sumptuous salons, where the paper on the wall had preserved all its freshness, and all the brightness of its gold lines; she loved these apartments, wherein she had reigned as Queen for so long a time.

She left them only when there was not an article of furniture there. When the men came to her and said,

"Mademoiselle, everything has gone now, but your bed," she glanced around her with a sigh, and followed her bed with a melancholy heart. As she crossed the sill, she had a new idea; she went to the concièrge, and said as she gave him a rouble;

"If any one comes to hire these rooms, do not conclude the bargain without notifying me, I know a person who wants them."

Pauline considered that about six weeks, were the *ne plus ultra* of her celibacy.

At Marthe Oghérof's she met with her match. Hardly had she thrown aside her wraps, than she wished to take the keys from the hands of her dear Princess; but the dear Princess only relinquished the unimportant keys, those of the linen closet and the store room; those of her desk, wardrobe and chiffonier, she kept in her own possession.

Poor Pauline! To be refused the power of thrusting her nose everywhere, of hunting through drawers and closets, was a terrible humiliation, as well as a mortal offence which she, at once, added to the pile of rubbish, which represented so many dead hopes in that corner of her heart consecrated to interments. And there was yet another disappointment,—Monsieur Mélaguire, comfortably established in his *rez-de-chaussée* did not appear to suffer from her absence. He came to visit Marthe, saw or didn't see Pauline, as it happened; smiled agreeably at her, but asked her no especial questions, in fact, talked only of an approaching thaw.

It was not of this, that this ambitious creature had dreamed. As she saw her prey slip through her fingers, she felt that her hatred of Marthe, was daily acquiring new strength. She detested all the Mélaguires, "ungrateful creatures," she called them, forgetting that they had given her six thousand roubles the morning that Nastia was married, the little bride having given them to her in a casket; but Marthe had the honor of occupying the foremost place in her hatred.

Was it not Marthe, in fact, for whom she had been betrayed by Michel Avéroef? Yes, betrayed! For she had succeeded in persuading herself that Michel had loved her first, and had turned his back upon her, in consequence of Marthe's coquetries. Why should she not believe this, since it was what she ardently wished to believe? And did not Marthe now compel her to feel, daily and hourly, that Mademoiselle Pauline was a mere vassal, an upper servant — one not even worthy of the honor of making the tea and the coffee, but who received her pittance in all humility from the hands of the mistress of the house. Marthe had a way of turning the key in the tea caddy, before rising from the table, which brought the color to the cheeks of Pauline, as if it were a premeditated insult.

After all, Mademoiselle Hopfer was most unjust toward Destiny, for had she been entrusted with all the keys, she would never have been able to study at her ease, the machinery of these two existences, slowly doing its appointed work at her side.

The Prince was perfectly happy. He rose late, and seemed to be always in the best of humors; he had an excellent appetite for his breakfast, after which he chatted for a few minutes with his wife, asked for commissions, and it would have been the height of injustice to accuse him of indifference, for no man in St. Petersburg understood better than he, how to match a stuff or select *bric-à-brac;* then he went out and passed the whole day, coming home at six o'clock for dinner, club days excepted, and after dinner disappeared, and was not seen until the next day.

Now, Pauline had discovered that the passage which communicated with the room of the Princess, from that of her husband, was locked on both sides.

"On both sides," repeated Pauline thoughtfully, her nose somewhat more elongated than usual. When her inferences were duly drawn, her nose returned to its normal dimensions, and she began "to find the joint" with the skill of an accomplished carver.

She soon deciphered the Prince as she thought, but Marthe was still a mystery to her. She would enter her bed-room and dressing-room, at the most unexpected hours, and always found the dear Princess reading, embroidering, or writing a note which she asked Pauline to despatch by the footman, and all this was done so openly and naturally, and even with a faint suggestion of irony, that Pauline would have given one of her very eyes, to find the secret flaw, which must eventually disfigure this fine diamond.

Some days after the marriage, Paul Avérœf came to see his Aunt, and found her entirely alone, which was a very rare thing. As he seated himself, he met so inquiring a gaze from the clear, honest eyes of the old lady, that he felt that the time for his confession had come.

"Aunt," he said, "you see before you a great sinner."

"Indeed! My dear nephew, has not the good Lord said that there is mercy for all sinners. Confess."

"You encourage me; but when you know the whole truth, you will probably be less indulgent."

"Speak, and we will see."

"Well then, I will go directly to the facts. I have committed a youthful error, of which I shall repent for the rest of my life; I have a daughter whom I am educating, and to whom I wish to give my name, and it is in the name of this dear little innocent, that I ask your love for the criminal."

"Is the mother living?" asked Madame Avœroef, with entire calmness.

"She is no more."

"Is she the child whom Michel took to you, eighteen or twenty months ago?"

"Yes, dear Aunt; the same."

"Bring her to me, my nephew."

Paul kissed with tender veneration, the hand which his grandmother extended to him with a royal gesture.

"Can it be that you, who are so strict and so exacting in the performance of all duties, will welcome my innocent child."

"You have said it, she is an innocent child. I exact only one thing, which is that she shall not know until her own marriage, and not then, if it can be avoided, that her mother was not married. A child must not sit in judgment on her mother, not even when that mother has sinned before her own conscience."

"Before the world, my dear Aunt, but not before her own conscience!" cried Paul. "Her mother was —"

"An honest woman? So much the better for her child; but we will never speak of her, nephew. Bring me your daughter as soon as you choose, she is an Avéroef, I will ignore the rest."

It was the coldest time of the whole winter, and several days elapsed before Paul ventured to risk his little girl out of doors.

The day that Serge was due at home, when his leave was on point of expiring, he determined to take the child to his Aunt's, as he did not dare to expose himself and her, to the questions of the young couple, who were as inquisitive and bold as the children they were in reality.

Marthe, who had come to pass the day with Madame Avéroef, was seated opposite the door, when the servant announced,

"Monsieur Paul Avéroef and his daughter."

Supposing there was a mistake in the name, she leaned a little forward, and looked at the door.

The child came in timidly, pushed on gently by her father, who encouraged her in a low voice. She crossed the salon in this way, and when within a few rods of the two ladies, stopped short, overwhelmed with confusion.

"Go on," said her father, "go and kiss your Aunt."

Marie had been drilled on her way, but she had not expected to see two ladies instead of one. She hesitated a moment, examined the two faces, and then, attracted instinctively by the brown hair and brilliant eyes of the Princess, she came forward gently, slipped her little hand into Marthe's, and presented her rosy face.

Marthe, much agitated, did not prevent her, but embraced her mechanically, as if she were in a dream, and followed her with her eyes, while Marie, led by her father, went to Madame Avéroef's side to make her excuses.

Those curls, those great limpid eyes, the oval face were all Michel's, but the lips had the peculiar curve, and the chin the dimple, which were both Paul's.

She looked from the father to the child, and then fell into profound thought. Her eyes were fixed on vacancy, and as she sat with her chin in the palm of her hand, she remembered Pauline's wicked, obsequious smile, on that memorable twentieth birthday. She turned deliberately toward Paul, and said without apparent emotion:

"This child is your daughter, sir?"

"Yes, Princess," he answered, with all a father's pride.

"And do you, yourself, attend to her education? She is charming, and I congratulate you. Was she with you, in Italy?"

"Certainly, of course."

"But she was born in Russia, I am sure. She speaks Russ too well to have acquired the language."

Paul looked earnestly at the Princess. The delicate color in Marthe's cheek was dashed with purple spots; a light shiver ran over her from time to time, and shook

13

her tightly clasped hands.   She awaited his response with a smile that concealed a secret anguish.

Without comprehending the truth, seeing only that this question was not dictated by a desire to be polite, nor yet by curiosity, he carefully weighed the words of his reply, and determined to state the exact facts.

"She was born in Russia," he said, "before my departure."

"And you took her with you, young as she was! Were you not afraid of the fatigues of the journey?"

"No, Princess; I did not take her with me, my brother Michel brought her, after she lost her mother, two years ago, in the coming month of May."

Marthe sank back in her chair, her hands dropped apart; her eyelids flickered a little, then she extended one hand toward the child, who came at once to her side.

"She is very pretty," she said to the astonished father.

Her voice vibrated, like a crystal cup under repeated shocks.   Suddenly, moved by an irresistible emotion, she seized the child in her arms, pressed her to her breast, and buried her face among her blonde curls, while tears streamed from her eyes.

Madame Avérœf started forward.   She had been an anxious spectator of the scene.   She hardly knew what to do, nor how to check further manifestations.

"I beg your pardon, sir," said the Princess, as she regained her composure, and released the child, "but I have no children," and she turned her face away to hide her blushes. Marthe had learned to tell a falsehood!

Madame Avérœf drew a long breath; the danger was averted for the time. Marthe was certainly a clever woman, and the old lady felt that the Princess would never forfeit her self-respect under the most difficult circumstances. Consequently, when Paul and his child had gone, she did not think it necessary to dissimulate further. She extended her arms to Marthe, who sank on a cushion at her feet and wept bitterly.

The two women did not exchange a single word. What was the use? When Marthe's tears were exhausted, she rose and resumed her seat near the window. Day-light was fading, and the salon was full of shadows. She was still silent, and it was Madame Avérœf who first spoke.

"The will of God be done! you feel this, my child, I am sure?" she said, gently.

"Amen!" answered Marthe in a faltering voice, but the word came from a firm heart.

Never since that fatal day had she been so light-hearted. Her soul was released from heavy chains. Now, within the innermost recesses of her heart, could she once more love and respect Michel Avérœf.

CHAPTER XXV.

THE RETURN OF THE BRIDE.

A joyous uproar was heard; light footsteps hurried through the next room. Nastia appeared in the door-way, rosy, smiling, apparently grown in height, and altogether majestic in the amplitude of her train and her *moire antique*.

"Wait for me!" cried Serge, in the distance, "we must go in together."

Nastia still on the threshold, kissed her hand to her new grandmother, and to her sister who did not dare to go and meet her, for fear of showing her reddened eyes and burning cheeks.

"Hurry!" she said, turning her head over one shoulder, with the gesture of a bird. "I am dying of impatience, and if you wait another minute, I shall go in without you."

Spurs were heard clattering over the floor; Serge, at last appeared, and snatching his wife's hand, he advanced with her to the old lady, who had risen to bless them, with the bread and the salt which stood ready at her side on a tray.

"I welcome you to your house; may you be always under the guardianship of the Lord," she said, solemnly. "Embrace me, my children. Now tell me where you have been?"

Nastia began to laugh.

"Hush!" she said, putting a finger on her lips; "it is a secret, and my husband has forbidden my telling it!"

"You shall know all about it, grandmother," said Serge, impatiently, "only you must wait a little. It is a secret."

"Very well," said his grandmother, smiling. "Play at hide and seek as long as it amuses you!"

Oghérof entered, very gallant toward his sister-in-law, whom he called Madame Avéroef with the greatest care. Nastia generally forgot to reply, when thus addressed, which amused the Prince excessively. Never had the dining-room resounded with gayer laughter, and the old servants seemed filled with surprise.

"What unwonted gayety!" said Madame Avéroef, during a moment of comparative calm; "it makes me feel young again to be surrounded by all these youth."

"Well, grandma, it will be always like this," said Serge, gayly, "and when we have children about us it will be gayer still!" Even Marthe could not resist the contagion of this gayety. Besides, notwithstanding the knowledge of the irreparable, it was a great comfort to be able to esteem again, where she had despised. Her soul was once more at rest, and the presence of her husband did not disturb her; the truth was, however, that he, for a long time, had counted for nothing in her life.

She returned home in this same state of mind. The

Prince had, as usual, disappeared about nine o'clock. She went to bed and slept profoundly.

She dreamed that she was walking on the shore of some river, and that she was waiting for Michel as on her twentieth birthday.

He came to meet her, transfigured and radiant, as she extended her hand, he said:

"No; it is only a dream, my hands are but two sunbeams, you cannot grasp them, but I shall linger here forever, and the flowers of your garden will never fade."

She stood before him in an ecstasy, while the warm sunshine penetrated her chilled and torpid heart, wrapping it in profound and delicious repose.

She awoke to daily life, charmed and soothed by her dream. Reality was not fair, but it seemed fairer to her eyes than the night before. She dressed slowly and went down to the dining-room, where her husband was already at breakfast.

Pauline, quickly followed; she had made a rule never to enter the dining-room before the Princess. These few moments of observation were very useful to her. She did not allow herself to be chilled by Marthe's indifference, which this especial morning seemed to her more contemptuous than disdainful. Without showing her impressions, she began her breakfast, picking here and there like a bird.

"Do you know, Marthe," said the Prince, "that I met Paul Avéroef yesterday, at the confectioners, with such a pretty little girl."

Pauline was greatly disturbed, and sat with her fork uplifted. She had utterly forgotten Paul Avérœf and his daughter, in the ardor of her new combinations. Was it possible! Were they really in St. Petersburg, and yet the governess had not been to see her, nor advised her of her presence. She calmed her indignation to listen to the reply which fell from the lips of the Princess.

"Yes, I saw her at Madame Avérœf's," said Marthe, "she is a lovely child and his daughter."

His daughter! Pauline felt a shock like that given by a battering ram to an old fortress. Marthe was so calm, and spoke so gently, that the companion ventured to glance in her direction. The Princess was quietly stirring her tea, without the smallest evidence of emotion.

"I did not know he had a daughter," said the Prince; "he was never married, I am sure, or can it be possible that he is a widower. I thought it was Michel who had a child in a left-handed sort of way. I am sure, I heard something about it, a while ago."

"It was the most bitter calumny," replied the Princess, in the same gentle voice, and with the same calm face; "malicious people spread this report merely to injure him."

"To injure him?" repeated the Prince, "and how?"

"By preventing him from marrying possibly, I don't know."

"Oh!" said the Prince, with a shrug of his shoulders.

He thought his wife very simple, but after all, she was right, as he admitted to himself. Nevertheless, it was not one child, nor yet several, who would have prevented his marrying.

"Then, the child was Paul's?"

"Yes, Monsieur Avéroef told me yesterday, that his brother had brought little Marie out to Italy, after her mother's death."

"Yes, to be sure—I remember it vaguely. Ah! Michel took her out to him, did he? That was a queer thing to do. I seem to see Michel in the character of a nurse."

Oghérof laughed aloud, and Marthe's heart was so light that she began to laugh, too. Pauline, seeing that she was the only serious one, uttered a little hard, nervous laugh. The Princess turned swiftly upon her.

"Are you ill, Pauline?" she asked.

"I, Princess? no, indeed. Why?"

"Because you laugh like a person who is about to have an attack of the nerves."

"No, indeed, I am perfectly well."

"So much the better!" said Marthe, indifferently, and she turned toward her husband to give him a few commissions.

Pauline got out of the dining-room as soon as she could, and hastily put on her out-of-door costume. Summoning her drojki, she took it by the hour; and driving to the *Bureau des adresses*, she found out exactly where Paul Avéroef resided. Once there, she penetrated to the kitchen by the servant's stairs, and asked for the governess, who presently appeared, and without evincing the least surprise, conducted Pauline to her own room.

Avérœf had just gone out with his daughter, and the opportunity was an excellent one for an explanation.

"How does it happen," said Pauline, in her most pathetic contralto, "thát you should behave toward me in this way? I drew you from your obscurity. I have obtained for you, the most unlooked-for emoluments in a good family, where you are well treated, who will give you a pension when you leave their service, and yet you betray me — me, your benefactress, your compatriot! Oh! Marguerite, this is not well done. Your first duty was to have warned me of your unexpected return."

"Pardon me, Mademoiselle Pauline," said the governess, politely, trying to check this effusion, which threatened to be somewhat lengthy.

The woman had become much more refined since she had been among cultivated people, her appearance and manners greatly improved.

"Pardon me, Mademoiselle Pauline, you speak of benefits, and of treason in the same breath; it is true that I am indebted to you for my entrée to this house, but since then, Monsieur Michel and Monsieur Avérœf have also become my benefactors, Monsieur Avérœf especially. When you told me to write to you all that was going on, I knew little of what my duties were, and I consented. But since then, I have learned that it is not right to gossip about my masters' affairs—masters who have been good to me."

"But I have been good to you also," interrupted Pauline, "I owed you nothing."

"I know that, Mademoiselle, but your goodness to me, demanded in exchange, things from me which I do not consider right, so long as these people are so kind to me, and only ask that I perform my duties faithfully toward them."

"Then you betray me—you betray your benefactress. Are you not ashamed of your ingratitude?"

"If it be absolutely necessary that I must betray some one, I prefer that it shall not be those who ask no evil thing of me, and who have always been kind to me."

"Ungrateful creature!" cried Pauline, indignantly.

"I prefer to be ungrateful to you, Mademoiselle, rather than to Monsieur Avérœf," replied Marguerite, firmly, as she rose.

Pauline left the house livid with rage and gall.

CHAPTER XXVI.

MARTHE'S SOLITARY DRIVE.

DURING this disastrous expedition of Pauline Hopfer, the Princess had gone out in a sleigh — she drove out of town absorbed in thought. She needed the spectacle of this expanse of immaculate snow to cool her hot anger.

Since the previous evening she had driven the recollection of Pauline from her mind, but the sight of the woman had raised a tempest in her soul. It was this wretched creature who, for some reason which she could not yet comprehend, had invented and circulated these calumnies against Michel; it was she who adroitly mingling truth and falsehood, had separated Michel and herself forever.

"And for what reason?" the Princess asked herself feverishly, over and over again. "Why should she hate either Michel or me?"

Alas! Marthe could never understand that one may hate those who overwhelm you with benefits, precisely because they are your benefactors, and that to certain ignoble souls, this necessity for gratitude is an ever recurring humiliation.

She understood, however, the danger of her position. and the horror with which this woman inspired her was constantly on the increase. She had restrained herself this morning, but would she always be able to exert the same self control?

"Madame Avérœf will come to my aid," she said to herself, "as soon as she understands what I need, and I shall not even be compelled to ask her."

This reasoning was not altogether satisfactory. The good sense, *les convenances*, and the absolute necessity of protecting her own honor and her husband's name, the certainty that if Pauline would be sent away with eclat, that she in revenge would soil the name of the Princess Oghérof, in one of those calumnious inventions of which some traces are always left—nothing of all this could induce her to face with resignation the necessity of sitting at her own table opposite this viper, and induce her to treat her with civil indifference. She wished to crush her under her foot, like some vile, unclean insect, and then turn her eyes from the repugnant spectacle.

She made the tour of the Isles without finding solace. As her coachman turned, and asked where she wished to go, a sudden thought came to the Princess.

"Drive along the river bank and past our old country house," she said.

The sleigh turned into the unfrequented road. The horse plunged through the snow, which in some places rose to his belly; a fine frozen mist flew about the sleigh, and deposited an impalpable diamond dust on Marthe's velvets and furs.

How little this road resembled that which she and her husband had taken, the day she left the paternal mansion! The river was no longer blue in the sunlight, the sycamores were no longer green. The snow, several feet in depth, made the landscape perfectly level, through which peered an occasional cluster of bushes, or the black top of a wall or fence.

At a turn of the road, she caught sight of the house in which she had been married. The house was inhabited. The bright, clean windows had white shades, and a path cut in the snow, led to the servants' quarters. The court-yard was carefully swept, and clouds of white smoke puffed from out the chimney.

"Strangers are here," said Marthe aloud, "they will love and suffer in their turn; may they never, like me, see their dreams of happiness fade away, as they look forth on this landscape!"

This melancholy thought was balm to the cruel, conflicting sentiments which tore the poor woman's heart to pieces. In fact when one is suffering, and begins to pity herself, the sting is lessened and the sorrow becomes dulled into repose. She passed her old home slowly, then along by the garden where she had watched for Michel. The summer sun had forever deserted her life.

"Never more!" thought the young creature, and tears fell fast behind her lace veil. "To Madame Avérœf's," she said to the coachman, who turned around and drove rapidly back to town.

Madame Avéroef was not alone: the house was full
of relations and friends. Marthe had the patience to
wait an entire hour, then seeing that all who departed
were speedily replaced by new comers, she approached
the old lady to take leave, and said in her ear:

"What must I do with Pauline?"

"Keep her, at whatever cost to yourself!" answered
Madame Avéroef in a tone which proved that she had
turned the question over and over in her mind.

"So be it then," murmured Marthe with a sigh.

"Do not forget that you are to come to-morrow night
to take tea with us," said the old lady, kissing her tenderly. "Every member of both families will be here to
do honor to the newly married pair." Marthe would
then see Michel, and she could not run to meet him,
and extend her hands with the exclamation:

"I know all! I love you, and I respect you." Oh!
the misery of not being independent, the agony of
bearing another's name, of being compelled to hold it
in respect, of not being able to act or speak without
drawing down on her husband the laughter and contempt of the world, and upon herself, dishonor.

If she had but waited, if she had been less proud
and less hasty! If she had but had sufficient confidence in Michel to give him time to come back and
explain himself! And here Pauline appeared again
among her thoughts, and poor Marthe almost loathed
her!

And her pride! Marthe had said to Sophie, "I

never repent;" which was true when she said it, but how was it now?

Her pride had crumbled to ashes under her feet, and she wished to erect a pedestal upon this ruin on which she could stand and call loudly to Michel,

" I accused you — forgive me ! "

But here the Prince interposed. Her husband, whom she had sworn to love faithfully !

And between these two guardians who drove her thus from Paradise, Marthe was crushed and vanquished. She bowed her knees and asked pardon of God for having doubted Michel's goodness, for having unjustly condemned an innocent man. There was her fault, but how great had been her chastisement !

She would speak to Michel nevertheless. She could not live, with the idea that this man looked upon her as a coquette, without heart or head.

"I will let him know that I have loved him," she said to herself: "I have destroyed his happiness and mine by miserable pride, and he cannot suppose that I attach any value to his love. I will therefore let him know, that I wounded myself to the heart, while striking at him, and that this wound will bleed all my life long."

She did not pursue this thought. There of course could be no question of love between the Princess Oghérof and Michel Avérœf. But the Princess could admit to Michel how great had been the errors of Marthe Mélaguire, and obtain his pardon. Here it was that she stopped; she went no further, but at once proceeded to execute her plan.

Sitting opposite Pauline at table, she found much difficulty in smothering her indignation, but the presence of her husband brought her unusual relief and created a wholesome diversion.

"Have you been out to-day?" asked Oghérof.

"Yes, as far as *Les Isles*. It was very pretty there, in its winter dress."

"Somewhat monotonous," answered the Prince, "but it was a very good thing for the young horses. The difficulty of trotting through the snow moderates their ardor. Have you seen your sister to-day?"

"No; we are invited there to-morrow evening."

"A party?"

"No, only the family."

The Prince gnawed his moustache for a minute or more, then he had an inspiration.

"I will take you there and leave you, as I have a business engagement."

"Do as you please," answered Marthe, eagerly, "do not disturb any of your arrangements on my account."

Pauline looked inquisitively at the Princess and then dropped her eyes on her plate again. She was somewhat uneasy, and expected some allusion or bitter, jesting remark, and steadied herself to receive them. To her surprise, the dinner passed without anything of the kind; the Prince departed as usual, when they rose from the table, and the two women spent the evening alone. Pauline would have given much to end the tête-à-tête which Marthe seemed inclined to prolong. And how many sentiments were struggling in what Mademoiselle Hopfer called her heart! Fear—rage at being obliged to fear: the desire of having an inevitable catastrophe over and done with, and dread at what was to follow. At this moment, Pauline remembered with considerable pleasure her six thousand roubles, for which, however, she felt not the smallest gratitude, and began to form certain plans as to her vengeance when she was dismissed from the house, and these thoughts were so sweet that they absorbed her entirely.

Marthe rose at last, and closed the book she was reading.

"Good night, Pauline Vassilscova," she said.

"Good night, Princess," was the companion's reply, as she awakened with a start from amid her castles in the air—"must I go with you to-morrow?"

"Just as you please," answered the Princess coldly. "My sister did not mention you particularly."

She left the room. Pauline, when she was alone, carried her hand to her cheek, as if she had received a blow. What! could it be possible that she was not mentioned by her ex-pupil who had been well under her control not three months previously.

"There is something going on," said this amiable personage, in order to console herself. "The Princess is too calm: she hides her game, but I am quite as cunning as she, as I will let her see."

14

CHAPTER XXVII.

RECONCILIATION.

THE apartments of the young people were brilliantly lighted. Flowers blossomed in the windows, on the étagères, and everywhere that a vase or a bouquet could be placed. The hangings were all new and fresh, and additional furniture gave a festal air to the rooms, which were in size and height precisely like those on the lower floor occupied by Madame Avérœf.

Monsieur Mélaguire was in the best of spirits: he beheld his two daughters both in white, and both beautiful, each with a handsome young officer as her husband, and his paternal heart swelled with joy.

"How beautiful you are!" he said to Marthe, "you look quite as young as your sister!"

Marthe in fact was transfigured. The pearly pallor of former days, with the soft rose tint in her cheeks, were again on the face that had so long been worn by illness and anxiety. All her being vibrated with youth and life: she laughed with the others, she went and came, tranquil and almost happy. From time to time she embraced her sister with an effusion to which poor Nastia had been unaccustomed for the last two years.

"How good and sweet you are!" said little Nastia,

"and how nice it is to know that you are cured! You are like yourself once more." At these words a shadow passed over the fair face of the Princess, but in a moment she smiled and pressed her sister's hand.

"Will you do me a favor!" murmured Nastia, "a very great favor? There is Michel, just come in with Paul Avérœf. Shake hands with him, it would make me happy."

Without a word Marthe drew a little aside, permitted the two brothers to pay their respects to the bride, then in a clear, full voice she said, as she extended her hand to the astonished young man:

"Monsieur Michel, we are now connections, let us congratulate each other."

Michel took her hand, raised it ceremoniously to his lips, and looked the Princess full in her face. With joyous eyes and blazing cheeks, she smiled at him, and giving her other hand to Paul, she said:

"Why did you not bring your lovely little daughter?"

Paul murmured a few words, and then the truth came to him in a sudden inspiration. He glanced at his brother, and his heart swelled with compassion and remorse. He guessed the sad romance of these two lives forever severed, and turned away, leaving them alone in this room full of people, who paid no heed to them.

Marthe seated herself upon a sofa. She trembled so that she could not stand. Michel stood before her.

"You are a good brother," she said, softly.

Her eyes finished her silence, and completed her meaning. Michel's heart thrilled with joy. At last the day had arrived, when he was restored to her esteem. Wings seemed to have been given to his delivered soul.

"It is a very long time since we have talked together," continued the Princess, with easy grace. She was so sure of herself, and so confident of the austerity of her victim, that she did not hesitate to say all this.

"It was all my fault," she continued, "will you forget my folly — my worse than folly."

"Oh! Madame," murmured Michel, "you can have little idea of what you are doing, of what you are restoring, or of what it has cost me to feel, that I was incurring your unmerited anger."

The lady's head drooped. These tones had been long unheard, this voice had not reached her ears since the day of their long separation; all this Past started to life again. She looked up at the young man, her eyes were submissive, almost supplicating.

"Your companion is watching us," said Michel, without raising his voice; "distrust her, she hates you."

Pauline, sheltered by an open door — she liked such outlooks — was watching them with eyes as keen as a carving knife.

Marthe answered by a nod, and rising, went to join Madame Avérœf, who was the centre of a group in which the young pair were flitting to and fro, performing their duties as hosts, with a good humor, only equalled by their inexperience. Laughing gayly they would disappear from time to time.

"I honestly believe they have gone into a corner, to kiss each other," said Madame Avérœf, with a smile.

"Come now, Serge, the moment has come!" said the Prince to his brother-in-law, catching him by the arm. "You shall not mock your family in this way. You must tell us where you spent the two weeks of your honeymoon."

"Never!" cried Nastia, who was not far off.

"Yes," said a chorus of voices, "you must confess now. Take each other by the hand, and own up!"

Serge, in the most obliging manner, took his wife's hand.

"Must I tell?" he asked her.

"Yes, tell — it makes no difference now."

"Well, then, most excellent friends and relatives, I, on the day of our marriage, carried my wife to —

He stopped and looked slowly about him.

"I carried her to *Les Isles*," he concluded, triumphantly, "where we slept in her old room, and dined in her own dining-room."

A general burst of laughter greeted this declaration. It was a simple solution of the mystery, of which no one had dreamed.

"And you remained there a whole fortnight without leaving the place?" said Sophie Leakine in an ironical tone. "You must be real lovers."

"I beg your pardon cousin, we went out every day."

"Where did you go? To see the wolves?"

"By no means, we had a lovely garden all to ourselves, where orange trees bloom and camelias thrive."

"And where we passed half the day," added Nastia.

"What on earth do you mean?" every body exclaimed.

"I mean the Botanical gardens," said Serge, with a profound bow, while Nastia curtseyed to the ground.

Every one was much amused at the originality of this idea, and yet the gardens were free to the whole world.

At this moment, Michel, who was taking his leave, approached Marthe, who said in a low voice,

"To-morrow, at two o'clock, at the Botanical gardens. I have many things to say to you."

Michel bowed profoundly, and went away without looking at the Princess. But in spite of his caution, Pauline had seen Marthe's lips move, and the color flush the young man's face.

"I have them at last," she said, "and they shall not escape me this time!"

She apparently thought that they had escaped her the first time!

CHAPTER XXVIII.

CONSERVATORIES AND CAUCASUS.

THE next day was absolutely cloudless. During the night, the frost had spread the most wonderful flowers over the window panes, and a slight fall of snow had veiled all the impurities of the streets. Marthe rose early, ordered the coachman to bring up a light sleigh, and at nine o'clock she left, while her husband, who had come in very late, was indulging in the most delightful dreams. She had no fear of being surprised, for she had no sense of guilt; as she drove through the streets she looked about her, ready to greet every well known face.

It was extremely cold; a half-congealed vapor formed a little cloud around the nostrils of her horse. The sidewalks recently swept and covered with fine sand, were two long yellow lines, the length of the street. Snow lay on every roof and spire, smoothing down all asperities, and dazzling the eyes with its whiteness.

The smoke came out of the chimney in huge clouds, black beneath and white above, which the wind quickly dissipated in capricious, iridescent flakes. Marthe drank in all this and enjoyed life intensely. The burthen which had weighed so heavily upon her for twenty months, was at last lifted by the hand of a child. She found the road long; the Néva, as she crossed it, seemed immense and infinite, an ocean of ice, on the further shore of which, truth and honor awaited her.

When she reached the door of the Botanical gardens, Marthe stopped a moment. The entire garden glittered in the sun like an enormous jewel casket. Not a tree, not a branch or twig that was not sheathed in ice, standing out against the clear, blue sky. It was like enormous reefs of coral piled up—coral of snowy whiteness, and miraculous growth.

Marthe took the wooden footpath, which led to the conservatories — the branches of the trees met above her head, an occasional bird as it flew, scattered a little of the frozen snow over the path, but the sound of its fluttering wings was all that was heard amid the white stillness of the wintry scene. This kingdom was ice— was Marthe's very own, in fact!

She entered the office of the Administration to ask some questions as to where to procure seeds and precious cuttings, then went on toward the glass houses.

She had not felt the smallest uneasiness since she had come out, but when she had beheld Michel Avérœf waiting for her, her heart suddenly failed.

Michel came forward, and the two exchanged a mute salutation. They entered the conservatory together, and all at once the most insignificant trifle brought the color to her cheeks: one of the employés, with a sulky face, handed her a pen with which visitors inscribe their names in the register kept for the purpose. She turned to Michel in a helpless sort of way, while he took the pen and wrote the first name that occurred to him. He then offered his arm to Marthe, who was both ashamed and troubled.

The first puff of air which came in their faces brought such an intensity of sweetness, such damp warmth and heavy perfumes, that Marthe was tempted to retreat at once. She had not foreseen any of these things when she bade Avéroef meet her in the gardens. She had merely said to herself, that the gardens must be very much deserted, if her sister had been able to come there every day for a fortnight, without meeting any one. But at the first step the necessity of concealment and deception, faced her in all its hideous ugliness. But Michel left her no time to think. They walked very slowly between two hedges of camellias in full flower. The youngest and the smallest of the plants were in front, while the others were arranged on shelves, one above the other, forming on the right a wall of leaves glossy and shining, while the branches were thickly covered with flowers, white, rose-colored, scarlet and mottled. Some were widely opened in their pride and beauty, others were half rolled up, indicating their recent bud by the yet unfolded pistils in the centre, while others were veritable buds, jealously enveloped in their brown sheaths, where a faint streak of red gave promise of the future. On the left a bank of rose-colored camellias in full bloom, went from the floor to the glass roof. Plants and flowers had strewn the earth beneath.

Marthe stood still, struck with admiration.

"I never saw so many flowers in my life," she said to Michel.

These words broke the ice. Each had dreaded the first word, and behold! the flowers were selected to dissipate the danger. They continued to talk as if no fatal gulf separated them from that happy time when they could speak to each other without embarrassment.

The employé followed with an indifferent, bored sort of air. He wondered, however, if these handsome young creatures were brother and sister, or two lovers who met in secret. But this, of course, was none of his business. He was employed merely to see that visitors did no harm to plants and flowers, and he did not intend to see anything else. Nevertheless, his presence annoyed Marthe intensely. She kept turning to see if he were still at her heels.

"Wait a moment," said Michel, who understood her meaning.

He opened a door, and Marthe restrained an exclamation of surprise.

Before them rose a high glass cupola, under which grew to a most gigantic size, bananas, dracenas and palm dates. The palms grew up toward the light, eager for the sun, and seeking in the skies, their absent country. Twice already had the roof been raised. The vigorous branches extended themselves, and had twice broken through the glass, and compelled civilization to make more room for them. Very soon it became necessary to give still more, for they continued to grow toward the blue sky, with indomitable perseverance. Beautiful tropical birds hid themselves among the dark and shining foliage. Shrubs and plants occupied every vacant place. Orange trees in full blossom filled the air with penetrating odor.

The guard approached a spring hidden under the leaves, a fountain began at once to play, falling in fine rain into its basin, with sweet and monotonous music. After having fulfilled this task, the man took a seat with the air of a person who knows that he is there for a long time, and that he can take his ease.

"We are by ourselves now," said Michel, "come this way."

He led the way to a staircase of wrought iron, half concealed among the plants. She followed him with her eyes fixed on the dark mass of shining leaves, as different in form as they were in tint. She looked at Michel, their eyes met, and this look put them in unison: the old days became suddenly part and parcel of the present, without either being able to see where the chain had been mended. They reached the head of the first flight of steps; an aerial balcony stretched before them, crossing the conservatory from one end to the other. They walked out upon it, and stood leaning upon the railing.

Above their heads was a second balcony or gallery,

so frail and delicate, that it looked as if no human foot could tread upon it. The great, deeply cut leaves of the cocoa palm made a shadow above the clear glass.

The sun and the blue sky were visible. Under their feet was a sea of verdure: dark points indicated great stems, and huge, tangled masses, while knotted stalks wound among long, varnished leaves. The trunks of the palms rose like slender columns covered with imbricated scales; the leaves of the bananas grew in large glossy wheels, torn apart by the too complete blossom of the plant—aloes and cactii imperiously waved their long needles. Here and there a withered stalk, the dull red of a cluster of half ripe fruit, the pale gold of an orange, the insolent scarlet of a flowering cactus, announced that the power of man had vanquished nature, and that in spite of the vicinity of St. Petersburg to the pole, winter was annihilated in this enchanting spot.

"It is spring here," said Michel, softly.

"Eternal spring," murmured Marthe, overwhelmed by sudden melancholy. She tried to exert herself and throw it off. Turning to Michel, with her arms still folded on the railing, she said:

"I wanted to see you, to tell you of the wrongs of which I have been guilty toward you, and to explain why and how, I was so mistaken."

Michel looked at her with that honest, penetrating gaze, which was one of his greatest charms.

She went on eagerly and without embarrassment, for e looked upon herself as fulfilling a duty.

"I wanted to see you that day; it was my birthday; it seemed to me that your presence would bring me happiness. I was never happy when I expected you until I saw you come, and that especial day I—"

Her voice faltered, she hesitated and then continued:

"You sent me a bouquet?"

"Yes."

"I never received it. That it was intercepted is clear. What was it that you wrote to my father from Mentone, in that letter which we never received?"

"I said to him, that as soon as I came back, I should lay before him a petition, which, if granted, would ensure the happiness of my whole life."

Marthe dropped her eyes, and after a moment's thought, said:

"The bouquet and the letter have been suppressed by the same person."

"And you suspect—"

"Pauline Hopfer. I am sure of it! The very day you left, she told me—"

Marthe could not continue—the absurdity of her whole conduct flashed over her. Was there ever such credulity as hers, and how well, Pauline had managed her!

"Go on—I beg you—we are here to speak to each other without concealment!" said Michel, no less agitated than herself.

"She told me that you had taken a child away with you, and that you had gone to join the mother." And Marthe drew a long breath.

"And you believed it!" cried Michel, indignantly.

"I believed it," repeated Marthe, her head drooping.

"But it was utterly preposterous."

"Yes, but—"

"But what?"

"I was jealous and I was credulous," she said, in a voice so low, that it could scarce be heard; he guessed rather than understood.

Profound silence reigned in the conservatory. The fountain alone kept up its musical drip, and seemed to be weeping over the irreparable. A dry leaf fell to the ground from a high branch.

Marthe lifted her head, her eyes were full of tears.

"Will you forgive me?" she said, "I am well punished."

"I have nothing to forgive," answered Michel, with a gentle sweetness, that went through to the sick heart of his companion. His voice was music to her ears.

"We are both victims," he said, "and some day, we together will punish our executioner," he added, with an angry light in his eyes. "If I had only not to do with a woman."

"Such a creature is no longer a woman," said Marthe; "she has dishonored the weakness of her sex."

Michel told in his turn, how he had been prevented from seeing her father earlier; his meeting with Oghérof, and the marriage of Sophie Leakine.

"My father would never have listened to you without the consent and approbation of yours," said Marthe, sadly. "It was our destiny!"

They relapsed into silence. Michel looked at his campanion, whose unseeing eyes were riveted on the masses of foliage about her.

"What was your bouquet?" she said, in a low voice, but without looking at Michel.

"Entirely white, all orange blossoms. It was intended to tell you, that I was compelled to keep silence, yet a little longer."

Marthe sighed, and continued to look down at the leaves.

"And now," continued Michel, in a low voice. "What do you wish me to do?"

She turned—her brave, sad eyes met his.

"You must leave St. Petersburg," she said, "so that I, who must stay here, may not run the daily risk of meeting you. I cannot speak to you as I have done"—she stopped—"and I cannot speak to you differently from now. You see that we must separate."

"For ever, do you mean?"

"For a long time, at all events. While you are unmarried—"

Michel shook his head. "I shall never marry," he said, firmly.

"So much the better," she answered, almost involuntarily. "While we are young, then—"

"You exact this?"

"I entreat it."

"I will obey!" replied the young man, pale with anguish, but as courageous as she. "I can not, however, leave St. Petersburg in twenty-four hours. I must have time to change my regiment, and until these arrangements are completed, what do you wish me to do?"

"I will go away. I can go to some distant land, and not return until next winter. And you, where do you think of going?"

"To Caucasus."

Marthe did not answer, her hand trembled and shook the frail balustrade.

"If I do not return," continued Michel, "you will sometimes think of me, and you will know, that from the first day to the last, I —"

"No, no;" cried Marthe, distractedly, "do not utter one word that I ought not to hear, I implore you."

He bowed and did not speak.

A noise was heard below, the door was thrown open, visitors had apparently arrived.

"We are lost," murmured the Princess, in agonized tones.

Michel hastily reassured her.

"There are two staircases," he said, "if any one comes up by the one, we will go down by the other. In the meantime, let us stay just where we are, it is the safest plan."

Half hidden by the huge tree, they stood breathlessly awaiting a sound or voice, which should guide them. The visitors also were apparently waiting for a moment, and then passed beneath the gallery on which stood

Marthe and Michel. The new comers were talking earnestly together. Suddenly a youthful laugh broke the silence.

"It is my sister!" whispered Marthe, turning very pale.

"Let us go up, Serge," said Nastia, in a caressing voice.

"Not to-day, my treasure," answered the young man, "Grandma will lecture us, if we are late for breakfast."

They departed with their arms closely interlaced, and softly whispering to each other.

Michel said not one word. Marthe turned her face all wet with tears, toward him.

"Yes; it might have been the same with us," he said in reply to her mute interrogation.

And a great tear dropped upon his gloved hand, unperceived by himself.

Marthe buried her face in her hands, and wept her heart away. Suddenly the fountain ceased to flow. The guard, who had apparently been asleep, considered that the visitors had been there sufficiently long.

"Adieu!" she said at last, drying her burning tears.

"Adieu," he repeated, looking at her as if he wished to carry her living image away with him.

He extended both his hands. She recoiled with terror.

"No, no," she said, "not even that! Do not let the least earthly stain rest on this morning. When we meet in the world, I will give you my hand, but not

15

here. Marthe Mélaguire will love you always, but ask
nothing from the Princess Oghérof!"

At this name, Michel frowned; the detested image
of the husband, had come to mar the sorrowful serenity
of their parting. Marthe understood him.

" The Prince is, and will remain a stranger to me,"
she said, without looking at her companion, " but I
bear his name, and I must not blush in his presence.
If his hand takes mine in a friendly grasp, he must
not find that another —"

"Then, you have nothing for me?" interrupted
Michel, hastily.

"Nothing," answered Marthe, her eyes bright with
feverish excitement. " Nothing in this world — in the
world beyond, my love everlastingly."

She threw out these words as she turned to go down
the stairs, they sounded almost like a cry of triumph.
He followed her in silence.

What could he say in reply, since she had forbidden
him to utter the only word possible for him.

She wished to leave at once, but their cicerone
insisted on their going through the huge building.
The Princess glided on swiftly, far in advance of
Michel; she did not look back, indeed she saw nothing.
All vainly did the hyacinths and tuberoses call her
with their perfumes — vainly did the orchids droop
their weird distorted forms before her. She passed on
without seeing them; arrived at the end, she turned
toward Michel. A tender, delicate verdure sur-

rounded them on all sides; it was like the robe with which April clothes the hedges and the lawns.

" It is forever, then?" she said to Michel.

"Forever! You are not alone in the world; but if danger ever threatens you, I will be at your side."

"Thanks," she said, softly. "Farewell."

She went out and almost ran to her sleigh.

Michel, utterly exhausted by such strong and varied emotions, lingered to regain composure. But in a few moments, he lifted his handsome head, and turned toward the Quai. He reached the Grande Néva, and crossed it on foot. When he arrived in the centre of the river, he stood still and looked about him. Before him, behind him, all about him, bristled huge masses of ice, half covered with snow. That year the river had been suddenly frozen and blocked. A violent wind had driven the ice together, and piled it high, making the river almost impassable. It was winter in all its horrible magnificence.

"Winter, eternal winter for me!" said Michel, in despair.

Under the blue sky, the domes of the churches glittered in the wintry sun. The gilt spires shine alike in December and July — silent testimony of the faith which fears no snow, nor tempests, but raises to heaven its fervent and incessant prayer.

"I believe in her," said the young man, half consoled. "I believe in her and she loves me! To Caucasus, then, if it must be!"

CHAPTER XXIX.

FRESH FIELDS AND PASTURES NEW.

WHEN the Princess entered her house, she found Pauline and her husband breakfasting together. The first was extremely reserved, and evidently on her guard; the second was sulky. The supper of the evening before, had not agreed with him!

"Have you been out this vile, cold morning?" said the Prince, sulkily. "I suppose you had no other way of taking cold. "Some of your charitable visits, I suppose! Deuce take all the poor people!"

"No, my friend," answered Marthe as she unfolded her napkin, "I have been to the Botanical Garden."

At these words Pauline launched an oblique glance at her dear Princess, and then dropped her eyes upon her plate.

"What a ridiculous idea," cried the Prince, shaking off his apathy. "You should have taken me with you."

"You were asleep, your valet said."

"It was a charming drive though. Was it Black you had?"

The Princess answered in the affirmative.

"He goes well on the ice, does he?"

"Yes, to perfection."

"I don't doubt it. We must go to the Garden again.

It is delightful there in winter. And there are the Gromof Conservatories. You have never been there, have you?"

"No—never."

"We will go very soon."

"Whenever you choose," said Marthe, laying her napkin over her lap.

The Prince went out as usual, but Pauline had noticed a peculiarity in Marthe's manner; a certain feverish haste in her replies, a sort of affectation in selecting some dainty bits, a pretence of appetite, while in reality her plate went away almost untouched.

Pauline on leaving the table, went out as she had done the day before, and called a drojki, not without the sad reflection that all these performances were expensive, and had as yet been of no benefit to her. But vengeance was a dear delight! At this recollection Pauline ceased to bargain, and started for the Botanical Garden, driven by a feverish dream, and conveyed by a big-bellied bay horse with a short trot. As soon as she reached the entrance she asked if the Princess Oghérof had dropped a bracelet in the Conservatory that morning between ten and eleven o'clock.

"None has been found," answered the man.

"No person of that name has been here," added the man with the pen.

"Then it was yesterday. I have perhaps made a mistake in the day. Permit me to look at the register."

The register was under her fingers, and seeing that no objection was made, she examined the scantily covered page which recorded all the names of the visitors for the week.

"I have been misinformed," she said; "I will go to Gromof."

She returned home in a very thoughtful mood. Her two expeditions had utterly failed. Had her star abandoned her? Should she never know where Marthe had spent that hour?

That her star had not abandoned her was however proved to her that same evening, when the young married pair dined with the Princess. During dinner Nastia turned to her sister and said:

"Why did we not meet you at the Botanical Garden this morning? We saw your Black at the door?"

Marthe smiled, but her lips were very white. "I saw you pass," she said, "I was in the large hot-house in the gallery."

"Why did you not call out to us?" asked Nastia in amazement, "we could have returned together."

"You seemed to be so eminently content with the companionship of each other, that I did not venture to disturb you," Marthe answered, still with a smile, "then I should have run the risk of making you late to breakfast, and of a scolding from Grandma."

"Oh! Serge," cried Nastia, "she heard us!"

"I heard only that," added Marthe, astonished at her own self possession. "How easily one learns to dissimulate," she said to herself with horror. "I am not lying but I am deceiving them as much as if I were, and how easily I do it!"

Pauline was at first astonished, then delighted, and drank in all this conversation.

"Why did you not tell me this morning?" said the Prince in a tone of gay reproach, "that you had seen our young lovers?"

"I did not know that they would care to have me divulge their secrets," answered the Princess. "Lovers are secretive by nature," she added in a tone of indifference, while at the same time she was thoroughly digusted with herself, and with her own duplicity.

Pauline was so excited that she lost her appetite. "Can it be?" she said to herself, "that she went to the Garden, and did not give her real name! If she did, it was of course because she did not wish to be recognized. I am convinced that she was on the gallery with Michel Averœf when these simpletons passed, and if they had looked up, they would have seen the two!"

Pauline shrugged her shoulders, filled with pity for human stupidity, and her appetite returned.

But what was her surprise when two or three days later, the thermometer having risen considerably, she heard Marthe announce her intention of repairing to one of her estates situated south of Moscow, to enjoy the spring in a less severe climate.

"What on earth does it mean? She is going away!"

said the companion to herself. "Going away just as
they are beginning to understand each other! And
she will take me with her, and Mélaguire will become
accustomed to doing without me!"

Marthe in fact had decided to take the companion
with her. The Prince had insisted upon it, he of
course knowing nothing of her repugnance, the cause
of which he should have been the last to know. Then
too, the Princess felt a vague uneasiness in the thought
of leaving Pauline among her people. She preferred
to keep her near at hand, that she might watch her.
As regarded the forgetfulness of Monsieur Mélaguire,
the thing was done; but Pauline, like sparrows in a
time of scarcity, still nourished some illusions with her
crumbs of hope.

This wretched Princess would never cease it seemed,
to thwart the projects of Mademoiselle Hopfer!
Pauline thought seriously of resisting, and remaining
at St. Petersburg, but under what possible pretext
should she do this? In vain, while her busy hands
methodically packed Marthe's dresses and skirts, did
she seek one; she could find none. The packing of
these trunks was a menial task, to which only the fact
that it opened to her wardrobes and closets hitherto
locked, reconciled her, and made her feel it less of a
humiliation to her ambitious spirit. Marthe had infinite trouble in reconciling those about her to her hurried departure. Nastia wept the vehement tears of her
childhood again, as she implored her sister not to leave

her. Monsieur Mélaguire in despair, did not know in what words to frame his entreaties to his child. Why could she not be induced to lay aside this fantastic whim?

"Why can't you come with me, dear father?" she said one day. "It would not greatly amuse you, but it would make me very happy."

"At this season, Marthe, with my rheumatism and my asthma! what can you be thinking of? Such a journey would be my death, as it certainly will be yours," he added despairingly. "I think your husband must be utterly crazy, to allow you to travel in such weather."

This general outcry saddened Marthe, without, however, shaking her resolution in any way. She found a firm ally in Madame Avéroef, her natural confidante in all family matters.

"Let the Princess do what she pleases," she said to all who would listen to her. "She knows very well what she is about: she has a good heart and a strong head, and I believe she is entirely right when she says that the air of St. Petersburg does not agree with her at this time. Do you want to see her ill once more, as she was last year?"

By dint of saying this over and over again, she finished by convincing people of the truth of what she said, and Marthe was able to occupy herself with her preparations for departure, without being impeded by oceans of tears.

When she went to take leave of her old friend, she found her alone.

"You have done wisely," said Madame Avérœf, "most wisely—but do not throw away your life: it does not belong to yourself alone, it is the property of those who love you. Think of your father."

"Fear nothing," answered Marthe, understanding at once the old lady's apprehensions,—"I will carefully guard my life. You are right; I do not belong to myself—I need solitude—I will come back soon, but please say nothing about it."

Madame Avérœf looked at her doubtfully.

"Yes," continued Marthe, "I shall come back soon—you know nothing?"

The old lady shook her head.

"He is going to join the army," Marthe added in a low voice.

A long silence followed. Madame Avérœf thought of those so dear to her who had been devoured by that inexorable army.

Marthe said hesitatingly:

"I want to see him once more, for the last time, here in your presence—it will do no wrong to any one."

Madame Avérœf hesitated. Strict morality certainly forbade her to sanction such a meeting, but these two had so much, and the future held no happiness in reserve for them."

"I will invite the whole family here, the evening before your departure," said the old lady, whose eyes were weary with the tears she had shed in her long life, and who understood all sorrows.

Marthe kissed her hands, and her heavy lids bravely held back the tears, only too ready to fall.

The designated day was not long in coming. One evening, at the end of February, all the family connection was assembled in Madame Avérœf's salon, to take leave of the Princess.

Every one was inclined to be sad; but they all said a thousand foolish things, as often happens when expectation is on the stretch, and nerves are over excited. Marthe laughed so heartily, that no one would have supposed her to be more than seventeen. Michel himself, seated at a distance from her, kept up the conversation throwing the ball to the Prince, who prided himself on the brilliancy of his sallies.

Madame Avérœf alone, silent and sad, looked on with a melancholy smile, but no one willingly looked toward her. Of those who laughed the most heartily, more than one would have burst into tears, had she been hastily recalled to the truth of the situation.

This fair woman, who was about to leave them, had been for years, the joy and the comfort of many of those present — to her sister, she had been a mother — to Monsieur Mélaguire, when the death of his wife had left him alone, embarrassed by two children and a house, she had been a ministering angel, the sweet counsellor, the tender mediator, the incarnation of peace and order, and of filial tenderness. Even those more distantly allied to the family had felt her influence; not one among them, but could recall a kind word spoken in secret, or the judicious aid of a word or a look; or a hint and advice delicately given, without assumption, and seeing her leave St. Petersburg so long before the coming of the Spring, which witnessed daily departures and facile separations, every heart was full, as if some great misfortune threatened the traveller. As the evening wore on, conversation languished, and every one grew sadder and sadder.

Marthe, at last, had herself the courage to give the signal for departure; she was to leave St. Petersburg at a very early hour in the morning.

"Au revoir," dear friends and relatives," she said, rising. "May God keep you in health and happiness. I hope to find you all well, when I return!"

Every voice replied to her with warm wishes for her welfare. Paul Avéroef who never saw her but with a pang, expressed his regrets very strongly.

"Do not pity me," she said, "I shall be infinitely happier away than here. Kiss your child for me," she added, as he pressed her hand.

Paul looked after her with a swelling heart, as she turned toward Michel.

"Farewell," she said.

"Farewell," answered the young man.

He bowed over the hand she extended, and kissed it deferentially. She moved on with lowered eyelids, and approached Madame Avéroef who took her in her arms.

"I shall never behold your face again, Marthe," she said in a low voice; "I am too old; I wish it had been my lot to see you all happy, before I am called away. This joy will not be mine. May God be your guide, my daughter. Heaven owes you a recompense." And her aged trembling hands blessed Marthe who went away pale, but calm. The last look in spite of herself, rested on Michel, who stood a little apart; her eyes dwelt on his face for a moment, and then turned away a stranger forevermore, to the joys of this world.

No one wished a happy and prosperous journey to Pauline.

CHAPTER XXX.

PAULINE'S VENOM.

LIKE a gallant cavalier, the Prince accompanied his wife on her journey. This indifferent husband, who lived as much of a stranger to Marthe as if they inhabited different hemispheres, would have considered himself unworthy of the name of a gentleman, had he allowed her to travel alone. He had quitted the gay and bustling life of St. Petersburg, for deserted highways and for icebound rivers, the severe frosts always to be expected with the beginning of March. Oghérof was a gentleman, and did not care to entrust to his domestics, the task of guarding the Princess, his wife.

The journey was long and fatiguing. They were compelled, owing to alternate rain and snow, to change their runners for wheels, at least ten times on this journey, and the travellers were compelled to wait and lose much time. It was not until the fifth day that they reached Moscow, and shortly after, beheld the Seignorial mansion, standing out upon the snow. A wide wall only separated them.

This half day was the most dangerous of the journey. The ice was so very thin that the rush of the current was seen underneath. How on earth was that heavy carriage to drive over that fragile surface! The little party crossed it on foot, while the ferryman sought a more solid passage with the domestics. This was found at last a full league below, but not without some difficulty, and it was not until toward evening that the Princess entered the house, she had selected for her voluntary isolation.

A gleam of sun pierced the rain clouds, and threw its yellow light through the great windows, bare of softening shades or curtains.

"The sun salutes you as Sovereign Lady," said the Prince, gallantly to his wife, as he offered her his hand to assist her from the carriage.

Marthe involuntarily thought of her wedding journey.

"It is to be hoped that he, too, does not remember it!" she said to herself, with sudden fright.

Pauline, who instinctively understood her fears, used all her skill to have them realized. During the next twenty-four hours, she did her best, and lavished upon the Prince the most ambiguous compliments.

"What an amiable husband," she said, "to abandon the town and all its pleasures, to bury himself alive with his wife!"

"But I do not propose to bury myself," answered the Prince, "I shall only stay here two weeks."

"A veritable wedding trip!" she said later, in a discreet under tone.

"You would be de trop, if that were the case, which of course, could never be," he added, with that gallantry which in him was simply mechanical.

Annoyed by these constant attacks, the Prince one day, turned upon Pauline.

"One would be inclined to think that this journey is stupid for you?" he said.

"Quite the contrary sir, it amuses me immensely, or at all events it amuses me as much as it does the Princess."

"I dare say. But you see," he continued, somewhat rudely; "you have certain advantages, if not pleasures in this excursion. Having no one to whom you can talk, you can hoard up the treasures of your wit and imagination for next winter. You can act the part of the prudent ant," and he turned his back upon her.

Pauline had nothing to say in reply, as before she had sufficiently collected her thoughts he had left the room.

A sudden rage filled her soul. She never had supposed it possible that she could hate Oghérof, so gay and courteous as he always was and yet these few words from him, had placed him on the list of those whom she would injure if she could. What luck was hers! She could strike two blows with one stone — injure two persons by the same adroit words — it was, indeed, a double joy.

"Besides," she said to herself, "the occasion is most favorable. I shall never find a better one!"

Pauline decided to play her last card, and made all her arrangements — purchased a pretty, light sledge,

and left it with the peasant who had sold it to her
When she went to buy sugar, she discovered that the
diligence for Moscow left twice a week; then she
gathered together a good deal of small change, and
sewed her own savings into the lining of the dress she
wore, with the precious gift of six thousand roubles,
which would enable her to injure with impunity the
daughter of her benefactor. When all these preparations were completed, she awaited the day that the
diligence was due.

That morning it so happened, the Prince was not in
the best of humors. Pauline's hints had not been
thrown away. The Prince looked at his wife attentively, and realized that she was as beautiful—if not
more beautiful—than ever before in her life. He said
so to the Princess, who turned a deaf ear to his words.
He took pains to please her, but she would not be
pleased. Two days of rain combined with her husband's
attentions, affected Marthe to such a degree, that she
shut herself up in her own rooms, for twenty-four
hours.

The Prince was quite in the mood to say to her and
to himself, that she was his wife, that he had married
her for love, and that if he had been guilty of some
faults toward her, they were no excuse for her, or
any reason, why they should offer to the world the
spectacle of a ménage united only by a regard for *les
convénances*. He was ready to make, for her, the
sacrifice of remaining in this Thébaïde, if the climate

16

suited her; but he thought she might, at least, speak to him in some other way than through a half-open door.

He had just reached this point, when Pauline entered to make the tea.

"Did the Princess pass a good night?" she asked, in the most dulcet tones.

"I know nothing about her!" answered the Prince, half angrily, but quickly controlling himself, he added,

"I hope, however, that she slept well, and is better; she was far from well last evening."

"So I thought," said the companion.

After rattling the teacups for at least ten minutes, a noise which was always especially irritating to the irritable nerves of the Prince, she placed the teapot on the tray, and said in a plaintive voice:

"Poor Princess! she is so sad!"

Oghérof looked at her in amazement. Pauline pretended not to notice his questioning glance.

"Prince, have you read yesterday's paper," she said, presently.

"No, I have not," answered Oghérof, who was walking up and down.

"Where is it, may I ask?" and Pauline turned over the music on the piano. "There are news in it of your friends and acquaintances."

"Of whom?" asked the Prince, mechanically.

"Young Grab is promoted to a captaincy in the horseguards in place of Monsieur Michel Avéroef, who goes at his own request to join the Caucasian army.

"Avéroef, going to Caucasus?" exclaimed the Prince, wheeling about hastily. "It is impossible. Where did you see it?"

He snatched the paper from Pauline's hands, and read the order aloud.

"Well! upon my word, what does this mean? Avéroef never opened his lips to me of this plan!"

"Oh, Prince; he of course would never mention it to you!" said Pauline, quietly.

"And why not, pray?"

The Prince, whose nerves were somewhat disturbed, spoke most abruptly, and in a more peremptory tone, than was his habit. Pauline did not reply, but began to rattle her teaspoons again.

"I ask you why," he repeated, stepping a little nearer.

Pauline pressed her hand on her waist to assure herself that the money was all safe, and then looking at the Prince with a deliberate air, she said:

"I don't know; and if I did know, I should not say, for it is none of my business!"

With lowered eyelids, brandishing the teapot in one hand, and the strainer in the other, she began to fill the cups; the Prince snatched her wrist, and forced her to set the teapot on the table somewhat promptly.

"Speak!" he said, sternly; "you have said too much to be silent now. Why is my wife sad, and why does Avéroef go to Caucasus?"

"But," said Pauline, "why do you connect these two things."

"Do you take me for an utter fool?" thundered the Prince. "I may be hair-brained, but I am no fool. You will say this moment just what you know, or just what you have invented, unless —— Speak, Pauline Vassilscova," he resumed, after a sudden pause, "do not make me forget that I am a man, and that you are only a woman."

"I must obey you, Prince; but you will bear me witness, that I speak at your commands. Heaven knows —"

"Will you speak?" cried Oghérof in a rage, bringing his hand down violently upon the table.

With her eyes lowered, and the corners of her mouth drawn down, Pauline told how Michel Avérœf had loved Marthe before her marriage; how Marthe had certainly returned this affection; how when he left for Italy, she had wept the whole day long, either in the garden or in her room.

"Wept?" said the Prince, who had listened calmly; "wept? and why?"

"Because the report was in circulation that Monsieur Avérœf took a child with him."

"Ah! yes, I know. Go on."

"Well, then, Prince, you can see from this, that the poor Princess already loved Monsieur Avérœf."

"Already," roared the Prince. "Then you have something else to say! But I am utterly mad to listen to the foolish chatter of servants! Do you know Mademoiselle, that you are an ignoble wretch, to come e with such gossip about my wife?"

"You may call me a wretch if you choose," answered Pauline, darting a look of hate upon him from her viper-like eyes; but it is no less true that your wife and Michel Avércef had a *rendezvous.* I have the proof in my possession."

"A *rendezvous?*" repeated the Prince, turning pale and drawing back.

"Yes, at the Botanical Gardens."

- "Nonsense! she met her sister there!"

"But she did not write her own name in the Register," cried Pauline triumphantly, "which proves that she was not alone in that gallery, which was so high that no one could see her. I have looked at the Register myself, and her name is not there! Why should it not be if she had nothing to conceal? Besides, I saw them make the appointment. Michel Avércef is your wife's lover, and she is sad because he has left her!"

Oghérof rushed toward Pauline, who was frightened, and put the table between her and the enraged man. The Prince stopped, ashamed of his outburst.

"I came very near disgracing myself," he said, "but you made me forget that you were a woman. Mademoiselle Hopfer, you are dismissed from my house."

"I do not see that my going alters the position of things," Pauline answered with her wicked laugh as she closed the door after her.

Oghérof with the greatest difficulty refrained from following her and wringing her neck. He restrained himself, however, and striding across the salon and through several rooms, he reached Marthe's chamber, of which the door stood open. He hesitated; perhaps his wife was not alone. And then, too, what was he to say. His hesitation was of short duration; he knocked twice and entered without waiting for a reply. The Princess stood before the mirror. Her magnificent hair, braided but not bound up, hung over her white peignoir down to her knees. She turned as her husband entered, and stared in astonishment, awaiting an explanation of this intrusion. The honest, frank eyes interrogated the Prince, who answered at once:

"Madame," he said, "I have just dismissed Pauline Hopfer from this house."

Marthe knew that the hour had come. She laid her hand on her heart to still its beating, and continued to look at her husband who continued hastily,

"She is an infamous calumniator! She dared to say that you have loved Michel Avérœf."

"This woman is a mischief maker and a slanderer, and was a disgrace to our roof," answered Marthe, "but in this case she told the truth—I have loved Michel Avérœf."

"And you dare say this to me?" asked the Prince, who was very pale. He spoke through his clenched teeth.

"I say it only to you," answered Marthe. "Had you asked me the question before marrying me, I would have said to you then, what I say to-day."

"Why are you not his wife then, instead of mine?"

"Because Pauline calumniated him then as she has me to-day, and compelled me to feel contempt for him."

"But this contempt was not of long duration?" asked the Prince with an effort, for he was choked with rage.

"It lasted until Paul Avérœf's return with the child, whose father Michel was accused of being.

"And since then?"

"It is my husband who questions me," answered Marthe, with dignity. "My husband has a right to do so, and I will answer! Since then, feeling that by my haughty pride I had caused him great pain, and wronged a man worthy of all esteem and consideration, I have shown him clearly the regret I felt for my precipitate conduct."

"You met him by appointment then? Is that what you mean?"

"Yes, Prince—I admit my fault. I should not have made this appointment, for it was I who asked it."

"And where was it?"

"At the Botanical Garden. I have concealed this from you, but I have told you no falsehood."

"And you cursed the obstacle that divided you—the husband who prevented you from being happy—and swore eternal affection?"

"We cursed no one—we separated forever. We were both too proud to sin. Had I even touched his hand, I would never have dared to put mine in yours."

Marthe extended her right hand to her husband with

so proud a gesture, that Oghérof's anger suddenly
changed. He took the little hand, and looked his wife
full in the face. She met his eyes without effrontery,
but with the calm assurance of innocence.

"He has left for Caucasus. Did you know it?"
said the Prince.

"And I asked you to bring me here," she answered
quietly.

Oghérof, subjugated and humiliated, bent his knee
before his wife.

"I ask your pardon for my suspicions, Marthe,"
he said, "but this viper has a way of speaking that
deprived me of my common sense."

"I know her," answered the Princess.

"Why have you kept her then?"

"Because I wished to avoid just what has happened.
Had you asked me a single question I was ready to tell
you the truth. Do you remember how difficult it was
for me to give you an affirmative reply?"

"Certainly, I remember. Ah! had I but known.
And now I am the only obstacle to your happiness.
My dear Marthe, do you detest me now?"

"No, Prince," answered Marthe, with some embarrassment; "I esteem you, and love you, as an honest
man and an excellent friend."

"But Michel—you love him still?"

"We are forever separated: he no longer exists
for me."

The Prince sighed.

"I see then that I must win you for the second time. But," he added with a start, "this woman is going. She will disseminate the calumnies she has already poured out to me. At all cost she must be silenced. Her interest or her fears must be played upon. I trust she has not yet gone."

He hurried out, but came back again.

"Marthe," he said, "you are a good woman? Michel Avérœf deserves you far better than I do. He is a steady fellow, and I am a very foolish one, but as Fate has given you to me, I will do my best to merit you!"

With a gesture of adieu he rushed away.

Marthe was utterly overcome at this new cross laid upon her shoulders. Must she now struggle against a growing love on the part of her husband? She looked about her in despair.

CHAPTER XXXI.

A DOUBLE TRAGEDY.

PAULINE lost no time. She had gained her end, and hastened to make good her retreat before the storm broke. She got possession of her sledge, bought and paid for in shining new roubles, a pretty little horse which the peasant sold her at a bargain, seated herself in her small equipage, with her valise under the seat, took up the reins, and started off in the best of spirits. What genius she had shown. At one blow she had made the Prince very unhappy, crushed the Princess, and probably started the ball which could not fail sooner or later to kill Avèrœf by the hand of the husband.

She excited her horse by shaking the reins upon his back — for in her haste she had forgotten her whip: but who is perfect?

She had gone quite a long distance. Behind her stretched the highway covered with dark tracks; it was now the end of March, and for some days a thaw had been doing its work with great rapidity. The clumsy trot of the little animal threw into Pauline's face a considerable quantity of mud and melted snow, but she did not care. In the life she had selected she would have many such things to bear.

"I had the last word," she repeated to herself over and over again.

She would have rubbed her hands joyously had she not been driving. She shook her reins instead, and the energetic little beast, revenged himself by throwing more mud in her face.

"Wait!" she said, "I shall not punish you, but I will sell you, and for a higher price than I paid for you!"

The river, hidden by a slender line of trees, rolled at the foot of a rough hill, down which Pauline drove with many precautions. At the bottom she looked up, and pulled in her steed with dismay.

Half of the ice had disappeared, and in its place ran a rapid stream, blue, clear, and gay in the sunshine; the other half, shaded by the trees, was still solid and fixed to the shore, forming a sort of bridge to the middle of the river, and when the end of this bridge was reached, what then? A ferry boat was on the other side, but the ice prevented it from reaching the other shore! What on earth was she to do?

Pauline hailed the ferryman, who having nothing to do, had gone to sleep in the barn, and he was long in awakening. But Pauline's voice was so piercing that it would have awakened the dead. The ferryman at last appeared, winking and blinking in the sunshine.

"How is one to get over?" she asked without any preamble.

"You can't get over," answered the man, "you must go home."

"Impossible! I am in the greatest haste. It is a very important matter. I will pay you well if you can find any way of getting me over."

The thought of an ample reward succeeded in thoroughly awakening the ferryman.

"There is one way," he said, "not very convenient, certainly, but the best I can think of."

"And what is that?"

"To go in the sleigh to the edge of the ice, I will bring the boat up, you will whip the horse up, and then "——

"The sledge will go on the boat?"

"Oh yes."

"And the ice will not break?"

"That happens sometimes, but if you are in a hurry you know "——

The gallop of a horse on the high road above was heard. Pauline felt a vague apprehension.

"Get your boat ready," she said, "I will try it."

The ferryman entered his skiff and took up the boat hook.

"There is too much water," he said, "the current is too strong. Wait a moment, I will go for my oars."

"Make haste," cried Pauline, "and I will give you a noble."

The galloping horse was heard coming nearer. The man came back with his oars, and began to row in an oblique direction, seeking a favorable spot for Pauline's attempt. At this moment Pauline, in a spasm of abject terror, beheld Oghérof not fifteen feet from her.

"Pauline," he cried, "wait! I must speak to you!"

"No," she answered, "I have done with you all."

"I have something to propose—"

"I will not listen," she answered, as she gathered up the reins.

The sledge started forth upon the ice.

"Much money!" said the Prince, driving his horse cautiously down the slope.

The boat approached—only a few feet were between it and the ice.

"Much money," repeated the Prince.

"My tastes are very modest," answered Pauline with a sneer, "I have all I need. Farewell!"

She was now midway on the ice.

"You shall not go," cried the Prince in a fury.

"I have proofs," said Pauline, without turning her head.

"They are false!"

"They will answer my purpose," said the companion maliciously. She had almost reached the boat.

"You shall give them to me!" and the Prince drove his horse on the fragile ice.

"We will cross together, it seems," answered Pauline with another sneer.

A shout rent the air—a sharp report—the ice was breaking around them. Mad with fear, Pauline struck her horse violently—the poor creature made one desperate leap and missed the boat, disappearing under it with the sledge. A large block of ice slowly floated over the place where Pauline had been a moment before.

The Prince mute with horror, stood as if frozen.

"Save her, Prince!" cried the ferryman; "it is not deep here."

Oghérof looked down into the blue water, where little ripples were slowly rising to the surface.

"She is a woman after all!" he said, "and my life is of so little consequence, Marthe would shed no tears. God have mercy on me!"

He drove his spurs into the horse to compel him to leap into the water, but the animal was afraid; he reared, a second report was heard, and a large rift spread from the shore—a gulf opened under his feet, and Oghérof disappeared. Twice did the cavalier and the horse rise to the surface, twice did the despairing ferryman hold out his oar. The third time, the horse exhausted, struggled to the shore, but he was riderless and alone!

Pauline could injure no one now, she slept forever at the bottom of the river.

Marthe was a widow.

CHAPTER XXXII.

WAS IT SUICIDE?

THE intelligence of this event, when it reached St. Petersburg, was received at first, with utter incredulity. That Alexander Oghérof, the bravest and the most skillful of all the young officers could have been drowned in crossing a river like any common peddler, seemed impossible. Monsieur Mélaguire was so overwhelmed that he could not speak. He could think only of Marthe.

"Poor Princess! poor Princess!" he said over and over again, "only two years married, and this is the end. They loved each other so fondly!"

He, with Serge and Nastia, hurried off to pay their last respects to the dead, and to bring Marthe back.

When the body of the Prince was carried to his late home, the young widow contemplated it without a tear falling from eyes dilated by the terrible shock. That handsome, manly face, unmarred by death, on which the toils and disappointments of life had as yet left no mark, had a certain fascination for her.

Vainly did they all entreat her to leave the room, she allowed herself to be led away, but an hour after, she was found there again, wrapped in the same tearless, wordless contemplation. She longed to tear from those pale lips—from those closed eyes, the last secret thought. A terrible doubt haunted her incessantly.

"Did he die wishing to avenge me, or did he kill himself because I did not love him?" she asked herself these two questions over and over again.

In the night she rose, and wrapped in a pelisse, she went again to that icy room, where the Prince lay, and there, while the Deacon, half asleep, recited in a monotonous voice the funeral verses by the light of the flickering candles, she again, questioned this face—this face to which she had been so indifferent, and now whose every line had to her stricken soul a new and terrible meaning. On her knees, by the side of the open coffin, with the stiff, cold folds of the cloth-of-gold pall pressing against her, she questioned God Most High. Her conscience told her that if she had not committed a crime, she had, at least, been guilty of an imprudence.

"Ought I then to have told a falsehood?" and this question from this poor stricken heart, beat at the gates of Heaven with impetuous eagerness. And prayer, incessant and passionate, brought her no peace; for she, who had been able to look at the shadow of evil, now struggled with remorse for an involuntary, but irreparable crime.

It was in this state that the travellers found Marthe on the third day after they left St. Petersburg, the fifth after the tragic event. She came to meet them with a pale and rigid countenance—hollow eyes and burning hands; her long mourning garments, trailing after her like a shroud. She had not aged in these five days, but she had become etherealized. She looked like one of those men who, devoured by some secret torture, move about the convent chapels, bearing a candle in the hand—hearing nothing, seeing nothing—mortal, but not terrestrial apparitions.

The ceremony took place the following day, amid a numerous crowd drawn from two hundred verstes around. Not for a long time had such magnificent obsequies been witnessed in that part of the country.

Pauline's remains, found the day after the accident had been at once interred in a corner of the cemetery, her faith not sanctioning the service of the Greek church.

After the burial, the visitors having left the house of mourning, the family assembled in the great hall—they were to consult together, and come to some decision.

Monsieur Mélaguire would not listen to the suggestion of leaving his daughter in the country. To all his supplications and remonstrances, the Princess answered with the same words:

"I cannot desert my husband's grave."

Did she hope to force the secret from the tomb by her prayers?

Vainly, did her sister and her brother-in-law, supplicate her to accompany them, and for the hundredth

17

time were using the same arguments, when a servant came to say to the Princess that the ferryman wished to see her?

"The ferryman, who is he?" asked the Princess, without turning her head.

"The ferryman who was at the river, the day—"

"Did any one see the accident?" interrupted Marthe, suddenly awakening to what was going on about her.

"Yes, your Highness, he saw it all, and he has come to bring you something he found."

"I thought there was no one present," said Marthe, after a brief silence. "How happens it, that I was not told before?"

"I beg your pardon, but your Highness was told at once; but you heard nothing said at that time, and since then, you have asked no questions."

"That is true," said the Princess; "very well, I will come."

She went toward the door, her relatives silently watching her. Suddenly, midway, she tottered and extended her arms, seeking support. She could not walk, her limbs, bent by her constant prayers, refused to bear her body, worn by fasting as it was. They placed her in an arm-chair, and Monsieur Mélaguire bade them send the ferryman to her.

"No," said Marthe, trying to rise; "no, I wish to see him alone."

"You shall not do it!" cried Monsieur Mélaguire, angrily. "It shall not be, that after losing my son-in-law, I shall lose my daughter, too. Bring the man here, and quickly!" he added, turning to the servant, and speaking authoritatively.

Marthe submissively bowed her head.

What did it matter after all, if this man accused her unconsciously, in the presence of her family. His mere account of what he had witnessed, might in itself be an accusation. Was not her fault one of those, which no earthly chatisement can fitly punish.

The ferryman entered, and stood near the door.

"You were there," began Monsieur Mélaguire.

"When the misfortune?"

"Yes," your Excellency.

"You were alone?"

"Entirely alone, your Excellency. I was asleep when the lady arrived."

"What did she say?"

"She asked if she could get over, and I told her no; that she must go back, and she said she must go on."

"But, why did you let her?" asked Monsieur Mélaguire, in a tone of reproach.

"Because, sir, we were all in the habit of doing just what I advised her to do, and no harm ever came. If we tumble into the water, we shake ourselves, and are none the worse; but the lady did not know how to drive her horse, and she was in too great a hurry, too."

"But, why was she in such a hurry?" interrupted Serge, who had listened attentively.

He had questioned the servants as soon as he

arrived, and had learned the probable cause of the misfortune, but it seemed to him that there was some mystery he could not fathom.

"She was in a hurry, sir, because his Highness, the deceased Prince, wished to prevent her from crossing the river."

"And why!"

"I don't know, I am sure," and the ferryman scratched his neck. "It was none of my business—"

"Go on, don't be afraid," said Monsieur Mélaguire, to encourage him.

Marthe listened, sitting erect in her chair, with her head bent down, and her hands clasped together.

"Well!" said the peasant, "when the Prince got up on the top of the hill, he called out to the lady, 'I want to speak to you, wait!' She answered 'no!' Then he went a little nearer and said, 'much money!' she said 'no' again. Then I did not understand what he said next to her, but she laughed; and she did not look at all good, just then, I declare to you!"

"The Prince got angry and tried to catch her. She whipped up her horse, and the ice cracked."

"And the Prince?"

"The Prince was on horseback."

"He did not throw himself in after her?"

"No," said the ferryman, hesitatingly. "No, he did not act as if he wished to jump into the water. I called out to him, Save her! save her! You know at such times, a man does not always know what he is doing, and, of course, I ought not to have said what I did; but he crossed himself and jumped in."

Marthe raised her head quickly, and looked at the man who went on.

"His horse did not like the water, and struggled like a very devil. They came up to the surface twice; I did all I could, I stretched out my oars and thought the Prince would catch them, and he nearly did once. The second time, the current had carried him too far. It was his horse that killed him; I am as sure of that as I am that I am a Christian."

Marthe's eyes were still riveted on the ferryman.

"Can you lift your hand and swear before God that you speak the truth?" she asked in a tone so strange, that every one felt a thrill of surprise.

"Before God," said the honest man, "as I value the health of my soul, I have spoken the truth!"

"He did not wish to make the leap, you say?"

"I did very wrong Madame, I know I did wrong," said the ferryman, in a troubled tone; "I said to him, 'jump! save the lady,' I should have tried to save her myself, but I had to hold the boat steady against the current. It was not my fault, but it was a great misfortune!"

"And he did not wish to go into the water?" said Marthe. "You are sure of that?"

"Indeed I am; who would like to plunge into the water, in the month of April," answered the man, in a sulky voice.

He began to regret having come.

Marthe said nothing, her white lips moved convulsively. Her fingers were so tightly clasped that they marked her thin hands with red spots.

"I found these," said the man; "at the bottom of the river," and he laid on the table a piece of a watch-chain, attached to which was a bunch of bréloques; among them a portrait of the Princess in a tiny locket.

Marthe made a little sign, and her father handed the man some money, saying as he did so,

" Thank you — you are an honest man."

" Shall I dismiss him ?" he asked his daughter.

"Wait a moment," was Marthe's reply. " You say that he struggled, and tried to catch your oars ? "

" Yes, Madame."

" Then, you believe it to be an accident ? "

" Of course it was!   He was such a handsome gentleman, and had so much to live for! "

" And it was to save the lady, that he jumped into the water ?   You are sure of that ? "

" Oh! yes, very sure ! "

Marthe rose, her fluttering hands snatched at the vacant air, and she fell unconscious. The evening of the same day, while Marthe, for the first time since her widowhood, was sleeping peacefully, Nastia drew Serge aside.

" Do you know," she said, "that I feel sure that Marthe thought the Prince killed himself ? "

Serge did not answer.

"And you," she asked, "what do you think?"

"About what?"

"Do you think Marthe believed what I say?"

"Yes I do," answered Serge, reluctantly.

"And, what do you think?"

"Why on earth should he have killed himself? No, indeed, I think nothing of the kind. He had everything in the world to make him perfectly happy."

Oghérof had never passed for a saint, and it was generally believed, that he was drowned in endeavoring to retain his mistress, who wished to leave him.

After some hours of repose, Marthe made no further objection to going back to St. Petersburg with her family, and the sad little party returned to town just as all the rest of the world were leaving it.

Madame Avéroef, after learning all she could, insisted on having Marthe with her, and installed herself as chief nurse, for the young widow was very feeble, and unable to leave her bed for many hours at a time. The conversation of this good woman, who had borne so many trials with such a courageous spirit, was to Marthe a supreme aid when her anguish seemed greater than she could bear. One day she made up her mind to speak openly to Madame Avéroef.

"It is possible that my husband did not kill himself," she concluded, after having repeated their last conversation, "but it is certain that he did not care at that moment to live. What in fact had he to expect from me? If, as is to be feared, his affection for me had returned, how miserable we should have been!"

"He might have found some other consolation possibly," thought Madame Avérœf, recalling the places which the Prince had been fond of frequenting. "God does everything for the best!" she said aloud. "You are young, and life is long. You have a right to be happy, since you were never false to your duties."

Saying this over and over again, she finished by convincing Marthe, who by degrees regained her health. Michel's name never passed her lips, but his memory was green in her heart. When she caught herself thinking of him, she drove the thought away, and reproached herself for daring to indulge in recollections rendered guilty by her recent widowhood. But it seemed to her sometimes that at the end of a long and dusty road, an oasis of verdure and running waters was opening before her.

She closed her eyes to shut out this vision, but the distant freshness penetrated each weary sense. She opened her eyes and the oasis was nearer than before, she had approached it unconsciously.

The day came when she realized that her thoughts reverted more than to any other season, to the winter preceding her marriage. That day she ceased her self-reproach and examination. Aided by her memory, she rearranged the old garnet-colored salon, and there passed her hours of solitude. Michel, whose invisible and silent presence she ignored, was nevertheless her constant companion.

CHAPTER XXXIII.

WAR AND ITS HORRORS.

THE Caucasian war was at last over, or, to speak more correctly, Shamyl was no longer at the head of the resisting forces. Some scattered bands still fought with the tenacity of despair. The contest, limited to a territory comparatively small, had the irritating charm of a party whose success is assumed, but whose final result is retarded just as one is on the point of grasping it. Intelligent, earnest officers were more than ever welcome, and Michel had no difficulty in negotiating an exchange. All was so quickly arranged that he was able to depart by the middle of March.

He left St. Petersburg in a calm and steadfast spirit. He had chosen Caucasus, because it was only there, among its struggles and dangers, that he could effectively serve his country. It was not, however, enthusiasm for a soldier's cause that had guided his choice. He knew very well that the service was one of great danger — hidden dangers and unforeseen surprises — within the depths of his heart this was not a matter of surprise to him. He had however not the smallest intention of allowing himself to be killed unnecessarily. He could by living, better evince his resignation and his courage, and there might come a day when Marthe would need him. Who could say? Such were his feelings when he went to take leave of his old aunt.

"Caucasus took my son from me," she said, "as Turkey did my husband. You will come back I hope, happier than you are to-day. There as here, my child, I know you will make the name of Avéroef honored."

Like an old Roman matron she did not flinch from this trial, but blessed Michel with a serene brow. She said to herself that the shortest martyrdoms were the best, and that Michel, expecting so little from life, would not have much to regret were he to lose it. And still deeper within her heart lay the secret joy that if these two young creatures were separated in this world, that their honor was untarnished.

The news of Prince Oghérofs death was a great shock to the whole connection, and to Madame Avéroef more than to any of the others. The sacrifice so courageously made had been useless! Her first impulse was to write to Michel to return, but a soldier cannot return in that way without having smelt powder, and she put a strong guard on herself, that she might not tempt her nephew.

Like most women, she knew little of the stringency of military discipline, and it was a week after the death of the Prince before she wrote to Michel.

Paul had not been so cautious. He wrote at once, "the Princess is a widow." He was about to say more and write freely, but after all what could he say? His brother had told him nothing. He therefore contented himself with the simple announcement.

Unfortunately Michel did not receive this letter. He reached his regiment only in time to march away with it, and the letter followed him from village to village without reaching him.

These eight days were eight days of constant fighting, for the heroic band among whom the young officer received his baptism of fire. A considerable number of rebels were massed into a place encircled by mountains, and from there started forth to make murderous incursions into the Russian camp.

Michel received a few scratches, and for a month thought of nothing but war. The fever had seized him and he determined to conquer: all his strength of mind and body, all the solid energy of his resolute character was turned toward this end, and he threw himself head foremost into the thickest of the danger, in such a way that the Colonel was obliged to reprove him for his temerity. The young man promised greater caution, but when the next skirmish arrived, circumstances were too strong for his resolutions.

One evening in May, the little troop which Michel commanded, were marching cautiously through a narrow valley. The Colonel had ordered a reconnoissance, as all the live stock of the regiment had been stolen the night before.

All seemed quiet. The torrent which the soldiers were following rolled its impatient waters over its rocky bed with a musical rhythm. At the bottom, from a narrow, dark gully, dropped a thread of silver,

which bathed a willow plantation at the foot of the
rock.

The narrow valley seemed to terminate here, and to
be bound by inaccessible rocks.

"Halt!" commanded Michel.

The butts of the muskets brought sharply to the
ground echoed loudly, and at the same moment a rain
of balls fell upon the little group, followed by a silence.
A cloud of blue smoke as it disappeared showed them a
narrow cleft in the rocks, through which only one person could pass at a time.

Avérœf counted his men, some of whom were
slightly wounded but none severely enough to prevent
walking. To engage with an invisible enemy was
useless, to await a second discharge of musketry was
senseless. The mountaineers were watching the troops,
but would they dare come down and attack them?

Michel ordered a retreat, and a second discharge
struck his Lieutenant in the arm, a young fellow who
had just left the military school of the district. The
poor fellow had lost much blood. Michel took him by
the arm, and while he covered with his body the retreat
of his men, he pressed the wound firmly together, and
when at last sheltered by a turn in the valley, he dressed
the young Lieutenant's wound, and returned to the
camp absorbed in thought.

After making his report, he awaited orders from his
Colonel.

"There are no orders," said his superior officer,

"no orders whatever, unless it be to double the senti-
nels."

Michel made a military salute and went back to his
tent. Ever since he had returned from this expedition
he was haunted by an irresistible desire to discover
the enemy himself. Without a word, he allowed the
usual arrangements for the night to be made, and then,
an hour after midnight, quickly left the camp to carry
out his plan.

He had nearly despaired at the difficulties of the
road through which they had come, but he had little
difficulty in finding the place where he had been
attacked. The fissure in the rock was twenty feet
from the ground. The moon was in its last quarter,
and the light therefore very faint. Assisting himself
with both feet and hands, he climbed up, and succeeded
in reaching a well-sheltered spot from which he could
see the fissure, which of course he expected to find
guarded—to his surprise it was not. The mountaineers had probably not expected so speedy a return.

With his hand on his dagger, for his pistol would
have betrayed him, he stole through the fissure. To
fire on the Russians, the enemies must have passed
closely against and behind each other, for three men
could not have stood face to face in front of the opening. Beyond, the gully grew wider, and Michel saw
before him, a few hundred yards away, a small fort on
a side hill.

The sky was whitening with the early morning light;

the young officer lying in the shadow of the rocks, watched this building from whose chimneys a little smoke ascended. Profound quiet reigned there, surrounded as it was on all sides, by the enemy. At the foot of the fort a spring issued from the rock and fell into a natural basin.

A woman enveloped in her white vail, descended the slope, a vase of antique shape upon her shoulder, filled her vase, and started up the long staircase hewn in the rocks. A huge tree shaded the walls, and the morning breeze rustled its foliage.

Michel, feeling a new, strange emotion, watched this woman with her amphora slowly climb the granite steps. Enemies were here, but also patriarchal life — children, too, probably, and yet he was planning how to come back, sack and burn this place—this nest of brigands, to be sure—but it was also a family nest.

A distant shot among the mountains recalled him to his military existence. He went back to the camp, and awakening his Colonel, told him of his discovery, and asked for instructions.

An hour later, the fissure in the rocks was in the possession of the Russians, and the first mountaineer who made the discovery was taken prisoner. An accidental discharge of his gun just as he was killed by a bayonet, brought out the men from the fort, and the fight took place on the plain.

The taking of this small fortress was not so small a matter as may be supposed. After some hard fighting, the men retreated behind the walls, but not without loss. Michel fought like a lion, with a melancholy undercurrent of thought from which he could not escape. Finally the fortress was taken and fired. As the red tongues licked the walls, a white form appeared on the roof, and extended supplicating arms towards the Russian troops. All the men who had not fled were taken. How was it that this woman alone had remained? Was there not in this fort some secret passage leading to some distant issue, as is often the case in places of this kind?

After her sudden appearance on the roof, the white form disappeared, but showed itself presently in the courtyard. The palisade of white planks began to blaze. The poor creature, habituated to the ferocity of her compatriots, dared not descend amid the Russian soldiers who made signs to her to trust them; she preferred death by the flames, rather than the tortures which she feared awaited her at their hands.

Mad with terror she tore her hair and wrung her hands. Michel threw himself over the wall.

"Avéroef!" they shouted on all sides, "the house is falling, come back!"

He did not hear. He reached the woman—threw her over his shoulder as he would a lamb, and tried to make his way back, just as the house fell—a mass of fire filling up the courtyard and cutting him off from the rest of the world.

A cry of horror escaped from every breast. Michel

had made himself beloved by all. The soldiers in consternation looked at the fiery furnace which had engulfed him. The smoke was rising slowly and the flames seemed to decrease in fierceness. The tree, crisped and twisted, still extended its dry limbs.

"Perhaps he is not dead," said the Colonel, "as soon as possible we will ascertain."

And a few hours later they began to search. All the débris were turned over, every stone was raised, but neither his body nor that of the woman he had endeavored to save, was to be found.

The Order of the day contained these words:

"*Died—Captain Avéroef—on the field of Honor.*"

The news reached St. Petersburg like a thunder clap.

Since his arrival at Caucasus, Michel had sent to his brother, several short letters written standing, in some brief interval of fighting. The colonel wrote to Paul; gave him some particulars in regard to the conduct of Captain Avéroef, and expressed the regret felt in the regiment at the loss of so good and brave an officer. Notwithstanding all this testimony, Michel's friends and family refused to credit his death. It seemed impossible to believe, that a friend so recently among them, could have died in this strange way, without a friend to throw upon his coffin a handful of earth.

"His body was not found," said Paul; "he is not dead!"

Sensible people shrugged their shoulders, and pitied this poor Monsieur Avéroef for cherishing such foolish illusions.

The family's first suspicions were aroused, when they saw the care with which Madame Avéroef concealed this sad intelligence from Marthe. Under the pretext of tender care for nerves which had already received so rude a shock, she established a sanitary cordon, and allowed no newspapers to go up to her without the most minute examination.

But she could not think of everything. The whole family went out to Karskoé-Sélo. Paul Avéroef went there occasionally to pass a day, but since the news from Caucasus, he went less frequently than before. He never spoke of his brother, and Marthe had not yet asked a question in regard to him; his deep mourning hindered him from breathing his brother's name among them. One day, at Marthe's request, he had brought his little girl. With a mother's care he had superintended the child's costume. She was all rose color and white.

Marie went to the garden with Marthe, to gather some flowers, and was chatting gayly with the Princess:

"You know," she said, suddenly, "I put on this rose-colored dress to come and see you, but it is too short."

"It is very pretty," said Marthe.

"It is too short," persisted the child, "but my governess said it was not worth while to have it lengthened."

"Why not?" asked the Princess, absently.

"Because I shall not wear it again this year. Since Uncle Michel died, I never wear anything but white."

Marthe struck to the heart, snatched the child's arm.

18

"Is your Uncle Michel dead?" she gasped.

"Yes—Oh!" said the little girl, suddenly remembering. "I was told not to speak of him before you, because you are sick. Please don't tell that I told you, or Papa will scold me!"

Marthe had suffered too much, not to be able to restrain all outward manifestations. She was able to bear the most cruel of blows in silence. Besides, she had felt for several weeks that something strange was going on about her. More than once she had noticed a sudden check in the conversation when she entered the room, or a change in the subject; but she had supposed that it was because they did not wish to remind her of Michel in the midst of her deep mourning. When this terrible blow struck full at her heart, she did not flinch. She went slowly back to the house leading the little one by the hand.

"Michel is dead," she said to Madame Avérœf, who turned very pale. "You could have told me, I am strong again."

"Who has told you this?" cried the old lady, terrified at seeing her so calm.

"What does it matter! I know it now. It is God's punishment. God is just, and I bow under the weight of his hand."

She passed on to her chamber, without Madame Avérœf daring to detain her.

We talk of martyrdom and tortures. Happy are those who see their blood run, and whose flesh cries out in agony. Death is near, and glory comes with it. But those, who in the silence of the night—in the long slumbrous summer days, look down into the depths of their desolated souls and see that implacable Destiny has torn everything from them, ruined and destroyed all, and they must go on to the end, with mourning in the Past and nothing in the Future—these are the true martyrs, and Death is slow in coming to their deliverance.

Marthe was not ill; this last shock changed her life entirely, and inspired her with supreme resolution. She devoted her attention to the entangled affairs of the Prince, and sought to bring order out of chaos. She passed half her nights over huge ledgers, comparing accounts, and finally declared that she must visit all the estates of the Prince before coming to any decision. There might be a great mistake in regard to the value of his land, she said, and before any sales were definitely settled, all must be clearly arranged.

In reality, she merely sought a pretext to leave these affectionate friends, whose tender solicitude harassed her. The care they took of her health, the necessity of composing her countenance in their presence, the impossibility of being alone, and weeping in peace, wherever she felt the need, rendered her daily life intolerable. She had renounced the joys of existence and would pass the rest of her life in expiating her faults, which had been punished with so heavy a hand; but she wished to be free, to suffer in her own way.

In this project, she had her ancient ally on her side—Madame Avèrœf, who fought and conquered all opposition.

"She is right," she said, "entirely right, and you are mere foolish children by her side. She is a woman who has lost her husband, a woman whom illness has brought more than once to the very doors of death; suddenly she arouses herself, wishes to busy herself with serious matters, to change her residence—things which it is eminently proper and wise that she should do, things which will distract and fortify her mind, and you wish to compel her to remain shut up, and to entrust strangers with the cares which concern her personally, and to live amid those scenes which recall to her every moment, precisely that which she wishes to avoid. You wish apparently, to see her fade away and die, merely to give yourselves the pleasure of keeping her close at your side a few weeks now. I am not so selfish, and, although I am the eldest of you all, I am glad to have her go; so fully persuaded am I, that she will come back to us cured."

Marthe left St. Petersburg about the end of July, first, to the vicinity of Moscow, and from there wherever her caprice dictated, for she had five or six estates to visit. She took with her only her maid, and a former Intendant of the Prince who had retired from his service with a pension, and who was greatly attached to her.

When she was seated alone in the compartment of the car, reserved for her, she dropped the window and drew a long breath. "At last," she said, "I can weep at my ease."

But the air was so delicious and the moonlight lay so softly on the landscape, that her heavy heart grew lighter by degrees. She did not weep, a tender melancholy filled her soul; but in this solitude—the friend of the unhappy, she felt a joy hitherto unknown—independence and liberty!

CHAPTER XXXIV.

RESURRECTION.

PAUL AVÉRŒF was right, Michel was not dead. He had spent six hours upon the rock in the rear of the fire with the woman he had sought to save, a serving woman, grown old and ugly in hard labor. The mountaineers, coming to visit the ruins put an end to their sufferings, and relieved them from the danger of their position, but they took Michel away as their prisoner. For a fortnight the young man did his best to escape, but was carefully guarded as a valuable hostage in case of an exchange of prisoners. He had no arms — his uniform had been taken from him, and he ran the risk of being ill treated by his own side before they recognised him.

This consideration did not deter him however, and one night he made his escape—was fired upon—an adroit aim fractured the clavicle, while numerous slighter wounds were inflicted by less able hands.

He reached the Russian camp after much useless wanderings in a most pitiable condition. The first sentinel he met, thought he had won at least another stripe by taking him prisoner. Treated like a spy at first, he succeeded finally in making himself knówn, and was at once reinstated in his position. But his wound gave him a right to a leave, and he hastened home with all the speed possible, in order to prove to his family, that the news of his death was premature.

On reaching the first post-house Michel opened his long accumulated correspondence. The first letter whose seal he broke, we must confess, was that of Madame Avéroef, brotherly affection lay dormant apparently, and the only words that he ever remembered were these, "Marthe is a widow." Michel was stunned, he turned to the date, read and re-read these three words, stuffed all his letters in his pocket, and ran to order post-horses.

Coming back, he read the other letters, which all confirmed the happy news. Happy, we say, for he accorded not one tear, nor yet a regret to the Prince. Man is selfish, Philosophers say!

The journey seemed long, and was long. The roads, however, were excellent at that season of the year. The August sun struck no terror to the soul of the young officer — fractures of the clavicle have one advantage, they do not necessarily prevent one from attending to one's affairs — but how many endless verstes must be conquered before he could behold a railway station. Fortunately his thoughts were of the sunniest. One thing alone disquieted him. How had Marthe received the news of his death? Of this he could know nothing until the end of May. An abyss separated him from the rest of the world. How carefully he examined the newspapers, with what dread he turned to the fourth page, lest he should find there a paragraph surrounding the name of his beloved.

One evening, all covered with dust, tanned and browned by military life and his journey, he entered his brother's room.

Paul, at first much startled, manifested his joy by extravagances unworthy of a man as *posé* as himself. He walked round and round Michel, touched him and shook him gently, to assure himself that it was his brother in the flesh, a little injured to be sure, but still living and well.

Then he took a chair in front of him, and looked at him as if he wished to devour him.

After the first explosion of joy, Michel was uneasy and restless; he did not know how to ask the question that burned on his lips. Paul came to his assistance.

"The Avérœfs and Mélaguires are at Karskoé-Sélo," he said.

And as Michel did not speak, he continued:

"The Princess left them two weeks ago, to visit her estates."

Michel's face elongated, as he asked:

"How long will she be gone?"

"No one knows. I am inclined to believe that she is travelling merely as a distraction."

"A distraction?" repeated Michel.

"Yes," Paul hesitated, "for some time she has not been herself."

"You mean since the accident which made her a

widow?" asked Michel, not knowing precisely what he said.

"No, ever since she learned, in spite of all our efforts to keep it from her, the false news of your death," said Paul, with a vague wonder as to how his brother would receive these words.

Michel was silent for a moment, but his eyes filled, and with an eloquent smile, he extended his hand to his brother, and the two hands were joined in one long grasp.

"She is not ill?" asked Michel, anxiously.

"No, not ill, but she has suffered a great deal and is killing herself thinking."

"Where is she now?"

"You must ask Madame Avérœf. She knows better than any one else, the thoughts and movements of the Princess."

"You will prepare Madame Avérœf at once," said Michel, "and to-morrow I will go and see her." The young man began to realize that he had been travelling for a month, and was thoroughly worn out. "Give me a bed somewhere, I can't move."

While a bed was being prepared, Paul endeavored to elicit from his brother, some details in regard to his sojourn with the army, and an account of the events which had had such grave consequences, but could gain no information.

"I am not sure," answered Michel, " that anything of the kind ever happened. At the time these events took place, if they took place at all, it was only my body that was present, my soul was afar off.

And he relapsed into a dream.

"My mind is utterly confused," he said, arousing himself. "I shall remember later, possibly. At all events, that part of my life is of no consequence, and I do not care to recall it!"

The next day, Paul started at an early hour for Karskoé-Sélo, agreeing to wait there for his brother, until three in the afternoon, when he should have had time to communicate his news without too great abruptness.

And when, at the hour indicated, Michel stepped from the car to the platform, he saw Serge Avéroef and his young wife awaiting him with joyful impatience.

Embraced and questioned, he hurried with them to Madame Avéroef's house, where she, with several clergymen, was awaiting him.

All through her life, she had attached infinite respect to the benediction of the cross in all solemn circumstances. It was then to the sound of the chants of the Church, that Michel crossed the threshold of the house, which was supposed never to receive him again.

The religious character of this welcome softened the emotions which human joy and suspense would have rendered too acute.

When the last notes died away with the smoke of incense, Madame Avéroef extended her arms to her nephew.

"My son was lost and I have found him!" she exclaimed in the language of Holy Writ. "War, at last, has restored to me one of my children! God be praised!"

Supported by Michel's arm, she returned to her chamber. whose cool darkness soon calmed her natural agitation. Nastia and Serge with their arms interlaced, watched their cousin with tender gladness. Monsieur Mélaguire was the one who had the greatest difficulty in believing that he saw Michel alive again. More than once he declared, that he was a delusion born of some old romance he had read in his boyhood. Finally, however, his doubts vanished, and his welcome was as cordial as ever.

When Michel had been interrogated on all that had happened, there was a long pause. It seemed as if no one had anything more to say.

Presently, Madame Avérœf announced that she had something important to say to Michel, and the others withdrew. It was quite time, for the constraint which Michel imposed upon himself, had altered the very tones of his voice, and drawn his features.

"Dear Aunt, talk to me of her!" he exclaimed, as soon as they were alone. "I cannot bear this silence any longer!"

With one word Madame Avérœf calmed him.

"She loves you," she answered.

Michel covered her hands with kisses.

"Be patient," added the old lady with a kind smile, "you will see her soon."

"Where is she?"

"I do not know precisely, but we will write at once and she will be here in a month."

"A month!" exclaimed the young man. "It is an eternity. Why not say twenty years?"

"Unless you go and find her."

"Which I propose to do," interrupted Michel, "if you will tell me in what corner of the world to look."

"We will speak of that later," said his aunt. "I too have much to tell you. First, did you know that Pauline was dead?"

"Pauline dead! No indeed. How and when?"

Madame Avérœf told Michel all that had happened after the Prince and Marthe had reached their country place up to the hour of the catastrophe. But she said as she finished her narration, that Marthe was terribly shocked by a discovery she made, as she was looking through Pauline's effects, to discover some address to which she might write, and apprise the family of this— this accident. In a casket which contained papers and jewels, Marthe discovered a bouquet of dried orange blossoms, and a letter from you directed to Monsieur Mélaguire and dated Mentone.

"My letter and my bouquet!" cried Michel. "The wretch!"

"She is no more," said the old lady, softly. "May God pardon her!"

Michel bowed his head, but he did not show any desire to join in this pious wish.

"And now, what are your plans?" said Madame Avéroef, after a long silence.

"Can you ask me? Ever since those four words written by your hands, 'Marthe is a widow,' opened a glimpse of Heaven before my dazzled eyes, I have had only one idea, to return and bear her in my arms so far away, that no one can ever tear her from me!"

"You will marry her, I presume, first," said his aunt, smiling at his passionate vehemence.

Michel laughed.

"That of course. And now I am going to ask Monsieur Mélaguire's permission, lest some new misfortune snatches the cup once more from my lips!"

"You are going now? My dear boy, think well what you do, for the worthy man might have an attack of apoplexy."

"He bore up under the attack made by Serge," answered Michel, gayly, "and I thought him hardened by this time."

"And when he has consented, what then?"

"Then you will tell me where to find Marthe, and I will go and bring her back to you."

"But you cannot marry at once. First, there are legal delays and then the *convénances!*"

"My dear Aunt," interrupted Michel, gravely, "I do not ask to marry Marthe at once, since, as you say, there are necessary delays, but I assure you if in any way I am prevented from being constantly with her, up to the time she becomes my wife, I will leave at once for the Caucasus, and will return, if I return at all, only when I am permitted to claim her hand."

Madame Avéroef looked at him, and saw that he meant what he said.

"As you will," she answered. "Certainly such an arrangement was never before heard of, but it seems to me that an Avéroef never marries like any one else!"

"Will you, Aunt, sustain my application to Monsieur Mélaguire?"

"I think you will find some difficulty at first in making him understand what you want, but that is only another reason why I should be present at the interview," said the old lady, not without a spark of malice.

CHAPTER XXXV.

ASTONISHMENT.

DURING this conversation, Monsieur Mélaguire was alone, and doing his best to accustom himself to the idea of Michel's resurrection. He said to himself that he should invite him as of yore to his Monday dinners. He had always enjoyed the society of the young man, and was really enchanted to have him alive, and at his side again.

Michel's gravity as he entered his presence, accompanied by Madame Avérœf, evidently disturbed the old gentleman, who offered seats with a look which seemed to indicate that he apprehended a new misfortune.

"It is two years and a half, sir," said Michel, as the three sat facing each other, "since I cherished the intention of asking the hand of Mademoiselle, your daughter. A happier man than I, obtained her hand. To-day, circumstances are in my favor once more, I have now the honor of asking the hand of your daughter, Marthe Palovna."

Monsieur Mélaguire was dumbfounded. The recollection of his daughter was just at this time so shrouded in crape and black garments, that it was impossible to realize that it was for her hand, that this application was made.

"But, Monsieur Michel, my daughter is a widow," he said, after some reflection.

"And it is precisely for that reason that I have the honor of asking her hand," answered Michel, unable to suppress a smile.

Madame Avérœf smiled behind her handkerchief.

"Ah yes, to be sure. But it is very odd; she is wearing mourning for her first husband."

It was easy to see that Mélaguire faced the question from a new point of view.

"Do they ever ask widows to marry again, before they are out of mourning?" he asked, turning toward Madame Avérœf.

"It is not the general custom, but we are occasionally obliged to close our eyes to an infraction of rules, in favor of Michel's earnest desire to ally himself to your family," the lady answered. "You will remember that he first sought this connection some time ago."

"And what was the obstacle to your application, then?" asked Mélaguire, setting himself squarely in his arm-chair.

"It was impossible for me at the moment to ask my father's consent, and I knew the importance you attached to etiquette."

"Very good, very good, and" Monsieur Mélaguire nodded approval, "and now?"

"I have had the grief of losing my father, and am entirely independent."

"But, a widow wearing crape, can't be married,"

cried Monsieur Mélaguire, suddenly brought back to reality. "Such a thing was never seen; and she is not here, either! How can you marry her?"

"I make my request this morning, sir, that I, with your consent, may go and bring her to you. As to the time of the marriage, her mourning is not eternal, and when *les convénances* permit."

"It is really a most singular idea — my daughter's— going off in this way, into the country, when she was so comfortable here!"

"Say yes, dear Monsieur Mélaguire, and I will bring her back to you in a fortnight."

"But I ask no better, sir," cried the good man; "you are the son-in-law I needed." Had he had ten sons-in-law, each would have been the one he needed! "But, suppose she will not have you?"

"Permit me to assure myself of her consent," urged Michel.

"It is really most extraordinary! I am sure I don't know what to say. I never heard anything like it before," repeated Mélaguire, utterly bewildered, "Prascovia Petrovna, get me out of this trouble. You see that I don't know what to do."

In another ten minutes, the desired consent was obtained. Michel and his future father-in-law shook hands cordially, and the other members of the family were summoned to hear the happy news.

"When do you go?" asked Paul.

"It will take me three days to arrange my affairs,"

19

answered Michel, counting on his fingers. "It is Wednesday to-day — Thursday, Friday, Saturday. I will leave Sunday."

"As soon as that!" they all exclaimed, as with one voice.

"I wish I could leave to-morrow," he answered, with a smile which illuminated his fine face. "Where is she?" he asked, turning to Madame Avéroef.

"Her last letter announced her intention of going to an estate she has in the district of Kazan, and from thence to a sort of farm in a wild spot among the woods, on the shores of the Volga, somewhere; but I really cannot tell you definitely."

"I will find her!" said Michel, gayly.

On the following Sunday, he left St. Petersburg, not this time with a heart half broken, but full of hope and gladness.

CHAPTER XXXVI.

THE VOLGA.

EIGHT days later, Michel descended the Volga on one of those great steamboats which run between Nijni, Novgorod and Astrakhan; not finding Marthe on her estate in the district of Kazan, which she had left, he went to seek her still further on, at that farm of which Madame Avéroef had spoken. At first absorbed in thought, he paid little heed to the landscape, but after passing Simborsk, he could not remove his eyes from the glorious view which opened before him.

The Volga is not an ordinary river running between two shores—mountainous or level; it is sometimes a tumultuous torrent—sometimes a lake. One morning, on leaving his cabin, Michel saw spread out before him, a limitless extent of blue and tranquil waters, the distant shores indicated merely by a faint undulating line of green; tiny islands of yellow sand looked like streaks of sunlight on the waters. An occasional cluster of shrubbery showed that the water was very shallow. Swans floated here and there in large flocks. Their white feathers scattered by their autumnal moulting lay like new fallen snow on the gentle ripples which washed over the sand, after the boat had passed.

The magnificent birds sailed along, not in the least

terrified by the steamboat, turning their graceful necks
to look at the great monster. Sometimes a sharp
whistle of the machinery put them all to flight; they
rose on their great outstretched wings, and hovering
for a moment, they flew towards their distant haunts,
where no human noise could disturb their savage
independence.

. Further on, the shores again drew nearer together;
the left bank was low and sandy, while the right rose
higher, their mountainous sides covered with purple
underbrush glowing in the autumnal sun.

Granite boulders clove the earth, and advanced
majestically toward the shore. The peaked rocks re-
appeared through the transparent water, and the width
was such, that the travellers with outstretched arms
could almost touch the shore while the boat swept
down the current.

And what beautiful water it was! Michel never
wearied of contemplating it: leaning over the side, he
saw the sharp prow cut this wonderful water sepa-
rating it in two curves: aqua marine in tint, or more
like an opal, pearly and fringed with a white foam that
looked crisp and delicate, like the lichen on the north
side of the trunks of trees, spared by the wood cutter
in the forests. The morning sun lighted these waves
with indescribable purity, and gave them richness of
tones. The curves spread and spread, forming a wave
which at last broke in foam on the calm waters, and
then rolled back into a translucent track, up to the

rock against which the waves beat with gathered force.

Michel remembered this beautiful water all his life through, and ten years later, he had only to close his eyes to see again the aqua marine curve open under the pressure of the prow, and unroll itself with the voluptuous grace of a fairy, who rises and shakes out the folds of her velvet mantle.

CHAPTER XXXVII.

A PRIMEVAL FOREST.

HILLS succeeded to hills, rising in rapid succession, separated by narrow ravines, down which roll the torrents from melting snow. An occasional cluster of huts built on piles were called villages. The number of inhabitants at the highest computation may have been thirty. A few boats were fastened to the piles, fishing nets and clothes were drying in the sun, and constituted the wealth of these simple people—true hermits of modern civilization.

Once or twice, Michel caught the gleam of the pointed roof of a church; after which for hours he saw nothing save a long stretch of low stunted willows which the cruel winds of Siberia never allow to grow to their full development.

"In what secluded corner of this virgin soil will Marthe be found?"—thought Avérœf, his eyes wandering from the summits of these hills, burned by the sun to ravines so deep in shadow, that the light of day never penetrated them. In what secret asylum must he look for her? And what are her thoughts in this solitude, not yet thoroughly explored by man, where more than one secret place of great beauty has been seen only by the white winged swans as they

sweep over the mountains in their indefatigable
pilgrimages.

And as the boat went on, the rocks were piled
higher and higher, the water grew deeper, while the
demi tints of evening succeeding to the high lights
of morning, lent to the blue water a mysterious
attraction. It was easy looking down into it in this
undecided hour, when the hills covered with heath were
purple in the setting sun, and stood out against the
pale violet sky. The ravines were as black and threat-
ening as if they had been the dens of terrible monsters.
The waves were sometimes blue, sometimes almost
black, and then so transparent, that one was tempted to
plunge in, to ascertain what made it so black, and yet at
the same time so clear, that one could see its depth.
Looking down it was easy to believe in the Undines.

Night came on, and the boat anchored at the foot of
a huge rock.

"What is the name of this rock?" asked Michel of
the pilot.

"It is called Oussolié," the man replied.

"I shall not see her until to-morrow," said Michel to
himself in some disappointment, for he had fixed his
heart on seeing her that night. The next day the day
had hardly tinted the sky with a pale gray, than the
boat was on its way again. Michel was on deck at
the first movement of the boat, and felt the fresh morning breeze blow full in his face.

"I shall see her to-day," he said, full of joy at the
mere thought.

Above the hills, the sky was rosy, but rosy as is the
cheek of a little child—soft and delicate, while directly
above, the last stars were fading away in a sky as blue
as flax blossoms, while a light fog, precursor of autumn,
rose slowly from the shore here and there, revealing a
bush or tree, disclosing a dark ravine, floating above a
clump of fir trees where they seemed to leave a few
scattered fragments, rising against the sides of a steep
rock like smoke. Sometimes a succession of granite
peaks pierced the cloud, a single flake of the fog, like
a feather from a gigantic swan, clung to one of the
peaks, as if to show that the greatest in this world are
not exempt from common distresses.

Suddenly the sun rose from behind the mountains
and inundated the Volga with dazzling light. It was
a conflagration of the river. The ripples created by
the morning wind were tinged with gold. The luminous wake of the boat was fringed with pearls. The
curve in front unrolled more deeply and more gor-
geous in color, and the scattered fog was transformed
into drops of dew on the hills, on the trees and furze,
on the boat and on Michel himself, who took off his
hat.

"Good morning, Sun! I salute you!" cried Michel,
"Good morning! Beautiful Day—Herald of my
happiness!"

He was alone—leaning over the rail, he drank in this
spectacle, so unlike any other in the whole world, and
one which will lose half its beauty, when man fully

explores it. What buildings or what ruins can compete with the magnificent silhouette of Oussolié and its companion rocks, thrown up like gigantic bastions by Nature, to defend her domains.

Michel was growing very impatient. At last he heard the name for which he was listening from the lips of the captain. They had reached the spot where he wished to land. Michel went for his valise while the boat described a short turn to avoid a sunken hull, at the entrance of a ravine.

When Michel went on shore, he found himself, to his great astonishment, entirely alone with a peasant, on the frail wharf, which shook as the steamboat took its way toward the Caspian sea.

"Is this Bogodai?" he asked of the peasant.

"No, sir, it is the station for Bogodai."

"And where is Bogodai?"

"Thirty-five verstes from here, sir."

"There is a village here I presume?"

"No, sir, there is no village."

"But where do you live?"

"Underneath here."

And the peasant pointed to a ladder which descended to the interior of the wharf, which was shut in and lighted by four narrow windows. This habitation bore a certain resemblance to the isbas on piles seen along the shores.

"Are you here alone?" asked Michel, considerably surprised.

"No, sir, I have a comrade, he has gone for wood now. What can I do for you?" asked the peasant with a dawning apprehension that this handsome young officer had not come there merely to talk with him.

"Do you know a farm called Mariévo which ought to be near this——?" Michel hesitated to find some suitable term.

"This station and the town of Bogodai?" he continued.

"Bogodai is not a town, sir, it is merely a great village with a church."

"A church, is that really so? I am delighted to hear it," continued Michel, somewhat nervously. "Well then, do you know the farm which goes by the name of Mariévo, and belonged to Prince Oghérof?"

"Certainly, sir, and a lady, the Princess herself, came about a fortnight ago, and is still there."

"Very good, how far away is it?"

"About fourteen verstes by the road. But why did you come here? You should have gone only as far as Oussolié, and then taken post horses."

"But why on earth!" cried Michel, in a state of exasperation, "do you have a station here if you do not use it?"

"We do, in spring and autumn for merchandise, but travellers never come this way. You have done a very odd thing, sir."

"It was certainly a very odd thing to look up a town on the map, and then get off at the landing nearest it.

But as I am here, tell me how to get to Mariévo. Have you a horse?"

"A horse?" repeated the peasant in a dazed sort of way, "what should I do with a horse!"

And what use indeed would a horse have been to him, to this man who lived on the fish he caught with his own hands, and on the black bread brought by the boat. What did any form of active life matter to this philosopher, since he could live without occupying himself with the exterior world?

"Can I go on foot?"

"Yes, sir, it is not very far, and my little boy can show you the road if you wish."

"Have you children living down there?" asked Michel in astonishment.

"Yes, sir, and a wife."

"Very well," said the young soldier, "lend me your boy as a guide."

He took up his valise gaily, and started off, accompanied by a little fellow not more than eight, who was lively enough, but so far as Michel could judge, absolutely dumb.

The road could hardly be called a road, it was merely the bed of a mountain torrent dried up by the heat of the summer sun. A thick border of willows already tinged with autumnal coloring, screened the thread of water that ran slowly in the middle of the brook. Since the spring the wheels of the télégues had worn a sort of path over the pebbles thrown up

by the high tides or freshets. Occasionally a point of
rock came out of the ground, and barred the passage
of the stream which then divided to the right and
the left, while the road followed the most direct
line, remorselessly crushing the young shoots.

After two hours of walking, which seemed to him
very long, Michel reached a plateau—the source of the
mountain stream, fed by a little lake—and a well trod-
den path showed that it was much visited. Hills rose
on all sides, some brown and bare, others veiled with
purple broom, and others still, covered with a
young growth of trees.

A thick grove of oaks with their foliage richly cut,
stood between two great rocks on either side of the
path like the guardians of some Hesperides.

"To the left," said the little guide, opening his lips
for the first time.

"You can speak then, can you?" said Michel,
filled with admiration for a child who was capable of
holding his tongue for two whole hours. "Here is a
rouble for you."

The child's face, previously bright with pride,
became very gloomy. He took the paper disdain-
fully, and turned it over and over, as if half inclined
to destroy it.

"That is for your father, take care of it," said
Michel perceiving that he was no longer at St. Petersburg, "and this is for you."

And he gave the boy a huge piece of copper. The

little fellow colored high with pleasure, clutched the clumsy money in both hands, and rushed like the wind in the direction of his home.

Michel, somewhat astonished at finding himself left in this absolute solitude, put his valise on the ground, seated himself upon it, and looked about him.

And this was the desert chosen by Marthe as her retreat! She was certain of finding there nothing which should remind her of the society from which she had fled. But from what wound, was this haughty spirit suffering so keenly, that she wished to hide her pain? Could not a woman mourn in peace less far from the abode of man, less far from all possibility of aid, in case of any trouble or illness?

At this idea, Michel started to his feet, shouldered his valise and turned to the left. Two hours more elapsed, the afternoon sun warmed the earth, thousands of grasshoppers skipped over the short grass— brown and slippery on the dry hill-sides. Occasionally Michel caught a glimpse of a flock of wild goats runing away toward the hills, that shut off the distant Volga. The young man felt no fatigue, for each step took him nearer to Marthe—Marthe ill,—possibly in peril!

When this idea had come to him, it took entire possession of his mind. He hurried on, and arrived at an enclosure surrounded by a hedge of young poplars, the first evidence of the presence of man which he had seen since he left the landing. He pushed open a gate that was simply latched, and walked up an avenue shaded by poplar trees, notwithstanding that two or three dogs made incredible efforts to break loose, not having learned, probably, in early youth, that the chain is part of the daily bread for dogs as well as for men.

At the noise made by these animals, a servant appeared. No pen can describe his amazement at seeing an officer of the Guards approaching with his valise in his hand.

"The Princess Oghérof?" asked Michel, touching his cap with his two fingers.

"She is within, sir," replied the old Intendant, "but permit me to ask how you came?"

"On foot," answered the young man.

The Intendant looked at him doubtfully.

"Whom shall I announce, sir?"

"Captain Avérœf, returned from Caucasus," said Michel, suddenly realising that surprises are not so agreeable, when one has domestics as intermediaries.

The old servant entered the house, and presently returned.

"The Princess is not here," he said, "she is probably walking in the garden, or at the back of the house. Shall I go and tell her?"

"No," answered the young man, "I will go to her myself—only," he added, with some hesitation, "I should like to make some change in my dress."

The servant took him into the house. Humble enough it was, only two rooms, one a chamber and a

dining-room with a passage-way between. Another
cabin contained the kitchen and two servants' rooms, of
which one was vacant, the Princess keeping her maid
with her at night. The farmer and his wife, the latter
acting as cook, inhabited another cabin, a little
further off.

The dining-room was furnished with four straw
chairs and a table of pine wood. A golden shrine in
one corner was the sole relief from this nudity. The
bed-room, the door of which stood open, was of nun-
like simplicity, with the exception of a dressing-case
that stood on the table, surrounded by its silver uten-
sils, and seemed the one vestige of civilization.

"What on earth is she doing here?" said Michel to
himself, more and more perplexed. He was very soon
ready. A little fresh water made him forget his
fatigue. He asked a few directions and went out. He
looked in every direction, but Marthe was not to be
seen. At last he opened a door recently cut in the
palisade, and found himself in the wilderness.

CHAPTER XXXVIII.

A BROKEN VOW.

A BROOK rippled through the valley, and leaped from rock to rock with a musical tinkle; here, as noisy as a bugle call—there, as gently as a mysterious whisper. A tall peak showed its granite under its garb of moss, sown thick with pink flowers, a few seeds of which had taken root on a little dust. It needs no more than this, for a rock to clothe itself in festal garb.

The sandy soil swept gently toward an opening, where the brook fell twenty feet or more into a shallow basin. There the path ended. Michel turned back, and followed the course of the brook. Two rocks nearly met and almost impeded his passage. A few flat stones permitted him to cross the brook without wetting his feet. Michel chose this direction, for at the season of the year of which we write, the night comes on apace. The rays of the setting sun flooded the narrow gorge, and fell on a young fir growing luxuriantly on the fine green turf. The rocks here spread, and made an open space on which the sunlight fell; at the other extremity, the brook fell with a soft sigh. Michel looked around, Marthe was there!

On the turf, leaning against the trunk of a tree, she

sat wrapt in thought. Her two hands were loosely clasped, and their whiteness stood out with startling force, against the black raiment falling about her in lustreless folds. Her face was calm, but sorrow and vigils had left their traces there. Her calmness was that of resignation.

Michel felt an emotion of fear as he looked at her. His heart which had beat high with joy and impatience, was suddenly chilled and fell like lead. How was he to tell this woman who had shed so many tears for him, that he was still living? Might not the shock be too great for her tender nerves.

Hesitating, anxious, and trembling with joy and fear, he stood motionless. Suddenly, Marthe turned her face toward him.

She looked at first without seeing who it was that stood there; and supposing it some one to say that she was wanted on business, she nodded. Then glancing up to the face, she started forward with one hand on her heart, the other supporting herself on the turf. Her great eyes opened wide, and she gazed at Michel in mortal terror, believing him to be an hallucination, and feeling that reason was escaping her.

Without a word, he rushed toward her, and fell at her feet, with his face buried in the folds of her dress.

Marthe seized his head between her hands, and looked him full in the eyes, at first incredulous and greatly agitated.

"Living!" she exclaimed, and she closed her eyes.

20

There was a long moment when she seemed to be fainting, but before Michel could make an effort to restore her, she recovered her senses, and looked at him, no more with terror, but with a joy mingled with remorse.

"Living!" she repeated. "It was not true then?"

"Almost," answered the young man. "Marthe, I love you!"

"I am a widow," she answered at once, brought back by these words to the hard realities of life.

"You are my wife!" cried Michel. "Who shall separate us again? I came here to seek you, and will never leave you again until the hour of death."

"Living!" repeated Marthe. "Ah! the tears I have shed for you." And at this thought, she burst into passionate weeping.

"All that is a bad dream," said Michel, taking from her face the hands with which she sought to hide her tears. "We will forget the Past—the Future is our own. We are at last united for ever."

Marthe drank in the sweet intoxication of his words. Her lashes were still bathed in tears, and her lids trembled, as she fixed her eyes on her lover, for whom she had mourned with such sincerity, and had now found again.

"I love you!" repeated Michel, drawing her toward him. "At last we shall be happy."

Marthe tore herself from his arms, and wrung her thin hands with a despairing gesture.

"No," she cried, "it is impossible."

"Impossible!"

"It was our love that killed my husband," she said, continuing to wring her hands nervously, "there is a death between us. It is impossible!"

Michel felt all his young blood boil in his veins.

"Impossible? And I have returned from Caucasus, wounded, sick! I have travelled two thousand leagues to find you, only to be told that it is impossible! Ever since the day that I knew you to be free, I have not drawn a breath without thinking of you, I have not once seen the sun rise without saying to myself, 'one day less!' and now you tell me that it is impossible! And yet we are both free to love each other before God and man. You love me and I love you and I say in my turn, 'it is impossible!' Try and repeat it after me; you will find that your lips refuse to utter the words."

Marthe shook her head as her eyes were fixed on vacancy before her.

"You see, Michel," she said,. slowly, "my husband died within the hour that I told him I had loved you —that I still loved you. I, at first, thought he had killed himself after hearing this, then I assured myself that his death was the result of an accident; but there are accidents that happen, only when one is weary of life. You see there is a death between us, nothing can change that fact."

"The Prince was an honest man," answered Michel.

"peace to his ashes! It is not my wish to blacken him in your eyes. But do you think he loved no one but you?"

Marthe remembered that morning at Ladoga, the day after her marriage, when she felt that nothing could efface the insult she had received.

She did not reply, but sat with her eyes still fixed on vacancy.

"And since his marriage—" continued Michel.

Marthe looked at her companion, reproachfully.

He hesitated, and then continued.

"If you had died—died of grief at not being loved as you merited, do you think the Prince would have sworn eternal fidelity to your memory?"

Marthe's head drooped. The sun was slowly going down; deep shadows and cool freshness filled the grove—under the trees it was already dark. Marthe took a step or two, and found herself opposite a fissure in the mountains, through which the lingering sunlight fell in one long luminous line.

Her dignified head stood out in profile, black against this golden light; the melancholy face crowned by masses of brown hair. Marthe looked back at her life, and this spot was an eloquent image of her Future. On one side, warmth and light—on the other, chill shadows, wherein the living soon become like the dead on whose graves they kneel.

Marthe's whole existence passed before her, from the day when she had waited for Michel in the garden, .

until the hour when she had learned of Michel's death, up to the present moment, and in spite of herself, her youthful heart expanded with ecstasy at the thought that he was there, living, breathing, loving—he whom she had wept as dead. Why then did she say again to this man whom she loved—"never," in such despairing tones.

"Marthe," answered Michel, in the tone of a husband and a master, "there is something in your heart which you do not tell me and which I have a right to know."

Marthe hesitated a moment.

"So be it," she said, "you shall know! When I learned of your death I made a vow to consecrate myself to God as soon as my father was no more, in expiation of my fault. I should not have loved any other man than my husband.

"Say rather that you should not have married any other man than the one you loved; there was your fault, it was not toward your husband nor toward God. It was toward me whose life you marred, and now you refuse me reparation!"

The sun disappeared. Marthe stood motionless, draped in her woolen dress, with its soft classic folds. Michel suddenly, without her being able to retreat, folded her in his arms. "Listen," he said, "God does not wish you to give yourself to him, since he has led me back to your feet that I may worship you to the end of my days. Your greatest fault was in doubting me. This fault you have expiated, and I, the one whom you injured, have forgiven you."

"Look!" and he pointed to the evening star. "At Caucasus, when I was a prisoner, expecting each day to be shot, I watched for that star and when it appeared it seemed to me that your eyes were upon me. I said to myself—Marthe promised to love me until death. And now, saved as it were by a miracle, I come to claim my reward. And will Marthe be faithless to her promise?"

He drew her gently toward him, and his lips rested on her hair, Marthe making no resistance, and seeming fascinated, as it were.

"Before promising anything to God," he said, "you promised me to love me always, and I——I love you."

Marthe started as if from a dream. She threw her arms around Michel's neck.

"I love you," she said softly, "can it be that we at last shall be happy?" she added slowly, and as if half asleep.

Michel answered only by a kiss.

THE END.

Mrs. Southworth's Work

ISHMAEL; or, IN THE DEPTHS. (Being "Self-Made; or, Out of Depth

SELF-RAISED; or, From the Depths. The Sequel to "Ishmael."

THE PHANTOM WEDDING; or, the Fall of the House of Flint.

THE "MOTHER-IN-LAW;" or, MARRIED IN HASTE.

THE MISSING BRIDE; or, MIRIAM, THE AVENGER.

VICTOR'S TRIUMPH. The Sequel to "A Beautiful Fiend."

A BEAUTIFUL FIEND; or, THROUGH THE FIRE.

THE LADY OF THE ISLE; or, THE ISLAND PRINCESS.

FAIR PLAY; or, BRITOMARTE, THE MAN-HATER.

HOW HE WON HER. The Sequel to "Fair Play."

THE CHANGED BRIDES ; or, Winning Her Way.

THE BRIDE'S FATE. The Sequel to "The Changed Brides."

CRUEL AS THE GRAVE; or, Hallow Eve Mystery.

TRIED FOR HER LIFE. The Sequel to "Cruel as the Grave."

THE CHRISTMAS GUEST; or, The Crime and the Curse.

THE LOST HEIR OF LINLITHGOW; or, The Brothers.

A NOBLE LORD. The Sequel to "The Lost Heir of Linlithgow.

THE FAMILY DOOM; or, THE SIN OF A COUNTESS.

THE MAIDEN WIDOW. The Sequel to "The Family Doom."

THE GIPSY'S PROPHECY; or, The Bride of an Evening.

THE FORTUNE SEEKER; or, Astrea, The Bridal Day.

THE THREE BEAUTIES ; or, SHANNONDALE.

FALLEN PRIDE; or, THE MOUNTAIN GIRL'S LOVE.

THE DISCARDED DAUGHTER; or, The Children of the Isle.

THE PRINCE OF DARKNESS; or, HICKORY HALL.

THE TWO SISTERS ; or, Virginia and Magdalene.

THE FATAL MARRIAGE; or, ORVILLE DEVILLE.

INDIA; or, THE PEARL OF PEARL RIVER.   THE CURSE OF CLIFT

THE WIDOW'S SON; or, LEFT ALONE.   THE WIFE'S VICTO

THE MYSTERY OF DARK HOLLOW.   THE SPECTRE LOVER

ALLWORTH ABBEY ; or, EUDORA.   THE ARTIST'S LOVE

THE BRIDAL EVE; or, ROSE ELMER.   THE FATAL SECRET.

VIVIA; or, THE SECRET OF POWER.   LOVE'S LABOR WO

THE HAUNTED HOMESTEAD.   THE LOST HEIRESS.

BRIDE OF LLEWELLYN.   THE DESERTED WIFE.   RETRIBUTI

T. B. PETERSON & BROTHERS, Philadelphia, Pa

THE PRINCESS OGHÉROF. *A Russian Love Story.* By *Henry Gréville.* Price 75 cents in paper, or $1.00 in cloth.

XÉNIE'S INHERITANCE. *A Russian Story.* By *Henry Gréville.* Price 75 cents in paper, or $1.00 in cloth.

THE TRIALS OF RAÏSSA. *By Henry Gréville,* author of "Dosia." Price 75 cents in paper, or $1.00 in cloth.

DOSIA. *A Russian Story.* By *Henry Gréville,* author of "Savéli's Expiation." Price 75 cents in paper, or $1.25 in cloth.

SAVELI'S EXPIATION. *A Russian Story.* By *Henry Gréville,* author of "Dosia." Price 50 cents in paper, or $1.00 in cloth.

BONNE-MARIE. *A Tale of Normandy and Paris.* By *Henry Gréville.* Price 50 cents in paper, or $1.00 in cloth.

PHILOMENE'S MARRIAGES. *By Henry Gréville,* author of "Dosia." Price 75 cents in paper, or $1.25 in cloth.

DOURNOF. *A Russian Novel.* By *Henry Gréville,* author of "Dosia." Price 50 cents in paper, or $1.00 in cloth.

PRETTY LITTLE COUNTESS ZINA. *By Henry Gréville,* author of "Dosia." Price 75 cents in paper, or $1.25 in cloth.

SONIA. *A Russian Story.* By *Henry Gréville,* author of "Savéli's Expiation." Price 50 cents in paper, or $1.00 in cloth.

MARRYING OFF A DAUGHTER. *By Henry Gréville,* author of "Dosia." Price 75 cents in paper, or $1.25 in cloth.

A FRIEND; or, L'AMI. *By Henry Gréville,* author of "Dosia." Price 50 cents in paper, or $1.00 in cloth.

MARKOF. *A Russian Novel.* By *Henry Gréville,* author of "Savéli's Expiation." Price 75 cents in paper, or $1.50 in cloth.

GABRIELLE; or, The House of Maureze. *By Henry Gréville.* Price 50 cents in paper, or $1.00 in cloth.

LUCIE RODEY. *A Society Novel.* By *Henry Gréville,* author of "Dosia." Price 50 cents in paper, or $1.00 in cloth.